"One of these days, a man is going to walk into your world and convince you to share your life with him,"

James said with authority.

"If you're talking about someone convincing me to marry him, no way," Stacy objected.

"Certainly you're not saying that one unfortunate experience has turned you off men for all time?"

"I like men. I enjoy their company, their companionship. But I don't want another serious involvement. Once was enough."

"He hurt you that badly?" James asked quietly.

Stacy suddenly became aware that she was on the verge of discussing her private life with the world's foremost contemporary sex expert. She had no intention of permitting James's professional eye to zero in on her. She'd be damned if she'd ever become one of his case histories!

Dear Reader,

Happy New Year, and many thanks for the notes and letters you've sent to the authors and editors of Silhouette **Special Edition** over the past twelve months. Although we seldom have time to write individual responses, I'd like to take this opportunity to let you know how much we value all your comments. Your praise and plaudits warm our hearts and give our efforts meaning; your questions and suggestions keep us on our toes as we continually strive to make each of our six monthly Silhouette **Special Edition** novels a truly significant romance-reading event.

Our authors and editors believe you deserve writing of the highest caliber, satisfying novelistic scope, and a profound emotional experience with each book you read. Your letters tell us that you've come to trust Silhouette **Special Edition** to deliver romance fiction of that quality, depth, and sensitivity time and time again. With the advent of the new year, we're renewing a pledge: to do our very best, month after month, edition after edition, to continue bringing you "romance you can believe in."

On behalf of all the authors and editors of Silhouette **Special Edition,**

Thanks again and best wishes,

Leslie Kazanjian,
Senior Editor

P.S. This month, ask your bookseller for *The Forever Rose*, a new historical novel by one of your Silhouette **Special Edition** favorites,
Curtiss Ann Matlock—the author has promised "family ties" to her next two contemporary novels, coming this year from Silhouette **Special Edition**!

MAGGI CHARLES

The Love Expert

Published by Silhouette Books New York

America's Publisher of Contemporary Romance

For Emilie Jacobson . . . for naming the book, and for lots of other things, too, tangible and intangible.

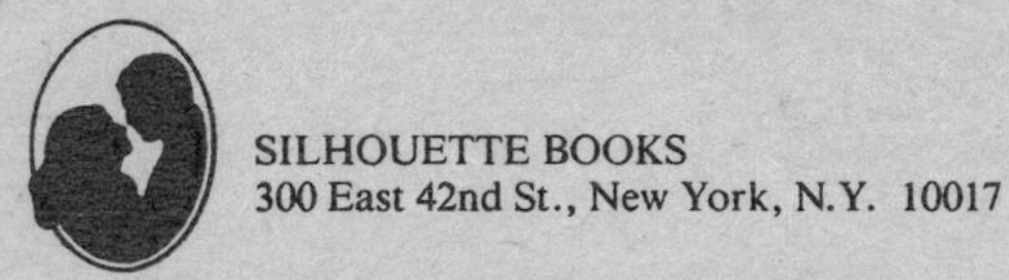

SILHOUETTE BOOKS
300 East 42nd St., New York, N.Y. 10017

ISBN: 0-373-09575-9

First Silhouette Books printing January 1990

Printed in the U.S.A.

Books by Maggi Charles

Silhouette Romance

Magic Crescendo #134

Silhouette Intimate Moments

Love's Other Language #90

Silhouette Special Edition

Love's Golden Shadow #23
Love's Tender Trial #45
The Mirror Image #158
That Special Sunday #258
Autumn Reckoning #269
Focus on Love #305
Yesterday's Tomorrow #336
Shadow on the Sun #362
The Star Seeker #381
Army Daughter #429
A Different Drummer #459
It Must Be Magic #479
Diamond Moods #497
A Man of Mystery #520
The Snow Image #546
The Love Expert #575

MAGGI CHARLES

wrote her first novel when she was eight, and fiction has been her true love ever since. She has written forty-plus romance and mystery novels and many short stories. The former newspaper reporter has also published dozens of articles, on travel, music, antiques and cooking. Maggi was born and raised in New York City. Now she and her writer husband live in a sprawling old house on Cape Cod. They have two sons and two grandchildren.

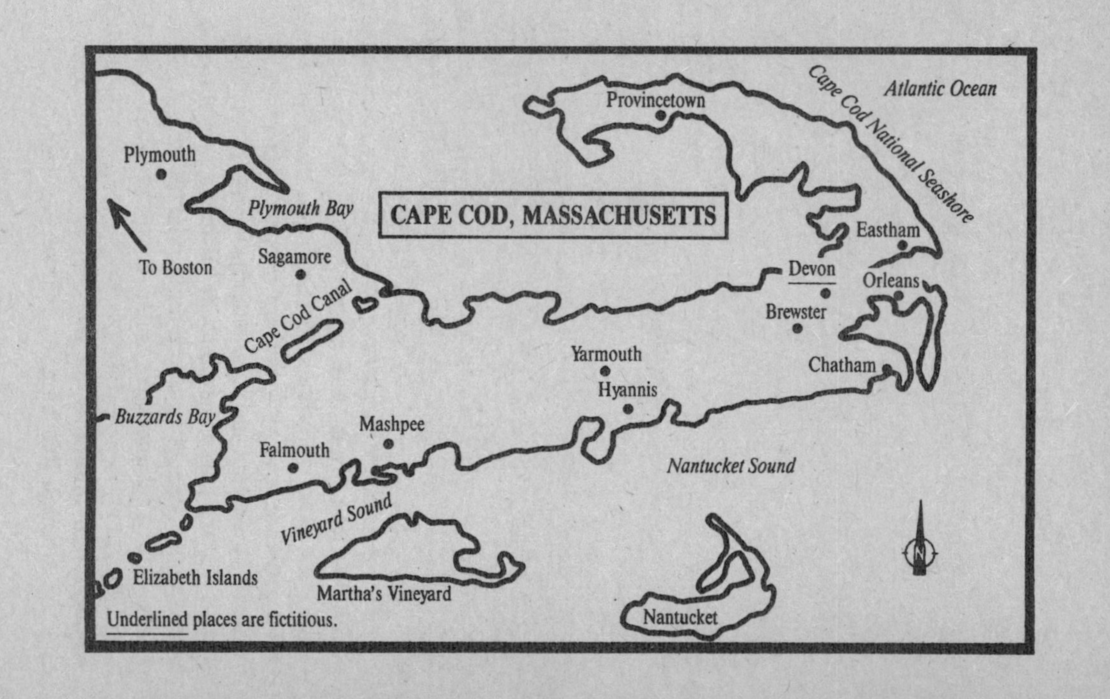
CAPE COD, MASSACHUSETTS
Atlantic Ocean
Cape Cod National Seashore
Provincetown
Plymouth
Plymouth Bay
To Boston
Sagamore
Cape Cod Canal
Eastham
Devon
Orleans
Brewster
Chatham
Yarmouth
Hyannis
Buzzards Bay
Mashpee
Falmouth
Nantucket Sound
Vineyard Sound
Elizabeth Islands
Martha's Vineyard
Nantucket
N
Underlined places are fictitious.

Prologue

It was a rainy afternoon in London. The streets were gray and glistening, the houses looked dark and damp, and here and there smoke spiraled from a chimney pot. The corner pub across the way was beginning to do a brisk business and, from her third-floor window in the aging Kensington hotel, Stacy stared wistfully at its wide entrance.

She wished she was walking through those venerable oaken swinging doors, making for the ladies' lounge. She wished she was ordering a pint of half-and-half, and maybe a Cornish pasty with some hot mustard to go with it. She'd be content to sit by herself, watching, listening, absorbing, enjoying the ambience. The English were good at letting people stay by themselves, when they looked as if they wanted it that way.

Instead...

She sniffed miserably, then indulged in a sneeze that rattled her bones. Reaching for a tissue, she bemoaned the fact that this was the day she was supposed to visit Stratford-upon-Avon for a tour of Shakespeare's birthplace. Instead, she was quite possibly on the verge of pneumonia.

She switched on the "telly," then perched on the edge of her plain, hard-mattressed bed. She still hadn't gotten used to the vagaries of English programming. There might be something, there might be nothing, but anything was better than suffering alone in silence.

A picture slowly swam into focus. It was an old television set, but the color was good, the picture surprisingly clear. So clear that Stacy blinked as she met the light gray eyes of the man whose face was filling the screen. Eyes as gray as London rain, she thought absently, staring into them while becoming possessed of the crazy notion that she and this man were communicating, that he was seeing her just as she was seeing him.

She leaned forward, and the camera backed away. The gray eyes receded, forcing her to become aware of the man's face in toto. It was an arresting face, intriguingly different. She sought for adjectives, because handsome was too trite a word to describe him. He was...exceptional.

She focused on his hair, a golden-brown shade that reminded her of autumn leaves in New England. It was thick, smooth hair, with just a hint of a wave. His eyebrows, slightly darker, arched over those fantastic gray eyes. His nose was rather prominent, like certain noses of the British aristocracy, and his high cheekbones appeared to have been sculpted. And then there was his mouth. It was an eloquent mouth, masculine, mature...and sensual.

"Possibly," he was saying with an accent reminiscent of all the dashing British actors she'd fallen in love with during her teen years, "I will be accused of being old-fashioned."

Stacy reached for another tissue, blew her nose violently, then leaned forward again. She was captivated by the man on the television set—by his presence, his sexiness, his voice, his confidence, and a whimsical tone that hinted of a good sense of humor. Her curiosity peaked as she wondered what he was going to say next.

He spoke slowly, as if this were something he'd weighed carefully. "My critics," he allowed, "may accuse me of reverting. But that's not so. I remain as much of a believer as ever in premarital sex—and, remember, I said premarital sex, not promiscuous sex. But I *have* slightly altered my opinion about a number of other aspects prevalent in today's relationships. . . ."

The camera withdrew slightly, and the lens angle discreetly widened so that the speaker became visible from the top of his smooth gold-brown head to the tips of his well-shod toes. As if aware of this added exposure, he shifted slightly and crossed one knee over the other. This small bit of action revealed long, well-proportioned legs, and a physique perfectly packaged in a stunning three-piece charcoal-gray suit.

In her absorption with his physical attributes, Stacy didn't at once realize what this exceptionally attractive individual was talking about. Then he paused, and in that pause his previous words filtered back to her.

Premarital sex. Promiscuous sex.

She leaned forward, curious. Who *was* he? And just what was this program all about?

The camera panned to the interviewer. He was an older man, his thin face stamped with cynicism.

"Doctor," he said with a small show of lofty amusement, "you will have to explain that statement rather in detail, you know. Else our listeners will be flooding us with letters and telephone calls."

Dr. Whoever He Was nodded gravely. "I should be glad to," he said graciously, "but one can't really do justice to the subject within the confines of a television program. Not even your program, Mr. Smythe."

"Are you suggesting our viewers rush out and buy your latest book?" Mr. Smythe countered snidely.

The guest of honor shook his head. "My next book will not be available for at least a year," he said smoothly. He was thoroughly in command of the situation. "Until then allow me simply to say that I have amended several of the concepts I expressed two years ago when *A Personal Sex Bible* was first published...."

A Personal Sex Bible!

This was Dr. James Ashley-Sinclair, the world's foremost authority on contemporary sexual relations?

Stacy nearly choked. She sniffed, blew her nose again and refocused. The camera lens was fixed on Mr. Smythe at that moment, which was just as well. She knew that were she to stare into Dr. Ashley-Sinclair's rainy-day eyes again she would feel as if he were undressing her!

She hadn't read *A Personal Sex Bible*, primarily because the issue of sexual relations was something she had deliberately been sidestepping. She had, though, read several articles about the book's author, including a detailed interview with Ashley-Sinclair that had appeared in the *New York Times*. In the interview he claimed to have written *A Personal Sex Bible* as a serious study, meant for the scientific rather than the lay community. His publisher had insisted on the flashy title. The fact that the book had soared to the top of the bestseller lists in his native England soon after its publication, and then had done the same thing across the Atlantic, was—so he'd stated—a source of great amazement to him.

Stacy didn't wonder at that. Since its publication, *A Personal Sex Bible* had been translated into everything from Japanese to Serbo-Croatian. The name Ashley-Sinclair was suddenly ranked with that of Kinsey, Peck, Buscaglia and a number of other authorities who dealt in the fields of sex, human relations or both.

The television program ended. Stacy, still sniffling, filled the electric teapot—one of the room's conveniences—with hot water. Yesterday she'd stopped at a small grocer's on Kensington High Street and bought a box of cookies—called biscuits in England, she reminded herself. She opened the box as she waited for the tea to brew.

This was her last day in London. Tomorrow—cold, pneumonia or whatever else notwithstanding—she was booked on a flight out of Heathrow. She'd come here on a brief, late September trip for the New York fashion house she represented, and she wished she could stay longer. Maybe because a part of her heritage was British—though Scottish rather than English—this island land intrigued her.

The short time away from New York, though, had sufficed to convince her that the moment for a decision about both her marriage and her future wasn't merely approaching. It had arrived!

She sighed, staring at the blank television screen as if she were about to meet Dr. Ashley-Sinclair's gray eyes again. She wished she was going to be around London long enough to attend one of his lectures, and maybe even have a personal consultation with him. Probably he would have been willing to see her because he was related to her employer, Kate Clarendon. She remembered Kate mentioning this one day as they passed a bookstore on Fifth Avenue that featured a window display of his treatise.

Dr. James Ashley-Sinclair. Stacy wondered if he were married and, if so, how *his* marriage was working.

Sipping her tea, she managed a feeble chuckle. What, she wondered, would it be like to be married to the world's foremost expert on sex?

Chapter One

Stacy spotted him immediately. He was standing in front of the speaker's podium, towering over the women who surrounded him.

She watched from the doorway, her lips twitching with an amusement she couldn't suppress. Dr. James Ashley-Sinclair appeared to have his hands full. Figuratively, if not literally.

She saw him glance around, as if seeking an escape route. Across the space of twenty-odd feet, their eyes met. Stacy was aware that by now she was grinning like the proverbial Cheshire cat. But it *was* rather fun seeing Kate Clarendon's famous cousin so patently ill at ease.

Remembering the man's relation to her boss, she wiped off the smile that was threatening to become a smirk. Reminding herself that she was here on business, Stacy proceeded across the ballroom of the Boston Ritz Carlton at a swift yet decorous pace, and wondered if she was going to have to shoulder aside some of Dr. Ashley-Sinclair's admirers in order to address the great man herself.

In the course of her brief safari, she became aware that he was still watching her, those gray eyes she had found so alluring on British television a year ago fixed squarely on her face.

"Dr. Ashley-Sinclair?" she queried, hoping her voice sounded as brisk and businesslike as she wanted it to sound. As she spoke, she touched the arm of the first of several women blocking her path of progress. The woman yielded reluctantly. The others also drew back, and Stacy found herself looking up at the world's foremost authority on sex. His face was several inches above her face and, right now, was wearing an expression that was a blend of curiosity and skepticism, mixed with wariness.

Stacy offered her hand. "I'm Stacy MacKenzie," she announced. "Kate Clarendon's representative."

James Ashley-Sinclair clasped his palm over hers, and Stacy tried to pretend the gesture evoked no reaction in her. But she would have been lying through her teeth if she succeeded, and she especially hated to lie to herself. The fact was, his touch made her want to shiver—but from warmth rather than cold, if that made sense.

"Ah, Miss MacKenzie," he said, his voice as soft and sexy and delightfully British as she remembered it. "I've been expecting you."

He took a step forward and clasped Stacy's arm. "Ladies," he said to his crowd of admirers, "thank you so much. This has been a pleasure." With that, he headed for the ballroom door, tugging Stacy along with a force that brooked no resistance.

There were other admirers waiting in the corridor. James Ashley-Sinclair exhibited considerable charm and patience as he swiftly wove his way among them, bestowing smiles and excuses. Downstairs, in the lobby, there were more clusters to push through or work around. But in minutes they were at the Arlington Street entrance of the Ritz, a doorman was summoning a taxi for them, and James Ashley-Sinclair was herding Stacy into the cab before she finally found her voice.

"Exactly where do you think we're going?" she asked.

To her surprise, Kate Clarendon's cousin leaned forward and gave the taxi driver a street address in Cambridge. "I'm not at the Ritz," he explained as the cab took off. "I've been staying with a friend in Cambridge. He's at Oxford ordinarily, but on a sabbatical at Harvard at the moment. We can pick up my luggage at his place before we go to Kate's."

"My car happens to be parked in a garage only a block or so from the Ritz," Stacy pointed out, not bothering to hide her annoyance. "I could have reclaimed the car first, and driven you to Cambridge."

"Does it matter?"

"Yes, because we'll be coming back into Boston at the height of rush-hour traffic, and getting out of town is going to be a mess," she informed him. "It's normally about a two-hour drive to Cape Cod. We'll probably be lucky if we make it in four."

"Are you from this area, Miss . . . MacKenzie, isn't it?" Dr. Ashley-Sinclair queried.

"Ms. MacKenzie," Stacy said firmly. "No, I'm not from this area, but I'm reasonably familiar with it."

He didn't comment, and after a moment she slanted a glance at him. He was looking out the window, so she had the chance to study him covertly. It was silly, but when she'd come face-to-face with him a while ago, she'd had the crazy feeling that he should recognize her, even as she'd recognized him. All because of her reaction last fall in

London, when she'd watched him on the television program. She still remembered vividly the way the camera had zoomed in for a close-up, and she'd met those gray eyes and felt as if he could see right through her....

Thank God, she thought suddenly, that the feeling had been fantasy rather than reality. Dr. James Ashley-Sinclair, by virtue of his fame—or should one say notoriety?—was not a person she would want to let into the innermost chambers of her secret heart.

She'd pretty well sealed off those chambers, anyway. For now, certainly. And she intended to keep them sealed until enough time passed so that she was sure all the pieces of the self she'd so carefully glued together were permanently welded. She'd seen friends get bitten by alleged lovebugs while they were still on the rebound from broken-up marriages, and the resulting romances—usually short-term ones—had only led to further heartaches.

Stacy didn't want any more heartache. She'd worked her way through betrayal, loss of face and loss of confidence. At the end of that tunnel she'd discovered a person she'd never fully known before—herself. She'd married young, lost so much of her identity in that marriage because of her husband's overpowering personality and equally overpowering conceit. Now she liked the person she'd become since she'd "found" herself, and she put a high value on her hard-won independence.

The cab crossed the Charles River into Cambridge and pulled up in front of an old frame house on a tree-shaded side street. "Would you prefer to wait in the cab, or would you rather come in?" James Ashley-Sinclair asked politely.

"Will it take you long to get your things together?" she queried.

"No. Bert will still be at class, so there won't be any farewells to say. I shall be quick, if you'd rather wait."

"I'd rather wait," she decided.

She sat back and waited. Soon the cabdriver engaged her in a conversation, which centered primarily on the weather.

"Looks like maybe we'll get the edge of that hurricane after all," he ventured.

"What hurricane?" Stacy asked.

"Helga. Saw a report on TV when I stopped for coffee an hour or so go. She's off the Carolinas. Looks like she might nip at the coast. On the other hand, could be she'll swing straight out to sea."

"I hope so," Stacy said. Coping with a hurricane was something she didn't need on her present agenda.

James Ashley-Sinclair appeared, carrying a couple of canvas-backed suitcases. He didn't say much, neither did Stacy, and the cabdriver—after a couple of glances in the rearview mirror at the two of them—kept silent, too.

The traffic was getting heavier, and it took a while to get back into Boston to the garage where Stacy had left her car. It took even longer to get out of Boston, and by the time they were heading south on the Fitzgerald Expressway, one of thousands of cars doing the same thing, the skies were becoming dark and ominous and the wind definitely was picking up.

"We may be in for a brew," Stacy warned.

"A brew?" her companion questioned.

"The cabdriver said there's a hurricane coming up the coast. The Cape, especially, may feel some of the force of it."

"In that event, would you rather remain in town and go down to Kate's place tomorrow?" James Ashley-Sinclair suggested.

Stacy vetoed the suggestion. "I'd almost rather be lost at sea at this point than to attempt to turn around and drive back into Boston," she told him frankly.

She was attempting to give her full time and attention to the demanding driving, but the man at her side was snitching his share, regardless. She began to wish she hadn't been so quick to acquiesce to Kate's request that she pick him up in Boston and chauffeur him down to Devon. He could have rented a car and made the trek himself. Or he could have flown into the Hyannis airport on the Cape and Kate could have arranged for someone to meet him there. Or he could have taken the bus. There were a number of choices that—in her opinion—would have been better than this one.

Kate's plan had made sense, though, because Stacy had needed to be in Boston anyway, in connection with a few details to be handled at the Kate's Kloset in Copley Place. And her next stop, as Kate Clarendon's troubleshooter, was Kate's Cape Cod Kloset in Devon. So there had been no good reason not to go along with Kate's request.

Life was sometimes so strange—and extremely unpredictable. *Had it been a year ago I would have welcomed the chance to talk to James Ashley-Sinclair,* Stacy admitted silently. *But not now. I've worked my way through my emotional maze, solved my problems, put my marriage behind me, and I'm doing just fine.*

"I'd be glad to drive, if you like," James Ashley-Sinclair suddenly suggested.

"Is my driving making you nervous?"

"No, no, not at all. I rather thought it might be making *you* nervous," he suggested. "You were just mumbling to yourself."

"Oh," Stacy said, and hoped she hadn't mumbled anything audible.

"I was wondering..."

"Yes?"

"Well, I thought it might be a good idea to turn on the wireless and see if there's an up-to-date advisory. The radio, that is."

"I was able to translate," Stacy said rather nastily. Then wondered why she was behaving like this. Why should she feel she needed to hoist her defenses up and lock them into place? James Ashley-Sinclair was being polite, but certainly he wasn't displaying any particular interest in her. As a person, as a woman, that is.

Stacy was accustomed to faster reactions from men, whether she liked them or not. Yet she wasn't surprised by the psychologist's seeming indifference. He was internationally famous, after all. A celebrity. He was used to meeting a variety of women, many of them as famous—and glamorous—as he was himself.

Also, from what she'd observed at the Ritz, women in general evidently fawned over him, swamped him with their attentions, and she imagined a time must come when ego trips would pale and ennui would settle in where female attention was concerned. Still, anyone deserved some time off from work, and it occurred to her that—as a result of his fame—women and work must be pretty synonymous in Ashley-Sinclair's life.

Stacy turned on the radio and within seconds was hearing the latest storm advisory. The outer fringe of Helga was already drenching the New Jersey coast, and there was a hurricane watch in effect extending through Cape Cod and the islands of Nantucket and Martha's Vineyard.

"I wonder why meteorologists always sound so *delighted* when they have a potentially catastrophic spate of weather to talk about," she said, switching the radio off again.

"Bad news is always more fascinating than good news," James Ashley-Sinclair observed.

Stacy took her eyes off the road long enough to cast a skeptical glance in his direction. "You really think that?"

"I know that," he informed her calmly. "Human nature," he added.

He saw a slight scowl cross her lovely face and was aware that she wasn't too pleased with his response. But then she hadn't seemed especially pleased with him since their initial handshake at the Ritz.

He'd observed her standing in the doorway, making no secret about her amusement at the sight of him. Or more probably, he amended, at the sight of a lone male surrounded by a bevy of clamoring females.

He'd noticed how quickly she'd changed faces and regained composure as she'd come over to him. It had taken a moment to realize that she was Kate's representative. Although Kate had said she'd be sending someone to the Ritz to pick him up, he hadn't expected an emissary such as Stacy MacKenzie.

Ms. MacKenzie. She'd been emphatic about that.

James glanced at Stacy's ring finger, found that she was wearing a sapphire cluster ring that had little in common with a wedding band, and wondered if she were single, widowed or divorced. Although the lack of a wedding ring wasn't necessarily definitive, he somehow doubted she was married now, but he suspected she had been. In fact, if the vibes she'd been sending in his direction were any clear-cut indication, he suspected she wasn't especially fond of men. He would say that Stacy was in all likelihood one of those unfortunate young women who had been burned—perhaps badly burned—by an experience with a man and thus had no intention of getting near the flame again.

That was too bad—because she was quite lovely to look at and he had no doubt she'd be heaven to hold, delightful to kiss. The lyrics of a song popular long before his time flitted through James's mind.

He'd noted, as they'd crossed the Ritz ballroom together, that the top of her head came barely to his shoulder. As she'd gotten into the cab ahead of him, he'd had the opportunity to regard her nicely curved figure and very good legs.

She dressed conservatively. She was wearing a jacket and skirt of a dark blue material, but the severity of her white blouse was softened by a lace jabot at the throat.

She wore rather large pearl button earrings, her only jewelry except for the sapphire ring. And the stones in the ring, James also had noticed, almost exactly matched the deep, intense blue of her eyes. She had a creamy complexion, nice features and thick, shoulder-length dark brown hair, styled with a fringe of bangs straight across her forehead.

She looked like a successful American career woman, probably in her late twenties, James assessed. And he wondered why there was something about this picture, this definition of her, that didn't quite ring true. He also wondered why she seemed to have taken an automatic dislike to him, especially since she didn't even know him.

Probably it was because of the damn book. The book inevitably inspired very definite reactions in people once they knew he was its author, though—particularly where women were concerned—the reactions were usually quite the contrary of the one he was getting from Stacy MacKenzie.

James wished he'd had the chance to meet his cousin's emissary under other conditions—at a time and a place where he was incognito, and she could have gotten to know him without first having been blocked by a lot of preconceived notions.

He was becoming pretty damn sick and tired of suffering from an identity loss, and of being eclipsed by a celebrity whom he often didn't even recognize as being himself.

The rain started a few miles north of Plymouth. Soon it was coming down in a thin, steady drizzle. "A hurricane rain," Stacy observed.

"How does one tell the difference?" James inquired politely.

Stacy's glance was cynical. Then she admitted to herself that probably it was the smooth quality of his voice and that devastating British accent that made her think he was asking simply for the sake of politeness. Possibly, she conceded, he actually might be interested in New England weather. Certainly the subject, with all its vagaries, was famous enough.

"Hurricanes are warm weather storms and so the rain accompanying them tends to be tropical in quality," she said. "It comes down like a blanket, thin at first, dropping straight and steadily. Then it gets heavier. Meantime, the wind starts to rise."

"Judging from the way the treetops are swaying over in that field, I'd say the wind has risen," James commented.

"That's a mere breeze compared to what we're apt to have later," Stacy informed him. "I've never experienced a serious storm in New England, but I have in Florida."

"Again," he said, "are you sure you don't want to turn back?"

"No. We're well on the way. Another hour, hour and a half, and we'll be there. There'd be no point in stopping now. Anyway, Kate will be expecting us."

"You think Kate's already in Devon?"

"She should be. She intended to drive from New York yesterday. So, though she may have encountered some peripheral rain, the storm as such should have posed no problem to her."

"It'll be good to see her," James said, and fell silent.

The comment, slight though it was, raised questions in Stacy. Kate had never said a great deal about her illustrious cousin, and now she wondered how close the two of them were.

Kate was in her mid-forties, and Stacy estimated that James Ashley-Sinclair was probably in his late thirties. A difference in age of maybe six or seven years, not much more than that. But six or seven years could be quite a gap when people were young, really young, that is. Also, Kate's father had been American, and she had spent most of her growing-up time in the United States, going to England with her mother mainly on holidays as a schoolgirl. Chances were that back in those years James Ashley-Sinclair would have been no more than a bothersome little boy cousin Kate might have preferred to ignore as much as possible.

He was the son of Kate's aunt—Kate's mother's sister, who had married a man with a title. Stacy did know that much. Kate hadn't said too much about the title, but she had said that her uncle by marriage had died some time ago. If James had inherited the title, he evidently didn't use it. Not, at least, professionally.

"I just saw a sign indicating there's a restaurant of some sort at the next turnoff," he said suddenly. "Do you suppose we could pause for a bite of something and a cup of coffee?"

She looked at him curiously. "You sound as if you're hungry."

"I am," he confessed. "I had breakfast at seven, plus a toasted bun they for some reason call an English muffin."

"You skipped lunch?"

"Lunch skipped me," he said with a smile. "By the time I thought I had a chance to take a forkful of whatever it was, I was called upon to speak. I've come to discover that eating and speaking don't usually jibe, if one's the principal speaker."

"Very well," Stacy said reluctantly. She wasn't anxious to stop, even for coffee. Common sense warned her that the best option available was to get to the mainland end of the highway as quickly as it was possible to do so with safety, and then over one of the bridges that crossed the Cap Cod Canal. She was recalling Kate mentioning that during a hurricane's near miss a few years back, the bridges across the canal had been closed by the governor's order. Should that happen, she and James Ashley-Sinclair would find themselves stranded on the wrong side of the water until the storm passed, a situation she really didn't want to have to deal with.

She parked as close to the small restaurant as she could. Luckily she and James both had raincoats with them, which they'd tossed onto the back seat. They struggled into them, then made a dash for shelter.

Stacy impatiently drank half a cup of coffee while James polished off two cups of the same beverage plus a cheeseburger and a thick slab of chocolate fudge cake. Meanwhile, a glance through the restaurant window showed her that the weather was worsening.

"I think I'd better give Kate a call and tell her it may take a while longer for us to get to Devon," she said decisively.

"Not a bad idea," James agreed.

Stacy found a public phone in the corridor outside the rest rooms, inserted change and dialed Kate's Devon number. The phone rang, and kept ringing. Finally, on the tenth ring, she hung up and redialed, since there was always the possibility she'd missed a digit. But, again, the phone rang and rang, and there was no answer.

"Probably Kate's gone out to lay in some extra supplies because of the storm," Stacy reported to James.

"Let's get another weather bulletin," he suggested, and once they were back in the car, he switched on the radio.

The meteorologist sounded a bit on the glum side as he reported that Helga had changed course, was heading for the open sea and so posed no further threat to either the Rhode Island coast or adjoining Massachusetts, including Cape Cod.

Fifteen minutes later Stacy was saying, "You could never prove that by me," as she grappled with the steering wheel of a car being buffeted by a full-fledged gale.

She was tired, out of sorts, Devon was still another thirty miles away, and the afternoon was waning. Darkness wasn't that far off.

Kate, who spent every moment she could tear away from her career in her Cape Cod Hideaway, had spoken often about this peninsula surrounded by water, and now Stacy remembered one of Kate's geography lessons. The Cape had been formed thousands of years ago by glaciers pushing toward the sea. The main highway followed the length of the peninsula's spinal ridge, a leftover from the ancient glaciers, and so it made sense to think that they might be taking more punishment from the wind here than they would on a less-exposed road.

Accordingly Stacy swung off the highway at the next exit and drove to the bay side of the Cape, where she followed a twisting state road that was considerably more protected.

The driving was still difficult, but nevertheless she had more time to think, epecially since James Ashley-Sinclair appeared to be absorbed in his own thoughts at the moment.

She concentrated on her real reason for having come to the Cape. Not merely to meet up with Kate's cousin—and deliver him to Kate—but to act in her capacity as chief troubleshooter for Kate's company.

Kate Clarendon had opened her first Kloset eight years ago, in one of the smaller Westchester County suburbs. She'd offered chic that certainly wasn't cheap, but was still affordable. Unlike many boutique-type dress shops, she didn't concentrate solely on sizes three to seven. She offered a reasonable range of sizes, and styles that ran a fair age and type gamut. But her clothes were just avant-garde enough to be interesting and, as Kate herself liked to put it, as "contemporary as yesterday." "Yesterday," she always added when she said that, "tends to become ultrafashionable. If not today, certainly tomorrow."

The Klosets had multiplied and now could be found in "smart" areas across the country. A number of them were in resorts, but carefully chosen resorts with enough permanent residency so that the Klosets could stay open most of the year rather than for just a short season.

Stacy had gone to work for Kate five years ago as a secretary. Her marriage had been faltering, and getting a job had literally saved her sanity.

She and her employer had immediately taken to each other. Kate had discovered that she didn't have to spell things out to Stacy in order for Stacy to catch on to her unique merchandising philosophies and to help her augment them.

The change in position to Kate's assistant and "troubleshooter" had come about because of need. Frequently, as the shops multiplied, a matter in one of the Klosets would crop up that required careful attention and a quick, efficient solution. Kate, needed on one front, often was involved on another. Once, when confronted with two critical situations at the same time, she'd sent Stacy to handle one of them. Stacy had been so good at effecting a perfect compromise between management and employees that the next week Kate had installed her in a new office and then had hired a secretary for *her*.

Now, for the past three years, she had been Kate Clarendon's right-hand woman. Kate had no qualms about giving Stacy responsibility, and Stacy had lived up to the trust time and time again.

This time it was the Cape Cod Kloset Kate was concerned about, but when she'd brought the matter up, Stacy hadn't agreed with her.

Sales *were* down in Kate's Cape Cod Kloset. But they'd briefly plummeted last year in the Key West Kloset, and Kate hadn't panicked then. Resort areas were always tricky. Sales trends rolled with the seasons, reflecting the influx of people into a particular location at a particular time.

"If you'd only wait a little longer before we start investigating," Stacy had admonished as they'd sat sipping sherry in Kate's Fifth Avenue condo a few days earlier. "It's always slow right after Labor Day. But then the Cape, according to our records, has a terrific Indian summer. In fact, sales were great right through Thanksgiving last year. Then there was a really outstanding week at Christmas...."

"Something is wrong, Stacy," Kate had retorted decisively. "I know what you're saying. Nevertheless, we've never had a shop show a loss for a major part of an entire year, and that's what the Cape Cod Kloset seems headed for. I really want you to look into this."

Now, watching the driving rain tattoo the car windshield, Stacy wished Kate hadn't been so anxious. Then she could have been comfortable in either her Manhattan apartment or her Manhattan office this rainy afternoon, and Kate could have met her cousin at the Ritz herself!

It seemed an eternity till she came to the Devon town line. She pulled off to the side of the road, fished in her purse and dragged out the directions Kate had written down for her. She'd never been to the Hideaway before, and Kate had admitted it wasn't the easiest place to find.

At her side, James Ashley-Sinclair asked, "Where are we?"

"Devon," Stacy said.

"Near Kate's house?"

"That's what I'm trying to figure out." She was studying Kate's makeshift map as she spoke and wondering how much sense of direction Kate had when it came to putting specifics down on paper.

"Let me see," James suggested, and she held out the crumpled piece of paper.

"It would seem," she said after a moment, "that we find Main Street and take a right. Then we drive almost to the ocean, but not quite. Kate says if you come to the parking lot for the town beach, you'll know you've gone too far. That, she has put down, is no big problem. She says, 'Just turn back and start scanning sharply. The lane to my place veers off to the right—the left, if you're reversing—and there's a discreet sign tacked to a pine tree that says The Hideaway in small letters.'"

"Well," Stacy suggested, "suppose I find Main Street, and then you find the lane."

"Good enough," James agreed.

But it wasn't that easy. The rain was coming down in torrents, and it was difficult to see objects such as small signs. By the time she'd passed several dirt side roads, Stacy felt certain she'd missed Kate's turn. "Hold on," James said suddenly. "There's a square something tacked to that pine tree you just passed."

Traffic was light. Very light. No one with an atom of brains would be out in weather like this, Stacy thought bitterly. She backed up, James peered, then opened the car door, got out and sprinted through the rain.

"That's it," he announced, climbing back into the car again. "Just take a turn here, and we should be at Kate's place in a jiffy."

Looking at the sandy lane stretching before her, Stacy wasn't so sure. It plunged directly into a section of pinewoods and tumbled underbrush that looked as primeval as it must have when the Wampanoag Indians inhabited this part of Massachusetts . . . and just as unnavigable.

Chapter Two

The rain had created deep puddles in the lane, strung out in sequence among the ruts. Aquatic stepping stones, they were brimming over. Stacy knew it would be easy to become bogged down in any one of them. It was equally easy to imagine the hassle of trying to back out, once she'd gone very far.

To make matters worse, the lane was edged with overgrown bramble bushes, providing nature's version of a barbed wire fence. Stacy's car was next to new, and the idea of acquiring a tic-tac-toe pattern scratch was something she didn't relish.

"Kate *does* believe in seclusion, doesn't she?" James Ashley-Sinclair commented.

Stacy didn't answer him. She was watching the rain rivulets run down her windshield to form a deltalike pattern. She was wondering what sort of place Kate's Hideaway was going to be—a shack perched on the edge of a sand cliff, just big enough to be comfortable for one? Kate had never been too specific about her sanctuary.

Stacy gave thought to heading back into town and finding accommodations—preferably in separate lodging places—for herself and her companion, and then trying again to contact Kate. On the other hand, she'd come this far under highly trying circumstances. It seemed a better idea to continue, to leave Kate's cousin at the Hideaway, and then to retreat to a nice, modern motel room, complete with hot shower and color TV.

"Can't be much farther," she muttered aloud, as much to herself as to James Ashley-Sinclair. She carefully negotiated the turn in the lane and, immediately, the car hit a puddle. A geyser spurted over the hood, causing the engine to cough and nearly die out. But under her frantic urging the engine sputtered to life again, and they plunged forward so suddenly that Stacy heard a muttered groan from her companion. The muffled word that followed sounded suspiciously like an oath, and she suspected he may have banged a knee or a shin on something, if not his handsome head.

The lane twisted and turned as it crawled up and over a series of undulating, brush-covered dunes. Stacy was beginning to think she'd stumbled onto an ephemeral path to nowhere when this semblance of a road ended so abruptly she had to slam on the brakes to avoid plunging into what appeared to be a stone wall covered with a mass of wild roses.

This time there was no doubt about James Ashley-Sinclair's reaction. He swore audibly, then said more mildly, "I guess we've arrived."

"Possibly," Stacy conceded. She buttoned up her dusty rose raincoat—one of the latest additions to Kate's fall line—and pulled its hood up over her head. The raincoat was made of a fabric that was reportedly impervious to water, yet soft and pliable to the touch. Stacy hoped there was veracity to a claim she hadn't expected to be testing so stringently.

She opened the car door, faced the downpour and started to climb out. In the process her elbow banged the steering wheel and hit the horn, which let forth a blast that sounded like an indignant banshee let loose. The sound so startled her she nearly slipped into the mud lake at her feet. And probably would have had it not been for the strong hand that quickly gripped her arm.

"Well," James Ashley-Sinclair said, "I'd say the horn took care of any questioning spirits who might be lurking around. Now, how does one get into Kate's place?"

It was a good question. There was no signpost suggesting an entranceway. Stacy, with James still holding her arm, began to fumble her way along the wall, trying to find an opening.

James chuckled. "Rather like playing blindman's buff, isn't it?" he queried amiably.

Irritated, Stacy wished he wouldn't be so damned *cheerful* under circumstances she, personally, was finding very trying.

The wild roses that covered the wall were only beginning to fade. As Stacy inadvertently touched a pastel petal, a thorn pierced her finger. Her "Damn!" was fervent, and James pulled her to a halt.

"What is it?" he asked.

"Nothing. Just a rose thorn," she said, and tugged away from him.

She was sucking the sore spot on her finger when, seconds later, she found a narrow gap in the stones. Wriggling through it, she followed an uneven flagstone path to the front door, painted blue-gray and centered with a large brass knocker fashioned as a sailing ship. The door was almost buried under an arborlike arrangement of even more wild roses. The roses were blurs of pink through the heavy rain, and Stacy gave them a respectful berth as she lifted the knocker and let it thud.

Silencc rcigned.

After what seemed a very long moment, she lifted the knocker and let it bang again. Nothing happened. "I'd say it's fairly obvious no one's home," James said, finally. "Do you have a key?"

"Oh, God," Stacy moaned. "Kate was so sure she'd be here when we got here I don't think it ever occurred to her to give me a key. You don't happen to have one?"

"No."

Stacy looked up at Kate's cousin and saw the rain streaming off his hair, cascading down his face and, she suspected, infiltrating the gap between his neck and his turned-up coat collar. It was both annoying and disconcerting to also see that he looked as handsome and self-possessed as if it were broad daylight on a sunny day and he was casually strolling around Hyde Park, or some other London landmark.

"Hold on," he instructed. "Try to huddle in the doorway if you can. I grant it's not very wide. I'll see if I can find a way to get in."

With that, James Ashley-Sinclair started off and in a moment was lost from sight.

Stacy tried to huddle, but Kate's doorway was, indeed narrow and offered very little in the way of protection. Wet and miserable, she was thinking about trying to find a way to get into the house herself when the front door opened so suddenly that she pitched into James's arms.

Again quick reaction time on his part kept her upright and—only because she was tired and her nerves were frazzled, she told herself—it actually felt good to be held by him. For a telltale moment she didn't mind depending on his strength, even though she was aware there was a quality to that strength—warm, insidious and very sensual—that could become too heady too easily.

James broke what Stacy was beginning to realize was becoming more of an embrace than a support measure. "Give me your macintosh and I'll put it somewhere to dry," he suggested.

She handed him the dusty rose raincoat. He had shrugged off his own raincoat, and held both dripping garments at arm's length. Watching him, Stacy asked, "How did you manage to get in here? Did you have to break a window or something?"

"No," he said. "The back door was unlocked. A typical Kate move, I'd say. I'm sure she doesn't run her Klosets the way she runs her life, but..." He broke off and laughed. "I'm afraid I may be telling tales out of school. Why don't you investigate and see if by any chance Kate has a fireplace?" he added, nodding toward a door opening off the foyer.

Stacy moved through the indicated door and immediately found herself in one of the most charming rooms she had ever seen. Large and almost square, Kate's living room had a low, beamed ceiling and wainscoting that came up halfway around the walls. The wainscoting was painted a warm apricot tone, while the walls were off-white. There were couches and chairs upholstered in deep ivory, handsome antique maple furniture, and paintings and bric-a-brac all of which looked choice. And Kate definitely had a fireplace. It was a focal point, centered against a long wall and framed by low bookcases on either side.

Kate's Hideaway most definitely wasn't a shack.

Stacy moved to the fireplace, and was gratified to see that there was a supply of logs stacked neatly in a black iron carrier. Nearby were some rolled up newspapers and, on one of the closest bookshelves, a box of long matches.

She piled logs into the fireplace, stuck a few newspapers here and there, touched matches to the newspapers, then sat back and waited for a warmth to come that would seep through her damp, chilled bones and make her feel human again.

Instead, black smoke belched forth into the room.

"You're not a country girl, are you?" James Ashley-Sinclair observed from behind her. "One opens the damper first, Stacy," he instructed, suiting action to the words. "Also, a bit of kindling's needed if you're to get a good blaze going. Here, let me."

Stacy moved aside and let him take over, surprised at the impact his easy use of her first name had on her. As he busied himself rearranging the logs and, finally, getting a good fire crackling, she studied the back of his well-shaped head...and even better-shaped body. He was broad-shouldered, narrow-waisted, and she already knew about his muscles from having been held in his arms.

He handled himself well, without the awkwardness of some tall men. There was a competence about the way he moved, the way his hands worked building the fire. He was strong, self-assured. Also, he was surprising her, though she couldn't put a "why" into precise words. Maybe it was that smooth British manner she'd seen demonstrated so vividly on television in London last fall that had made her think James Ashley-Sinclair would be a rather diffident individual. He hadn't seemed the type to want to soil his hands with such menial tasks as making a fire.

He got to his feet, and Stacy suddenly was aware of cool gray eyes studying her a shade too intently. But his conversation remained on the level. "I saw no sign of another car when I went around to the back of the house. And I rather doubt Kate would still be uptown shopping."

"What are you saying?"

"I'm inclined to think Kate never made it to the Cape."

"That's impossible," Stacy protested.

"Why? The storm may have been worse in New York. God knows the driving was bad enough as it was. Kate may have decided to exercise a little caution and to wait for better weather."

He let that register before continuing. "Why don't you try to call her again? There's a phone in the kitchen."

Stacy dialed Kate's home number in Manhattan. There was no answer. She glanced at her watch and verified that it was too late to reach anyone at the main office of Kate's Klosets, Ltd. Frustrated, she mumbled, "I don't understand this."

She had thought she was alone in the room and was startled by James's voice. "Well, possibly she put in somewhere because of the rain and she'll either be coming along shortly or she'll call us," he said.

Us. It suddenly struck Stacy that—with Kate absent from the scene—this was becoming a very "us" situation.

She saw James foraging through cupboards, and after a moment he triumphantly brought forth a bottle of Scotch.

"Ah," he said, "just what we need to take the chill off." He searched for glasses, found two, and poured out amber liquid. Then he crossed the kitchen and handed one of the glasses to Stacy. "Cheers," he said, clicking his glass to hers.

"Cheers," she responded rather weakly, and welcomed the whisky's fire as it trickled down her throat. James, she noted, had taken his wet shoes off and was going around barefoot. He had also divested himself of his jacket and discarded his necktie. Though he looked slightly rumpled, there was still that autocratic air about him that she found both fascinating and annoying. He seemed so totally in command, so very much at ease. She wished she could emulate him.

As it was, she was tense, her nerves were shrieking, and she was praying to God that Kate would suddenly burst through the kitchen door. Being alone with James Ashley-Sinclair was putting her on edge, and she wondered why she was reacting to him like this? Because he was the most attractive man she'd been around for a long, long time? Or was it because he had written that damn book, *A Personal Sex Bible*, giving people everywhere—women especially—the conviction that he knew all there was to know about what was, after all, one of life's most basic subjects.

Thinking about his book made her uncomfortable. It was disconcerting to contemplate being stranded in a Cape Cod cottage with a man who would know exactly how you ticked without knowing *you* at all. It made her feel rather ill to suspect that James must be expertly acquainted with every atom in a woman's body, to say nothing of her mind, and the intricate way her emotions worked. And that went for women as a species. Any and every woman. Every vein, every pore, every susceptible bit of flesh, every secret place...

She clamped a lid on her thoughts and took another hefty sip of Scotch.

James, she saw, was again foraging through the cupboards. "Kate keeps a reasonably good supply of tinned goods," he announced. "We won't go hungry tonight at least."

He moved toward the refrigerator. "We're lucky that everything's on and in working order," he observed. "There's ice, should you want it. I've never seen an American who can survive too long without ice. Also, some rolls and such in the freezer. Hungry?"

"No," Stacy managed.

"Well, then, why don't we wait a bit before we make some major decisions about what to have for our supper? You're shivering. Why don't you take off those wet shoes and come dry out in front of the fire?"

It was a logical suggestion. Also, it was stupid to think there could be anything erotic about squishing your feet out of your shoes and pattering along to the fireside behind a tall, handsome Englishman who might be fun to be marooned with—if he weren't an internationally acclaimed authority in a field she scrupulously wished to avoid.

She stretched out before the fire in one armchair, and James did the same in its counterpart. A round piecrust table stood between them. He'd added a couple of logs to the fire, and it blazed beautifully, the flames sending out a lovely orange-gold warmth.

"I gathered from Kate," he said suddenly, "that you had an appointment here on the Cape. That is to say, you didn't drive down here just for the sake of transporting me."

"Kate wanted me to touch bases with her shops both here and in Boston," Stacy admitted. "I saw the Boston people this morning, I plan to look in on Kate's Cape Cod Kloset tomorrow."

"And then?"

"Well, I hope I'll be able to start back to New York by early afternoon."

"So soon?"

"There's no reason to stay longer unless a real problem develops at the Cape Cod Kloset, and I don't anticipate that."

"Kate," Kate's cousin said, "calls you her trouble-shooter."

"Yes, I know. That's primarily what I do. The more stores Kate opens, the more problems crop up from time to time. There's a kind of ratio to it."

"Yes, I can imagine," he agreed. "Rather amazing, isn't it, the success Kate's had with her shops?"

"Not necessarily," Stacy said. "Kate's very astute when it comes to merchandising. She has an uncanny sense of timing, too. She's always a pulse beat ahead of the market, knows what people are going to want even before they know themselves. Also, the clothes she offers are good, fairly priced, excellent values."

"You should be doing her public relations for her," James Ashley-Sinclair observed rather dryly.

"I've no time for that," Stacy answered promptly. "Anyway she has an excellent agency to handle her PR."

James rose. "I should have brought the bottle in here with me," he said. "May I refill your glass?"

Stacy was still toying with her Scotch. "No, thank you," she said. She was remembering that she had eaten very little that day, and although she wasn't consciously hungry, the last thing she wanted was to get into an alcoholic haze with this man around.

When he came back, this time bringing the bottle with him, she decided it was time to switch the tables and to focus some of the conversation on him. Smoothly—she hoped—she asked, "Will you be staying on the Cape long?"

To her surprise, James Ashley-Sinclair seemed slightly disconcerted by her question. "I don't know," he confessed. "The lecture today was the last in my current tour, for which I'm thankful." There was a dangerously disarming quality to his slight smile. "I don't think I was ever cut out for life on a podium," he admitted.

"What makes you say that?"

"I don't like pontificating, for one thing," he said to her surprise. "Also, I don't like standing up and speaking in front of a lot of people. I'm a psychologist, not an actor, and I've come to think there has to be a fair touch of the thespian in a good speaker."

"From what I've heard," Kate couldn't resist saying, "I would gather you're a very good speaker. Also I..." She broke off, not wanting to go any farther.

She soon saw that James wasn't about to offer her an easy escape route. "Yes?" he encouraged.

"Well," Stacy admitted uncomfortably, "I saw you on television in London last fall."

"You were in London last fall?"

"Yes."

"Did Kate know that?"

"Of course. I was in London on business for her."

"I'll be damned," James said. "I wonder why she didn't tell me?"

"She knew I was...pretty much in a mood to be alone," Stacy said. She added hastily, "That's to say...I really didn't want to see anyone, meet anyone."

"Why?" he asked bluntly.

Was he always so direct? "My marriage was breaking up," she said hesitantly.

"I see." He paused, then asked, "And did it break up?"

"Yes."

"You're now divorced?"

"Yes." Stacy flinched slightly as she said that, because divorce was a word she'd always hated. Her parents had divorced when she was sixteen, and the resulting trauma for both her and her sister had been intense. She'd been so determined to make a success of marriage when her time came, but it hadn't worked that way. It took two, she knew now. Two people who loved each other enough to work their way through the multiple difficulties of joining forces and trying to make a life together. And she doubted there was a marriage in the world free of such difficulties. Triumph came when one surmounted the obstacles, went past them.

So-called love, when compounded largely of sexual attraction, could be very blinding. That had been her problem. She'd fancied herself madly in love with Paul Delacorte whom she'd met when she was taking a journalism course in college and he'd come to give a lecture on "The Media and the Public." She'd been so fascinated by the man, a highly successful journalist himself, that she didn't remember a word he'd said. Later they'd sat next to each other at a dinner given in his honor, Stacy having drawn that coveted privilege because she was editor of the college magazine. And that had been the beginning of a romance that flared beautifully, then eventually died in a fizzle, leaving little more than a heap of ashes behind it.

There hadn't even been many of the ashes left by the time she'd flown to the Virgin Islands last June and acquired her divorce. Then she'd stayed on for a while on Saint John, needing to begin cementing together the allegorical pieces of herself, a self that had been badly shattered over the seven years of her unsuccessful marriage. Only then had she returned to New York, and to her office at Kate's Klosets, Ltd.

Remembering this, she also remembered that she had been trying to turn the tables on James Ashley-Sinclair, where questions were concerned, with little success thus far. "Did what you were saying a few minutes ago—about not liking public speaking that is—mean that you're not going on any more lecture tours?" she asked.

"I don't know what I'm going to do," he confessed. "I don't have any more lecture tours, per se, on my agenda, though I do have a lecture to give in New York in early November before I go back to England. But that gives me over a month of what should be freedom. Right now I need a quiet place in which I can think and work," he admitted. "It's come to the point where there's such pressure in England that it's very difficult for me to work there any longer.

"Anyway," he continued, "I appealed to Kate. She suggested the Hideaway, since she said she wouldn't be using it herself for a while. Kate's assured me I'll have privacy here. Which is what I need desperately if I'm to accomplish the work I need to accomplish within the next fortnight or so."

"Work?"

He nodded. "Writing, as a matter of fact. Unfortunately—or so I feel at this point—I've gotten myself into some contractual obligations that must be fulfilled. Which means I now need to put a considerable amount of material into some sort of order, and to clarify my thoughts on a number of matters, as well."

He stood up again as he said that, and his tall figure became silhouetted by the flickering firelight. "If you'll excuse me," he said, "I have to make a quick call to London. I'll only be a few minutes. Then we can investigate the larder again and decide what we'll have to eat."

Stacy sat for a while in front of the fire after James left the room. As the flames started to dwindle, she wondered who Kate's handsome cousin was calling in London. Whoever it was, he was taking his good time about talking to them. The minutes ticked away. The last of the flames vanished, leaving charred logs and glowing embers.

Restless, she got to her feet and wandered around the room. Kate's collection of decorative items was impressive. Two brass candlesticks, obviously antique, flanked either side of the mantel. A satin glass vase on an end table picked up the apricot tone of the wainscoting. There was an old pine cranberry scoop, a Pairpoint paperweight, and tossed casually on a coffee table, Dr. Ashley-Sinclair's famous tome.

Stacy turned to the flyleaf. He'd written a dedication in a free-flowing hand. "To my favorite cousin, Kate...who has long known all my follies and foibles. May she forever keep them secret! Love, James."

His follies and foibles?

Stacy continued her pilgrimage across the room to the windows at its far end, concealed by floor-to-ceiling, nubby silk, sand-colored drapes. Tugging aside a corner of the drapes, she peeked out a view so spectacular that she automatically reached for the pull rope and yanked the curtains completely open.

There was just enough light to see the Atlantic pounding furiously below the steep, sandy cliff atop which the house was built. Through the driving rain the ocean was majestic in its fury, the wind whipping the waves to a mountainous froth. Stacy spied a sodden path that led from the rear of the house to the cliff top, and saw the edge of a wooden stair rail poking up. That must mean there were steps leading down to the beach.

For a sudden, oddly exhilarating moment she was tempted to dash out of the house and challenge the wind and rain. She could imagine descending the steps to stand at the water's edge, being buffeted by the force of the storm, the cold salt spray from the churning waves stinging her face. She threw back her head, imagining the wind blowing her hair....

James Ashley-Sinclair, just entering the room, saw her and stopped. She was an appealing figure, standing like that, as if prepared to meet some very special challenge head-on.

As they had talked in front of the fire, he had sensed a repression about Stacy and wondered whether he was the cause of it or if she was like that with all men. Chances were she was gun-shy because of an unhappy marriage and a divorce she may not have wanted. In which case she automatically would have lumped him with all the other males in the world. On the other hand, he had a strong feeling that the effect he was having on Stacy MacKenzie was personal—and might be quite different if it weren't for his book.

He wished the chance might arise for him to talk to her about the book. He found himself wanting to tell her how it had changed his life in many ways he didn't welcome. Fame had its rewards, he wasn't denying that, and it was easy for even the most modest of men to become affected by a continuing series of ego trips. But there were also times when fame—his kind of fame, anyway—was a millstone around his neck. And, he thought ruefully, Stacy MacKenzie just might let him drown before she took pity on him and attempted to discover the real James Ashley-Sinclair under the layers of papier-mâché publicity.

Again he wished they could have met "incognito." Again he wondered why Kate hadn't told him Stacy would be in London last fall, so he could have rung her up wherever she was staying. He could have said, "Hello there, my name is James. I'm a cousin of Kate Clarendon's, and she said you were going to be in town for a few days...."

But then, he reminded himself, she probably already would have seen him on the blasted telly.

He moved, and a floorboard creaked. Instantly Stacy swung around to face him.

"I opened up a couple of tins of soup and put the contents on to heat, and I popped some rolls into the oven," he said. "Why not come along to the kitchen? It's quite cosy out there now."

Stacy took a good look at the kitchen, this time around. It was pine-paneled and heated by a wood stove, which James had going, and which threw out a surprising amount of warmth. There was a lovely old pine table in the center of the floor, flanked by four almost-matching chairs. There was a hand-braided rug under the table and a rocker in the corner. Copper utensils hung from the wall. The spice rack was well stocked. The total effect was perfect.

She became aware of an aroma filtering through the air and, with a slightly lifted eyebrow, queried, "Is that coffee? I would have thought you'd be making tea."

"You prefer tea?"

"No, but I thought you would."

"Because I'm English?" He looked slightly annoyed. "Matter of fact," he informed her, "I detest tea."

He handed her a mug of hot, strong coffee and, with a growing sense of unreality, Stacy stirred cream and sugar into it as she watched the world's foremost authority on sexual relationships ladle soup into two china bowls.

"I checked out the accommodations," he informed her as they ate.

It dawned on her that unless Kate suddenly appeared on the scene, she was going to be spending tonight here alone with this man.

"Oh," she managed.

"There are three bedrooms upstairs," he said, "plus a full bath. There's also a WC—a toilet and sink, that is—just off the foyer. I'd rather like to shower before I call it a night. After that you can consider the upstairs bath as your own, should you want to soak in a hot tub for a while. You might like the bedroom nearest the stairs. It's the warmest. All right?"

"All right," she nodded. Then asked, "What about Kate? Do you know which room is hers?"

"No, but it doesn't really matter. After I spoke to London, I checked with a friend of Kate's in New York whom I felt might know her whereabouts. It seems that Kate tried to reach you in Boston from the airport—Kennedy airport, that is—but failed."

"What was Kate doing at Kennedy?"

"She was on her way to Miami."

"Miami?"

James nodded. "Her friend said that a designer from Madrid she's been wanting to meet with phoned her and said he'd be in Miami for a few days visiting a sister."

"Carlos Monteros de los Molinos?"

"Sounds right."

"He's the hottest designer in Europe," Stacy said. "Kate has been *praying* she could get to him so that he'd give her an exclusive on the distribution of his clothes in the States."

"Well, evidently he contacted her and wanted to see her, and there was a limited time slot involved, so she agreed to make the flight south," Kate's cousin reported imperturbably. "I'm sure this must have been enormously important to Kate, as you suggest, or she would have been here as she said. Probably she viewed it as only a slight delay in her overall plan. But, in any event..." James Ashley-Sinclair smiled his most disarming smile. "That rather leaves just the two of us, doesn't it?"

Chapter Three

Stacy drove the length of Seafarer's Way—one of Devon's two major shopping streets—then reversed directions and went all the way back to Main Street. In doing so she passed Kate's Kloset twice.

Perturbed, she drove out of the center of town, following signs to Snow Harbor on Cape Cod Bay. On this late September morning the parking lot was almost deserted. Stacy had her choice of spaces, and selected a spot next to a pier. The digital clock on the car's dashboard showed that it was four minutes before ten. Ten o'clock on a weekday morning and Kate's Kloset still wasn't open for business.

It was a bright and sunny morning. Hurricane Helga was already becoming a memory to coastal New England, having finally exhausted her fury far out in the Atlantic. Stacy watched sea gulls soar overhead, then focused on a trawler making its way through the narrow channel that led to the bay.

She vented a troubled sigh. She was beginning to get a gut feeling that there might be some real trouble involved at the shop, after all. Obviously Kate had already had that feeling, or she wouldn't have been so insistent about this trip.

Stacy had never doubted her employer's astuteness. Kate was both clever and sharp. Still, she wished that Kate, just this one time, had been wrong. If she ran into a can of worms here, it would mean staying on in Devon until she could effect some kind of a resolution.

Ordinarily that wouldn't have presented a problem. But the thought of sharing the Hideaway with James Ashley-Sinclair for more than a minimal length of time was disquieting, if not out of the question entirely. He'd come here, after all, because he both wanted and needed privacy so that he could accomplish some important work. Yet, if she *did* have to stay on for a few days, she was sure he'd politely disclaim the suggestion her presence might be a nuisance to him and would protest her moving to a motel or an inn.

She had no illusions that he'd *want* her to stay around. Rather, she felt certain that it would be a question of his suffering her presence, because he knew she played an important role in his favorite cousin's life.

Stacy watched a formation of Canada geese fly past and thought about last night. If—even subconciously—she'd expected James Ashley-Sinclair to become flirtatious and bothersome, she'd only been flattering herself, she admitted wryly. She'd discovered—almost as much to her chagrin as to her relief—that she might as well have been sharing living quarters with a brother.

Certainly her feelings about their situation and those of Kate's distinguished relative hadn't been on the same wavelength when it came time to go to bed. He had been friendly but cool. She, on the other hand, had suddenly realized he'd be sleeping just down the hall from her, and that knowledge had hit her with all the force of a sledge-hammer.

Previously they'd shared a soup-and-rolls supper, topped off with slices of a frozen apple pie James had found in Kate's freezer and promptly insisted upon baking. They'd also shared the cleanup stint, then had watched the news on TV, after which they had yawned together over a popular mystery program.

By the time the program was over, the idea of spending the night in the same house with this man was making Stacy squirm. She was relieved when James excused himself to go take his shower.

He came back downstairs wearing pajamas and a blue wool bathrobe, casually belted. His hair was damp, he looked fresh and squeaky clean, and Stacy—to her distress—felt something twist around inside her like a tight rubber band. She tried to tell herself that maybe it was indigestion, but she recognized that as self-deception of the sorriest kind. What she was feeling was simply, desire... something she hadn't felt for a long, long time.

When James suggested a nightcap, she stammered her refusal and allowed she thought she'd better turn in.

"You do look tired," he agreed calmly. "This has been a long day for you. Well, then, good night. I'll be watching the telly a while longer if you need anything."

Stacy beat a hasty retreat, took a quick shower instead of the leisurely bath her companion had suggested earlier, then slipped on her nightgown and snuggled under the covers of Kate's four-poster bed, pulling the blankets right up to her chin.

She was aware of the faint noise of the television set coming from downstairs. She was even more aware of the man who must be sitting in front of it. She still couldn't understand her out-of-character reaction to him, and was annoyed at herself for being attracted to him—especially when it was easy to see that he had no personal interest in her whatsoever. Professional interest maybe—from what she'd read about James Ashley-Sinclair, and what she'd observed of him with his admirers at the Ritz today, Stacy felt sure that women automatically became professional fodder to him, subjects of clinical interest. But personally James—though polite, even friendly—also maintained a certain aloofness, a *separateness*, that she was beginning to think must be a basic part of his character.

It was just as well, she told herself. The world in which he moved and the world in which she moved might as well have been two different universes. Suppose some vibes *had* been ignited between the two of them. She'd be in danger of becoming just one more case history to him, but she didn't need that.

What she was feeling about him, Stacy told herself firmly, was simply a fascination because he was so out of her league. The forbidden fruit syndrome. In this case, fortunately for her, there seemed very little chance that she was going to be tempted to sample that fruit.

This morning she hadn't seen James at all, though the fresh pot of coffee on the stove was evidence that he was up and around somewhere. As she drank two cups of his brew before heading off to town, Stacy had wondered where he might be at such an early hour. Then she brushed her speculations aside to concentrate on the task at hand.

Now, looking out over Cape Cod Bay, she warned herself she mustn't be too hard on Colleen Reynolds until all the facts were in. She had met Mrs. Reynolds briefly several months ago when the Cape Kloset manager had visited New York for a conference with Kate. She remembered her as an attractive, pleasant and efficient woman, and she'd certainly done very well with the shop until this past season.

The shop, of course, *should* have been opened at nine o'clock sharp. That was the rule for all of Kate's Klosets, wherever their location. Kate didn't impose many rules—preferring to leave individual guidelines to the local women she hired as managers. But she expected those she did impose to be followed. So it was strange to think that Colleen Reynolds would be so lax, even though the "high season," as such, was over till another year. Still, Mrs. Reynolds herself had made it plain that more and more people were coming to the Cape each year in the off-season, and the resident population was constantly expanding. There were always potential customers to be serviced. So...

Stop jumping to conclusions! Stacy chided herself.

A short while later she drove back to Seafarer's Way and parked near the shop. The moment she approached the entrance, she knew something was decidedly wrong.

"Drab," she muttered under her breath... and Kate's Klosets were *never* drab. Here, though, the window displays lacked the sparkling original verve that was a company trademark. A two-piece, coffee-toned knit wool dress sagged in a corner. The outfit was basically chic, Stacy noted with a frown, but the way the dress was displayed made it look droopy. A plaid suit in the opposite corner fared no better. Then there was a season-spanning coat that was right with the fashion but lost its appeal because of the way the fabric was bunched together. A lovely skirt, matched with a blouse of entirely the wrong color, a poorly placed grouping of accessories . . .

Stacy analyzed the window displays item by item, and before she was even half finished she knew that Kate Clarendon would be furious were she to see this for herself. It was just as well Kate had taken off for Miami!

Inside, the story was the same. Surveying the merchandise, Stacy wondered what could have gone wrong. How could the same clothes that stood out so terrifically in other settings appear so dowdy here?

The visual impact of merchandise was a combination of display, arrangement and lighting, carried out with liberal dashes of imagination. Also, there was a decided joy in working with beautiful clothes and accessories, and it showed in display results. But joy was an ingredient completely lacking on these particular premises. And where was the music that was supposed to greet customers as they entered and relax them as they browsed?

At that moment the music came on. Or, rather, a dominating sound was heard, the blare of a local pop radio station, not the light classical tapes that Kate provided for the morning hours.

Stacy was beginning to stew despite herself. But the sight of the woman approaching her arrested her anger.

Colleen Reynolds was considerably thinner than Stacy remembered her being last winter in New York. And in place of the engaging smile Stacy recalled, there was a harried frown. The shadows under Mrs. Reynolds's large brown eyes testified to a lack of sleep, and the creases that lined her brow seemed engraved there.

She was wearing a loose-fitting taupe dress that did nothing for her figure or coloring. In fact, it was difficult to imagine that the garment had come from Kate's stock—

though salespersons were urged to wear the fashions they were selling.

As the manager confronted Stacy, there was a questioning expression on her face. Stacy knew the other woman recognized her but couldn't place her. She thrust out her hand. "Hello, Mrs. Reynolds. I'm Stacy MacKenzie. We met at Kate's office in New York," she said, smiling brightly.

Alarm showed briefly on Colleen Reynolds's face. Then she mustered a weak smile and said, "Well, hello, Ms. MacKenzie. What brings you to Devon?"

Was there apprehension in the question? Or, Stacy asked herself, was she being overimaginative? "I had to be in Boston on business, so Kate suggested I come down and vacation at her Hideaway for a couple of days," she fibbed.

"How nice," Colleen Reynolds said, but the tightness in her voice alerted Stacy to the fact that this unexpected visit was anything but nice for her. "Come back to my office, won't you?" she added. "I have a pot of coffee brewing."

On their way through the store Stacy observed that there was only one saleslady in evidence—a middle-aged woman who looked pleasant enough, but very definitely wasn't wearing Kate's Kloset clothes.

Colleen Reynolds's small office in the rear of the shop looked as if Hurricane Helga had paid it a personal visit. There were papers and folders and boxes of clothing—both opened and unopened—strewn everywhere.

"I'm sorry about this mess," Colleen apologized as she cleared off a seat for Stacy. "I'm right in the middle of working up my report for New York, and doing inventory, and . . . well, there's no end to the paperwork." She found two coffee mugs and asked, "Do you take cream or sugar?"

"Thanks, black will be fine."

Stacy took the mug Colleen offered her, sipped quickly, then sat back. After two cups of James Ashley-Sinclair's potent brew, she hardly needed any more caffeine. Her nerves were already protesting.

Colleen's chair squeaked as she sat down behind the disaster on her desk. Funny... the sound seemed to sum up everything wrong with the store. The running mechanism that usually functioned so smoothly in all of Kate's Klosets had somehow run out of oil in Devon.

Damn! Stacy cursed silently. *Why did I have to walk in on what threatens to be a real mess?*

Silence filled the space between the two women for an awkward moment. Then Colleen, making an obvious effort to be polite, asked, "When did you arrive in town?"

"Last night," Stacy replied.

"You drove down from Boston in all that rain?"

"Yes. It wasn't raining that much when I started out. I admit, though, I'm glad Helga didn't come any closer."

Colleen nodded absently. For a few minutes they chatted about safe subjects such as the weather. Then Colleen's question came suddenly. "How long do you plan to stay?"

"I'm not sure," Stacy murmured evasively. "That depends on a couple of things."

"Well... perhaps we might have dinner one evening, if you're free."

The suggestion wasn't made ungraciously, but Stacy had no doubt that Colleen Reynolds had made it out of politeness and hoped to hear a negative reply.

"How about dinner tomorrow night?" she suggested.

There was no immediate answer to the question, and Stacy began to feel as if she were watching someone else's mental wheels turning. Colleen Reynolds seemed about to say something, evidently thought better of it, and finally said, "That would be fine."

Stacy stood. Colleen trailed after her to the door of the shop. Two customers came in and started to browse. The saleslady maintained a discreet distance, which wasn't the Kate's Kloset way. One always offered assistance to a customer, *then* let that customer browse, if that's what was wanted. There was a difference between being helpful to a customer and becoming a pest, and Kate's employees were well schooled in recognizing that difference.

At the door Stacy asked lightly, "How's business this time of year?"

"Quite good," Colleen Reynolds said quickly, but she sounded more defensive than confident. "Things always slow down for a while after Labor Day, of course."

Stacy nodded. "Yes. Well . . . thanks for the coffee, and I'll be in touch tomorrow."

She felt certain, as she walked back to her car, that the store manager's eyes were following her every step of the way. As she drove back across town toward the beach road and Kate's Hideaway, she wondered if maybe she'd hedged too much. She didn't think so. Her off-the-cuff analysis was that Colleen Reynolds was a nervous, frightened woman. Whether her problems were caused by difficulties with the shop, or whether they stemmed from something else entirely, remained to be seen.

Clearly more time was needed. Time in which to get a grip on the situation while at the same time managing to establish a rapport with the store manager so that the woman would feel she could bring her problems out into the open without necessarily jeopardizing her job.

Why did something like this have to come up now of all times? Stacy groaned as she turned onto the lane that led to Kate's Hideaway and jounced over the potholes.

Driving the lane, at least, was a lot easier today than it had been yesterday. The transition in the weather was really astonishing. Yesterday it had been pouring, the wind had been howling, there had been a hurricane just off the coast. But today was sunny and beautiful. The sky looked like freshly washed blue silk decorated with fleecy cotton puffs. The spikes of goldenrod along the lane were as bright as freshly minted gold, and the air was vintage New England.

The gap in the stone wall was clearly visible today, and Stacy was tempted to pick some of the wild roses, then remembered their thorns. She let herself into the house, encountering a quiet that made her feel sure James Ashley-Sinclair wasn't around, and that knowledge gave her an unexpected sense of loss.

She went into the living room, searching for signs of his occupancy, and saw a sweater tossed on a chair. Probably he'd gone for a walk on the beach, or maybe a run. Perhaps he was one of those individuals who had to get in a daily jog.

She wondered if he'd be back for lunch, and thinking about lunch made her realize she'd yet to eat anything today. She headed for the kitchen, suddenly hungry, and decided it was her turn to raid Kate's larder, and maybe rustle up some food for James, as well.

Questions about Kate's fascinating cousin arose again, and she was absorbed in thinking about them as, nearing the kitchen door, she suddenly heard the sound of running water. On the threshold she came to an abrupt halt. James—clad only in a thick terry robe—was standing at the kitchen sink, his right hand plunged under the water tap, and even from this distance Stacy could see that the water was running red!

Her heart pounded as she spanned the distance between them. "My God," she rasped, "what have you done to yourself?"

"Cut my finger," he informed her, using a tone one might use with a child who wasn't overly bright. "I'm trying to get the blasted thing to stop bleeding."

"I'd say that's more than a casual cut," Stacy observed, peering at it. "You've gashed yourself."

"Call it what you will," James muttered. "Now that you're here, fetch a towel, will you?"

Stacy found a clean dish towel in a kitchen drawer and handed it to him. He quickly wrapped the cloth around his hand but, even so, a telltale red stain rapidly began to seep through.

"You're going to need stitches," Stacy diagnosed.

He glared at her. "The hell I am!"

"James, don't be an idiot."

"I'm not an idiot. It's only a stupid cut, damn it. Pour me a shot of whisky like a good girl, will you?"

It was Stacy's turn to glare. "Stop patronizing me!" she snapped, and then stood stock-still, not quite believing she'd spoken to him like that. But years of having her ex-husband talk down to her had taken a toll. In London a year ago, she had made up her mind to end her marriage, and she had sworn to herself she'd never again let a man take a superior tone with her.

"It wasn't my intention to patronize you," James said stiffly.

"Okay," she said. She handed him a second clean dish towel, then added, "I'm not going to give you any whisky. Liquor might have an effect on any medication they may give you."

"*Who* may give me?"

Stacy was already at the phone, checking the directory for the local police number. Dialing, she asked for information about local medical facilities and was directed to a clinic in the center of town. With that, she turned to James and said, "Let's get going."

She noted that he was a couple of shades paler than he was ordinarily, and his lips were compressed into a tight line. She had no doubt that the gash was hurting like hell. She also had no doubt that James Ashley-Sinclair was about to prove he could be extremely stubborn.

She gave him a long look, then nodded. "All right," she said. "I'll see what I can do about finding a physician who makes house calls."

"Don't be ridiculous," he stated loftily.

"That," Stacy said, "is your right hand you've damaged, if that fact hasn't already dawned on you."

"So?"

"Don't you write with your right hand?"

"That's beside the point."

The red stain was growing. "James," Stacy said, beginning to be honestly worried about him, "there's no need for a display of machismo."

"The last thing in the world that interests me, Stacy, is putting on a display of machismo."

"Well, then, it's no sign of weakness to seek medical help."

"Don't you think I know that?"

"Then why are you being so pigheaded?"

To her surprise, he chuckled. "I have to admit that some Americanisms are apt," he conceded. "Okay, if you must, lead me to your slaughterhouse."

She scowled as she surveyed him. "I don't think that's very funny."

"Funny or not, I can't stop the bleeding, so I admit the cut needs some attention. Give me a chance to put on some jeans and a shirt and I'll go willingly."

The third towel was blood-soaked by the time they reached the clinic, and one look at it gained James immediate admission to the emergency treatment room. Before Stacy could say more than a word or two, the patient had identified himself only as James Ashley.

His idea of incognito, she thought with a smile.

With James out of sight, Stacy settled down on a couch in the small reception area and discovered that her knees were shaking. She'd never been too great at dealing with accidents. The sight of blood had always upset her, and the sight of James's blood had upset her more than she liked to admit.

Time passed. She flipped through the pages of a dog-eared magazine, but her focus wasn't on the pages she was trying to read but on the man now being treated. She hoped he hadn't injured his hand too badly. It was important that he be able to write, to get his thoughts down on paper whether by quill pen or typewriter or computer. Whatever he used, a certain amount of manual dexterity was certain to be involved.

"Are you here for treatment, too?" a voice above her asked.

Stacy looked up into the face of a young doctor wearing a long white coat, and shook her head.

"You came with Mr. Ashley?" he asked her.

"Yes."

"He's fine," the doctor said reassuringly. He sat down next to Stacy. "That's a fairly deep cut he has," he added. "It took a few stitches. We gave him a local anesthetic, but once it wears off the finger'll probably throb, so I'm going to turn these pills over to you. Your cousin can take two when he gets home and two at four-hour intervals thereafter."

He held out a small vial, and Stacy automatically reached for it. She was about to tell him she and "James Ashley" weren't related when the great man himself appeared in the doorway of the treatment area.

"So there you are," he said. "I see you've met Dr. Adams."

"Yes, I've just given your cousin instructions about the medication," the doctor said.

"Then you'd better also inform her as to whether or not whisky is permitted," James said, "or she won't let me have a drink."

The doctor grinned. "A shot or two will do no harm," he promised, "as long as you don't drive."

"Capital," James proclaimed. "And I thank you for everything."

"My pleasure," he was assured. "Incidentally, keep that bandage dry if you take a shower, okay? We'll remove the stitches in about a week, and your finger should soon be as good as new."

"We'll remove the stitches in about a week." The doctor's words kept repeating themselves over and over to Stacy as she went out to the car with James.

A week!

Before she could open the car door for him, he went around to the driver's side and opened her door for her. Though perhaps a shade paler than usual, he once again looked totally in command.

Nevertheless, as she took her place behind the wheel, she couldn't resist saying rather triumphantly, "Well, now do you believe this trip was necessary?"

"Yes, ma'am," James Ashley-Sinclair said with suspicious meekness.

She glanced at him quickly and saw that he was smiling at her, and there was a new quality to this smile. James hadn't merely switched it on. He was really looking at her, and suddenly she felt as if a Fourth of July sparkler had been lit between the two of them and there were little hot, white stars going off all over the place.

"Thanks," James Ashley-Sinclair said.

Stacy, momentarily, was too disconcerted to ask him what he was thanking her for.

Chapter Four

Stacy and James were silent on the drive back to Kate's Hideaway. Then, as soon as they were in the house, Stacy went out to the kitchen, got down the bottle of Scotch and poured out a hefty drink for James.

She expected him to go into the living room, possibly to lie down on the couch and try to rest a bit. Instead, she turned to see that he had come into the kitchen and was watching her, a vestige of that smile that had affected her so much lingering on his handsome face. As she handed him the drink, he raised a quizzical eyebrow and said, "This is what I call cooperation." Then, with a mock frown, he added, "What, no ice?"

"For that," Stacy informed him, "the next time I make you a drink, it'll be half an ounce of whisky over a glassful of rocks."

"Have mercy on me," he protested, and took a man-size swig of the Scotch. He pulled out a chair and sat down at the kitchen table. Stacy started an inspection of the fridge contents, then of the cabinet shelves, but she was so aware of his eyes on her that she nearly dropped a can of chicken soup on her foot.

"Looks like we'll have to settle for this for lunch," she said to James, brandishing the can.

"Fine," he said.

"I think I'd better do some shopping this afternoon," she added.

"There's really enough around here to do me for the time being," James said. "It does occur to me that before you leave, though, I'd better make arrangements to rent a car, so I can get around." He stopped and surveyed her, the last trace of the smile fading from his face. "Am I mistaken in reading something into what you just said?" he asked her. "That is to say, are you thinking of staying on yourself?"

"Temporarily," Stacy said, busying herself with opening the can of soup so that she didn't have to look at him.

"Did you encounter more of a problem than you expected at Kate's shop here?"

"Yes," she said, glad he'd evidently assumed her reason for staying on at the Hideaway was purely a business one. Actually, she couldn't possibly have walked out and left him alone. There was always a chance the cut could become infected. He could wake up in the night with a raging fever. Anyway, anyone with a heavily bandaged hand was bound to be helpless to some extent.

She stole a glance at James and knew it would be deluding herself to pretend he needed her around, bandaged hand or no bandaged hand. She'd never seen a man who looked *less* helpless.

It was true, however, that she should stay on in Devon for business reasons. There was a definite problem at the

Cape Kloset, and she only hoped it was one that could be solved fairly fast. Then she could get back to New York and put her life on an even keel again.

Again she was surprised at how easily her personal boat had been rocked by James Ashley-Sinclair, especially since the "rocking" had been so inadvertent on his part. She could imagine what a veritable tempest he could unleash if he half tried.

James, sitting at the table polishing off the last of his Scotch, watched Stacy working her way through some sort of quandary as she heated the soup and made a stack of toast. She looked lovely today. Her long wavy dark hair was brushed loosely around her shoulders, making her look younger than the more severe coiffure she'd been wearing yesterday. Her deep blue dress, made of some sort of knit material, was close to the color of her eyes. He suspected the dress was a Kate Kloset original. The lines were very good. It was free flowing—at least he supposed that was what one called something that didn't hug the body tightly, and yet showed up all the excellent attributes of that body at the same time.

He narrowed his eyes. Stacy, he estimated, must be about five-four, the top of her head just about came to his chin. In relation to his own height, he considered her on the short side—but she was very well put together. *Very* well put together, he mused appreciatively.

He wished he knew more about her. She was recently divorced, she'd divulged that much, but he was certain she wasn't the type of woman to go beyond simple statements into deep, personal revelations—not without considerable prodding, and he warned himself that under no conditions must he start to prod.

That would be taking a decided professional advantage, because—James thought rather grimly—he *was* good at his chosen work, basically good, despite the fact that all the blatant publicity over his book had rather buried his practical competence in his field.

True, his prime interest in psychology was in the areas of what he rather loosely considered research and exploration. But in order to accomplish both, in order to gain the knowledge, insight and experience ever to have been able to write his book in the first place, he'd done his homework as a practicing psychologist. The human psyche never failed to fascinate and astonish him. Understanding people and their emotions and trying to help them cope with both themselves and what life dealt out to them was a continuing challenge.

He'd had to give up a lot of that challenge since the publication of *A Personal Sex Bible*. He'd become so much in demand as a lecturer he'd had to shelve, for the time being, what had always been a limited private practice anyway.

As it was, it amused him to think of the prices women all over the world would pay him for the kind of analysis he'd love to do for Stacy MacKenzie . . . for free.

He was so immersed in thought about her that he was startled when she suddenly plopped a bowlful of chicken soup down in front of him, then placed a mound of toast at its side.

James devoured two bowls of soup and ate all the toast and agreed to Stacy's suggestion that she warm up a piece of the pie left over from supper last night. He was equally agreeable when she set about making a fresh pot of coffee. Meantime, disdaining any offer of help from him, she took their soup dishes over to the sink and started rinsing them off. "Hmm," she said after a moment.

James was watching her back—she had a nice, erect carriage, squared shoulders—and telling himself it would be what his cousin Kate would call very dirty pool were he to track Kate down by phone in Miami and ask her to fill him in on a few things about her assistant. He heard her "Hmm" and asked, "What is it?"

"Evidently," Stacy said, "we've no hot water."

"I know," James said, nodding.

She swung around. "You know? Why didn't you say something?"

"I'm sorry," he said. "It totally slipped my mind. You see, that's what caused me to cut my finger."

"What?"

"I got up early this morning and went for a walk around the place to see if the storm had done any damage," he explained. "You'd left by the time I came back. I sat here at the kitchen table and tried to pull my thoughts together." He smiled ruefully. "But they didn't want to be pulled. It was my intention to begin to map out a definite plan—a daily program—for dealing with the work I need to do. You see, I'm way overdue on my deadline for my second book. But, sitting here, I discovered there were simply too many cobwebs cluttering my mind to let me get down to details. So..."

He paused, not surprised at the perplexed expression on Stacy's face. She had every right to question how what he was telling her could possibly have anything to do with their not having hot water.

"I know," he said apologetically. "The hot water. Well, I decided after a time to go for a run. Running's not a serious hobby with me, but it is an excellent way to reactivate the brain cells when they get a bit on the soggy side. I ran along the beach, and then, after I got back, I went to take a shower. Midway through I felt as if I'd suddenly been plunged into a glacial pool. The shower water was frigid."

James paused again, aware that he was taking an awfully long time about getting down to the simple facts. As if to confirm this, Stacy tapped her fingers rather impatiently on the kitchen sink.

He went on, "I put on a robe and headed for the cellar, where I assumed I would find the water heater. I shortly discovered that the only access to the cellar is a wooden bulkhead at the side of the house. The bulkhead happens to be badly in need of repair and, as I tugged the hatch open, one door section broke off its hinges. So I set that aside and started down what can best be called a makeshift ladder. I'd only taken two steps when the rung I was standing on gave way. I lunged out instinctively to stop the fall and my hand snagged on the jagged edge of an old pipe protruding from the cellar wall."

"A *rusty* pipe?" Stacy asked, horrified.

"I'd rather think it's probably rusty."

"Did you tell them that at the clinic? You might need a tetanus shot—"

"I told them," James said, "and they gave me a tetanus shot. But . . . I'm afraid none of that solved the original problem. I never got near the water heater. Ergo...we still have no hot water."

"Hmm," Stacy said yet again, and went in search of the phone book.

"I wish Kate had left a list of people she gets to do her repair work," she said as she thumbed through the classified pages. She looked up. "Maybe there is one."

"I wouldn't count on it," James said dryly. "I know my cousin, bless her. Kate may be remarkably organized in her business life, but on personal grounds . . ."

Stacy didn't answer that. The fact was that while Kate was a genius at what she did, she was *not* all that organized in her business life. Which was one reason why Stacy was holding her present job.

She found three plumbers listed in Devon, only to have the first one tell her it would probably be a week before he could get around to the Hideaway. The second one said laconically that he just might be able to look the situation over the day after tomorrow. The third man was more obliging, but even so it was a couple of hours before he arrived at the scene to state, after inspection, that the problem wasn't a plumbing one.

"Furnace is out of oil," he informed Stacy. "You better get that ladder replaced, too, lady. Better still, put in some steps and get a new door on that bulkhead, otherwise someone's apt to break his neck."

Someone nearly had, Stacy thought direly, and for a moment wondered what she would have done if she'd come back to find James sprawled at the foot of the bulkhead ladder.

Fortunately Kate had a calendar on the kitchen wall that had come to her courtesy of a local oil company. Stacy put in an emergency call to the company, and an hour or so later she and James heard the rumble of a heavy truck coming up the lane.

By then James had a fire going in the living room, for the house had become quite chilly. Stacy left him to go meet the delivery man, who was lugging a heavy hose around the side of the house.

The delivery man was big and husky and looked as if he had lost any trace of good humor years back. His dark hair was shot through with gray, and his heavy-featured face was creased in a scowl. Not a pleasant man, Stacy thought as she greeted him and watched him start the oil flowing into an outside pipe set into the ground about ten feet from the side of the house.

The refueling completed, he screwed the top back on the pipe. "Guess I'd better start up the furnace for you. She'll need to be primed after running out like that." He was moving around toward the bulkhead as he spoke, and Stacy followed him. "Ms. Clarendon done anything about that bulkhead ladder?" he asked over his shoulder.

"No," Stacy said.

"One of these days she's going to get herself sued," the oil man predicted grimly as he swung the unbroken part of the hatch open.

Stacy took advantage of the opportunity to peer down the bulkhead ladder, and she was appalled. It was, indeed, fortunate that James—or someone else—hadn't fallen straight to the bottom with consequences she didn't even want to contemplate.

The oil man, in parting, gave her a receipt. It wasn't until she was inside the house again that she read it and saw he'd scrawled the name "Al Reynolds" across the bottom.

A relative of Colleen Reynolds? she wondered. Maybe Colleen's husband? If so, he didn't look as if he'd be an easy man to live with.

James was at the phone in the kitchen when Stacy walked into that room, and she realized he was once again talking to someone in London. It was after five and was getting dusky outside. She estimated the time difference and realized it would be after ten, in London. Late for a business call. Was there a woman in the great sex expert's life?

She had to smile at her own question. *A* woman in James Ashley-Sinclair's life? There must be a lot of women in his life, but the big issue was whether there was someone really important to him.

Could a woman have a relationship with James without feeling like a captured butterfly? Could one become involved with him without feeling like a specimen on a microscope slide, certain to be examined in precise, clinical detail? How was James Ashley-Sinclair where his own emotions were involved? Did he handle them better than most people? Did he ever really let go? Was he capable of love, real love? They said that if one worked in a candy store long enough, even a chocoholic lost the appetite for chocolate. Did the same thing apply to people who were such experts in the field of sex and relationships that, in the final analysis, all that was left was the capacity to be objective?

Would James Ashley-Sinclair *analyze* a woman even as he made love to her?

He glanced up at precisely the moment Stacy posed that question to herself, and their eyes met. She had no idea how she must be looking at that instant. She knew she'd never been much good at camouflage. Too often her face gave her away. She saw a strange expression creep into his gray eyes and knew she'd just unwittingly telegraphed something to him.

James hung up the phone—Stacy had been so immersed in her thoughts she hadn't even heard his final comments—and, to her surprise, he said abruptly, "Would you care to go for a walk on the beach?"

She automatically glanced at his bandaged hand. "Do you really think you should—"

"Stacy," he interrupted, "a cut finger really doesn't immobilize one, you know." He sounded both amused and annoyed.

She nodded. "I could do with some fresh air and exercise," she admitted.

They put on warm coats and left the house by the kitchen door, walking around to the bluff where the long flight of wooden steps led down to the beach. It was still light enough to see. "At least Kate's beach access is in better shape than the access to her cellar," James observed. "I checked, incidentally, just a minute ago. We already have hot water."

"Well," Stacy said with a slight smile, "I guess we'll have to give Kate points for her heating system."

"I give Kate points for a lot of things," James said, but he didn't elaborate.

They started out across the beach to the hard, firm sand below the tidal line. "Did you and Kate spend much time together when you were growing up, James?" Stacy asked.

"She used to come to England each summer," James said. "My family has a country place in Warwickshire, and she used to stay there with us. She's a few years older than I am, and the difference in those earlier years seemed greater than it does now. But she was a great deal of fun, Kate has something of the eternal child about her. She becomes genuinely excited and enthusiastic about so many things. I envy her that," he finished quietly.

"I know what you mean," Stacy said, equally quiet. "I envy her, too."

She was aware of the sharp, sidelong glance he gave her, but she wasn't about to elaborate. And James seemed content to fall silent.

The tide was coming in, and the sea was still churned up from yesterday's storm. The waves crested and crashed down, edging farther and farther along the glistening stretch of sand below the tide line. When Stacy and James turned to walk back to the Hideaway, they had to seek higher ground. Here the sand was deep and soft and the going considerably harder.

By the time they reached the foot of the steps, Stacy was feeling as if she'd had a fair workout, and she stopped for a moment to catch her breath. Darkness had been encroaching on their return trek. Now a new moon slivered the sky, and the stars were white and brilliant yet remote. She didn't feel as if she could reach up and pluck a star from this September sky.

"I say, have I worn you out?" James asked.

"No, no," she said quickly. "I need more exercise, that's all. I've been doing a fair bit of traveling for Kate lately, and that precludes getting in swimming, or an occasional game of tennis, or even going through my usual boring daily calisthenic routine to the accompaniment of a videotape."

He chuckled, then suddenly pictured Stacy—probably attired in leotards—doing her calisthenics. The temperature suddenly seemed about twenty degrees warmer.

Fate intervened—or so James told himself—because as Stacy started up the steps she stumbled, and reaching out to clasp her arm was instinctive. But, once she had steadied herself, he didn't remove his restraining arm. He could feel Stacy tense, but she didn't draw away from him, either. Rather, she half turned, and he gently nudged her to complete the turn. Even standing on the first step, the top of her head still barely came to his nose and, as he leaned over, James felt her soft hair brush his chin, and then his cheeks.

He kissed her gently, tenderly, deliberately holding back. He knew that—for reasons he still needed to find out about—Stacy had raised obstacles in her path when it came to men, and it wouldn't do to try to knock them over too swiftly.

Stacy still didn't try to move away from him, but neither did she really participate in the kiss. She was the recipient, and not entirely an unwilling recipient—James was certain—but she gave nothing of herself.

James stepped back, feeling neither victory nor defeat, and tried to make out Stacy's features in the darkness. But he couldn't see her clearly, so he couldn't honestly tell if he had pleased her or displeased her, and that admission brought with it some irony. What would his public think of him now if they could see him floundering like a schoolboy over kissing a woman who was beginning to be quite an enigma to him?

He reached in his coat pocket and brought forth a flashlight. "I brought a torch to light the way back," he told Stacy, and shone the beam on the steps for her.

She went up the steps slowly but steadily, those squared shoulders seeming especially erect to James. Outside the kitchen door he had to say something to her.

"That," he said, "the kiss, that is, was a way of saying thank you. For your help and consideration today. You were very kind."

Stacy busied herself in the kitchen, opening up a large can of beef stew that would have to make do for their dinner. Thanks to the hot water crisis, she'd never gotten around to going to the supermarket that afternoon and stocking up on provisions, as she'd intended to do.

James's kiss had taken her totally by surprise. She hadn't been expecting that kind of an overture from him—if it could be called an overture. Probably his action had been exactly what he'd said it had been, she thought wryly. A gesture. A way of saying thanks.

There were some tins of biscuits in the freezer, and she baked them as she heated the stew. James did full justice to the makeshift meal—he had an extremely healthy appetite, she noted, and she wondered how he managed to stay so slim if he ate like this all the time. Not that he'd had much of quality to eat, here in Kate's Hideaway, but she'd managed to provide him with plenty of quantity.

She wondered where he lived in London and if he had a cook to prepare meals for him. She knew, from the bits of information Kate had vouchsafed about him from time to time, that he came from a wealthy family and had never wanted for much of anything.

She wondered if he lived alone. If he went to London's famed theaters very often. If he liked Shakespeare and ever went to Stratford-upon-Avon.

She wondered what kind of art he liked, and what kind of music. If he had any interest at all in such things as American baseball. Shc was a devoted Yankees fan.

She wondered . . .

She made herself stop wondering and concentrated on cleaning up their supper dishes, having refused James's offer of help. She didn't want him to risk banging his finger on something and certainly didn't want him to get the bandage wet.

James came to the door. "What do you know," he said. "Kate has a sneaky little liquor supply in that nice old maple cabinet in the living room." He held up a bottle of brandy. "Shall we indulge?" he suggested. "Seems to me I spotted a couple of snifters amid the glassware."

Brandy, sitting in front of a fire on a September night in a Cape Cod house with this man? Stacy warned herself she should know better, but it was awfully early to say that she thought she should head upstairs and go to bed. And she was no more in the mood for television than she suspected James was.

He had been scanning the shelves where the glassware was kept and now triumphantly produced two snifters.

"Kate," he said as he poured, "does have good taste, I must say." He sniffed appreciatively. "This is excellent."

Stacy wasn't a brandy connoisseur. But, as she took a small sip of the brandy, she had to admit to James that it went down well.

She followed him into the living room and curled up on one end of the couch. James put a cassette in the stereo. The soft, sweet strains of "Greensleeves" filtered into the room.

James sat down on the opposite end of the couch and stretched his long legs out in front of him. "There is something so haunting about that piece," he said, nodding toward the stereo. "At least I find it so. Do you?"

"Yes," she said, staring at the golden flames that were leaping in the fireplace as she tried not to say any more. Because the fact was that "Greensleeves" had always had a profound emotional effect on her. There was something so poignant and so intrinsically beautiful about it....

"I'm sorry," James said. "Probably I should have chosen something else."

She glanced at him swiftly. "Why do you say that?"

"Because you look so sad, and it wasn't my intent to cause you to look sad. Unhappy memories, Stacy?"

"Not exactly. But long ago, when we'd all be home for Christmas—my parents, my sister Anne and I—we used to open our presents on Christmas Eve, and my father would always put some music on. 'Greensleeves' was one of his favorites, and it became one of mine."

"Your father's not living, Stacy?"

She shook her head. "No. My parents broke up. They divorced when I was sixteen, and my sister Anne was almost twenty. My mother remarried. She and my stepfather live in Arizona. Anne married and divorced. A couple of years ago she married again. She and her husband presently live in Alaska, so we don't see much of each other. My father had a fatal coronary about two years after the divorce. He wasn't the one who wanted it. But then I guess it's always one person who gets hurt the most, isn't it?"

She let the words trail off, wondering how she'd ever come to say so much in answer to a simple question. Did James have some kind of insidious, subliminal technique for ferreting information out of a person?

To her surprise, he provided information of his own. "My parents didn't divorce, but it might have been better if they had," he said quietly. "I was the last of four children—I have three sisters, all considerably older than I am, and we've never been at all close. Anyway, by the time I arrived, I would say that if there had ever been any genuine love between my parents it had become converted into something I can only think of as scrupulous politeness. I can remember, as a child, my mother having a suite in our London town house renovated for her own use—her own bedroom, dressing room, parlor. I doubt if from that moment on she and my father ever occupied the same quarters. But then it was quite a formal household, anyway. My father was a barrister, and he also took an active role in the House of Lords."

So there was a title involved, Stacy thought.

"He was extremely busy with his profession and with politics. My mother was an excellent hostess. She never faltered in her role as a grand dame. But when he died—eight years ago now—I doubt she shed a tear."

"Is your mother still living?"

He nodded. "Yes. She considers the London town house her place of residence, but she spends her winters either in the south of France or the south of Spain. When she's in England she also visits around quite a bit with my three sisters. And she allows ample time in which to pursue her present goal."

"Her present goal?"

James smiled. "She yearns to marry me off to the woman of her choice," he told Stacy.

Chapter Five

Why did a telephone always ring at the entirely wrong moment?

Stacy swore silently as she went out to the kitchen to answer the jangling summons. James had just intrigued her with that statement about his mother's prime objective. Now she wondered if she'd ever be able to get him back on the subject again.

She said, "Hello," and heard a familiar voice bubble back. "Stacy, you're not going to believe this. Carlos has capitulated. Totally capitulated. He's giving us an exclusive, and wait till you see some of his new designs. Fantastic, absolutely fantastic. Stacy, isn't this fabulous?"

Stacy had sometimes been tempted to get out a stopwatch and time Kate Clarendon when she was in this kind of mood. Kate's words tumbled out one after the other. Then she brought herself up short. "Well?" she asked her troubleshooter and assistant. "Aren't you going to say something?"

Stacy laughed. Kate never seemed to realize that when she got going she seldom gave another person a chance to say much of anything. "That *is* fabulous, Kate," she said, and meant it. "I know this is something you've wanted for a long time."

"Forever," Kate asserted dramatically. Then she paused and said more mildly. "I gather you and James rendezvoused without any problem. He called Betty Osborne in New York yesterday to find out where I was, and she said he was calling from the Cape."

Betty Osborne was one of the models Kate used frequently at fashion shows, a tall and stunning brunette. Naturally, Stacy thought wryly, James would be bound to know her. Maybe she'd even provided him with some of the information for his famous book.

Nasty, nasty, she chided herself. "Is everything all right up there?" she heard Kate ask.

She hesitated, then decided there was really no point in telling Kate right now that they'd arrived in a near-hurricane with no house key, that they'd run out of hot water and that James had cut himself badly trying to get to the water heater, which had necessitated a trip to the medical clinic in town. Nor did she see the need to tell Kate what a hard time she'd had getting a plumber to come to the house and that it probably was true if Kate didn't do something about her blasted bulkhead and the ladder to the cellar that she would, one day, find herself facing a lawsuit.

"Is everything all right?" Kate asked again. "Have you touched bases with Colleen Reynolds?"

Stacy decided to concentrate on the second question. "I went over to the Cape Cod Kloset this morning," she said.

"And?"

"I think," Stacy admitted, "that there are some problems." She didn't want to go into specific details about the late opening hours and the general ambience in the shop—or lack thereof. Right now that would only upset Kate and take the edge off her victory in having acquired an exclusive from the Spanish designer.

She continued carefully. "Mrs. Reynolds and I are going to have dinner together, probably tomorrow night. I think I need to get to know her better. Then I can better deal with the situation. I suspect there may be a personal problem involved, which may be causing her not exactly to neglect business, but to fail to perform at her best. Nothing to worry too much about, Kate. It can be straightened out," she said, and hoped she was right.

"Well," Kate said, "you'll handle it. I'm sure. This is an important one, Stacy, so take all the time you want. We have an excellent market there on the Cape, and I don't think we've tapped into it as much as we can. I like Colleen Reynolds personally, and she's been an excellent manager until recently. She's a sharp businesswoman. That's why I, too, have felt it must be a personal problem if she's slipping. So tread carefully. I know I don't need to tell you that, but I'll say it anyway. Let Colleen assume you're taking a fall vacation at the Hideaway."

"You do realize, don't you, Kate, that your cousin has come here to work?" Stacy asked.

"What's that have to do with anything?"

"Kate, Kate, the man came here because he wants privacy. Your place is charming, but it's not that huge. If I stay here, I see no way James can have the solitude he wants and probably needs."

"Nonsense," Kate said. "There's plenty of room at the Hideaway for both of you."

Was there? Stacy was afraid that even if she and James were alone in a place as big as Buckingham Palace, she'd somehow be aware of his presence.

"I could move to a motel," she said tentatively.

"That would be ridiculous," Kate said quickly. "Colleen knows I have a place there. It would be your obvious choice for a vacation spot."

"Yes...I've already mentioned I'm staying here to her," Stacy admitted.

"Well, then, you certainly can't change now. Speaking of James—might I speak to him, please?"

Stacy summoned James, then went back into the living room. He'd put some more logs on the fire so that it was blazing nicely. He'd shut off the stereo, though. No soft music enhanced the atmosphere. Maybe "Greensleeves" had provided a bit too much nostalgia for both of them.

James came back, but this time he sat down in an armchair, edging the chair around slightly so that he was facing her. "Kate said you seem to feel you'll be in my way if you stay on here," he said, looking her straight in the eye. "Did you tell her that?"

"Well . . . not in so many words," Stacy hedged.

"Obviously the implication was there. She pointed out that I could use one of the upstairs bedrooms as my 'ivory tower,' as she put it. She said I could set up a desk—seems she has a desk among some other furniture up in the attic here—for the word processor or typewriter or whatever I elect to use. I told her I really didn't need a damn ivory tower," he finished.

He sounded, if not angry, definitely displeased. Stacy felt she was being put on the defensive, and she didn't like being put on the defensive. Putting her on the defensive had been a consistent habit of her husband's, and, with the divorce, she'd promised herself that no one was ever going to make her take little guilt trips again.

"Look," she told James, "all I said was that you came up here so you could work in peace and quiet, and the Hideaway isn't all that big."

"Evidently you inferred you thought you'd be in my way." He was stony-faced as he stated, "You are not in my way."

Stacy couldn't repress a smile. "James," she reminded him, "you haven't even started to work yet."

"So?"

"So how do you know whether I'd be in your way or not? The situation hasn't been tested."

"I should say the answer to that is fairly obvious, Stacy. I believe I'm capable of making my own judgments when it comes to whether or not I'd find working conditions suitable," he insisted with a certain hauteur that caused Stacy to feel as if she were being put in her place by a voice of considerable authority.

"Well," she said resentfully, "excuse *me*."

James caught the resentment and realized he must have sounded like a pompous ass. Stacy's deep blue eyes were sparkling, giving him a new clue to her personality. Stacy, he saw, had a rather easily aroused temper, and he suspected it was a hot temper that she'd either learned to suppress as she grew up or, maybe, had been forced to suppress by someone who'd tried to mold her. Her ex-husband? It was an educated guess that didn't take a degree in psychology to hazard, but he'd bet it was the right one.

"That small speech of mine was actually intended as a compliment," he said carefully. "At best it came out as a backhanded one. But the fact is it doesn't take long to sense whether or not one can be comfortable around another person. To be honest, I know few people I'd want to have to share a house with when I have work to do that requires a lot of in-depth thinking in relatively little time. But I've no qualms about sharing this place with you. Not that it's mine to share, anyway. You've as much right here as I, probably more." James rose on that last sentence and picked up his empty brandy snifter. "Do you play Scrabble, by any chance?" he asked. "I notice Kate has a game."

It was a welcome diversion. They took the Scrabble board out to the kitchen, refilled the brandy snifters and settled in for a genuine contest. Had she been asked, Stacy would have said she was certain she couldn't beat him. That—she would have been equally quick to add—wasn't due to any inferiority complex on her part but because she recognized James Ashley-Sinclair's exceptional intelligence and was sure he'd run rings around her when it came to tallying up a Scrabble score.

To her surprise, she won the first game by a margin of fifty points. James won the second one. At that, he looked up at her, eyes twinkling, and suggested, "A tie breaker?"

"Definitely," Stacy said.

The tie breaker, to their mutual amazement, resulted in precisely what they didn't want: a tie. By then it was midnight, and they packed the tiles away, promising each other a return engagement the next night.

There was a warm camaraderie between them as Stacy bid James good-night and started up the stairs. The stairs were steep, old Cape Cod style, with a sturdy length of thick rope replacing a more conventional banister. Stacy turned midway to find James looking up, and watching her. She suddenly became aware of a strong tug that made her want to reverse her direction, go back down the stairs to him, throw her arms around him and bury her face against his shoulder. She wanted his nearness and his warmth and his masculine strength. Beyond that she wanted more, and she knew it. James Ashley-Sinclair was arousing some very potent feelings in her that had absolutely no place in her current life scheme. She was afraid if he were to beckon right now she'd go to him, and that she didn't like. She'd worked too hard to get control of her own destiny. Furthermore, she'd be an idiot to let herself become emotionally involved with a man who had even less place in his life for her than she had in hers for him.

But logic, while great, could fail dismally when faced with far more basic forces, Stacy thought ruefully. She knew that if James beckoned that finger right now, she would slide straight down the stairs to him, regardless of the future consequences.

"Good night," she said, as if she hadn't already said it once, and started up the stairs again.

James's voice halted her. "You're very lovely," he said.

Stacy stared down at him, wild birds suddenly starting to flutter in her chest. She could feel their imaginary wings beating, and the effect was both frantic and erotic.

"Very lovely," James repeated quietly. And before she could move, before she could answer, he added, "Your husband must have been the most total of fools."

The sun was spattering golden notes over the Atlantic when Stacy woke up. She stood at her bedroom window for a time, looking out at the incredible view of sand, water, sky and sun. Despite the fact that she knew danger lurked on her emotional threshold in the presence of James Ashley-Sinclair, she felt more relaxed, more *content*, somehow, than she had in a long while.

She dressed in jeans and a bright yellow sweater, then went downstairs. James was sitting at the kitchen table, the classified section in the telephone book spread out in front of him, and he looked abjectly miserable.

"What is it?" she asked him quickly.

"I," he said, closing the phone book and thrusting it aside, "have caused an absolute disaster for myself."

The way he broadened the *a* in disaster made his British accent especially evident, and Stacy knew that every time she heard an Englishman speak for the rest of her life she was going to think of only one person.

She advanced slowly into the room and asked, "What do you mean?"

"I set about looking up places that rent typewriters, or word processors, or whatever," he said, indicating the phone book. "I happened to use my hand as a guide instead of a pencil, which was extremely foolish. Inadvertently I pressed down on this—" he grimaced as he held out his stiffly bandaged finger "—and it's a wonder you didn't hear my yelp upstairs."

"Well," Stacy asked reasonably, "what did you expect would happen? You've had that cut less than twenty-four hours, James, and the doctor said it was a deep one. No matter how fast a healer you may be, you can't expect to use the finger as a pointer for a while yet."

"I can't expect to use the finger period for a while yet," he corrected unhappily.

"That seems logical to me," Stacy agreed. There was a can of orange juice concentrate in Kate's freezer. Stacy opened it and mixed the contents with water as she waited for James's answer. When he remained silent, she turned around to see him sitting very erect, his mouth set in a tight line. "Well?" she asked him.

His words were clipped; he did, indeed, sound very British this morning. "Does it occur to you," he asked her, "that this is my *index* finger we're talking about, and the blasted cut extends clear to the tip of it? All right, so I should have known not to put any pressure on it. I grant you that. But exactly what do you think I'd be doing if I were to try to type or use a word processor?"

"Oh," Stacy said.

"Exactly," James agreed grimly. "Oh."

"You're saying you're not going to be able to put your material together, type up notes, write what needs to be written, that sort of thing?"

"Precisely."

Stacy placed a glass of orange juice in front of him. "Well," she said, "that's not exactly the end of the world, you know."

"Not the end of the world, no," he agreed. "Just damn inconvenient at this particular time."

Stacy sat down at the table across from him and said, "There are solutions, you know."

"Such as?"

"We'll get the local paper and look in the want ads. Probably there's someone eager to get some secretarial work. Or maybe a temporary help service. I really doubt you'll have any trouble finding someone to take your dictation."

"I don't want to find anyone to take my dictation," James informed her.

"Well, perhaps you could dictate into a recording machine," she suggested. "We could pick up one of the mini-recorders. They're pretty terrific. You could even walk up and down the beach, if you like, and hold the thing in the palm of your hand and just talk into it. Each tiny cassette takes a whole hour of dictation."

"Which I would then give to some willing individual who would type what I'd done?"

"Yes," Stacy said.

"No," James said.

She didn't know him very well, Stacy realized. Regardless, she wouldn't have expected him to be so stubborn. "James, life is full of compromises," she said, becoming impatient with him.

That got his attention. He raised a cynical eyebrow. "Do tell."

"Look, this is such a tiny compromise. You might do better with professional help, anyway, rather than trying this on your own. You probably use some archaic hunt-and-peck system."

"Yes, I do exactly that," he agreed, "but at least *I* do it."

"You must turn your material over for final typing, don't you?"

"Yes, of course I do. But I have a secretary in London who handles those kinds of details for me. That is to say, she farms out my manuscript material to typists. I already have a good bit of the manuscript with me, but there's a long way to go and . . ."

"Yes?"

"No need to bother you with this," he said abruptly, and there, again, was that hauteur that made Stacy feel as if she were being shut out.

Then it occurred to her that maybe James Ashley-Sinclair wasn't accustomed to confiding his problems to someone else. Maybe he was so used to being on the listening end where problems were concerned that he kept his bottled up inside him. Perhaps that occasional aloofness was actually a kind of camouflage. . . .

Hey! she protested, stopping herself short. *Who's the psychologist here?*

"Is there any particular reason why you're against getting help when you need it?" she asked. "Hiring a secretary or typist isn't that wild a suggestion. Most people in your position would do it automatically."

"The hell they would," James said flatly.

"Just what are you saying, James?"

"I don't want some strange woman coming in here to take dictation from me," he said. "For one thing, I would find it extremely difficult to formulate my thoughts in front of a perfect stranger. For another thing, the moment she—and I presume it would be a she—discovered who I am, history would start repeating itself, and I'd find it impossible to continue with my work. The reason I asked Kate if I could use her Hideaway in the first place was so that I could get away from women, damn it," James finished belligerently.

Stacy couldn't help it. She grinned. James looked up and saw the grin. "I can imagine how that came across," he said stiffly. "The fact is..."

Stacy's grin widened. "The fact is," she picked up, "you come across like a super guru to most women, don't you, James? Well, what can you honestly expect, having written a book with the title, *A Personal Sex Bible*?"

"The title was my publisher's, not mine," James grated. "I should have suspected something. I should have realized that my publisher—who'd lost a fair bit of money the previous year—needed to recoup and saw my book as a way of doing so. I wrote the book as a scientific treatise for my peers, damn it, not as a sex education course for laymen. I went along with the publisher because the title didn't seem that important to me. What I'd been concentrating on was the information between the covers. No one was more surprised than I when, overnight, I became a celebrity, an internationally famous sex expert. Can't you imagine the position that puts a man in? Every woman I meet thinks I can tell her how and where to find the man of her dreams, and what to do with him once she's found him. Even in this supposedly enlightened age, your sex, my dear Stacy—much as most of them may deny it—clings to the knight in shining armor concept that, I'm sure, had no validity even when knighthood was in flower. They want the impossible and they expect me to help them find it."

"And do you, frequently, sometimes come to represent that impossible knight, James?" Stacy asked him softly.

He gave her a scathing look and muttered an expletive under his breath that astonished her. James Ashley-Sinclair, she saw—though briefly, she was sure—seemed in danger of losing his cool.

She felt a slight twinge of sympathy for him, but only a slight one. He'd put himself in this position after all. He'd accepted the fame and fortune that had come with the publication of *A Personal Sex Bible*. In fact, he was going a step farther. He was here in Devon to finish up a sequel to that book. Stacy voiced her thoughts. "You get what you ask for, James," she told him.

His gray eyes were cold. "And just what do you mean by that?"

"You could have turned your back on the whole thing if it was so distasteful to you. The fame, the publicity. Rather, it seems to me that by going on lecture tours and television programs you merely fanned it."

"It wasn't my intention to fan anything, Stacy," he said wearily. "Initially I simply didn't see where it all was heading, and by the time I did realize what was happening, it was already too late. Perhaps I was naive, but I had the rather altruistic idea that once the book was out and was so eagerly accepted by the public, that maybe there was as great a need for it as my publisher claimed when he ventured into such a large first printing with it. Though I hadn't intended the book to be a popular publication, as

I've told you, I did begin to feel maybe it might really help people."

"Perhaps you were right," Stacy said honestly. "Probably you were right," she amended.

He looked at her skeptically. "Do you really believe that?"

"I don't know. Maybe if your book hadn't had such a provocative title no one would ever have read it."

"Thanks a lot."

"Maybe, on the other hand," she continued, "what you're saying is really what people want to hear."

"What do you think?" he asked suddenly.

"What do you mean?"

"Well," he persisted, "what was your reaction? Your personal reaction?"

"To your book?"

"Yes."

"I haven't read your book, James," Stacy said and, to her astonishment, James Ashley-Sinclair burst out laughing.

He laughed until there were tears in his eyes, then he said, "That's wonderful. Absolutely wonderful. Make me a promise, will you, Stacy?"

"What?" she asked suspiciously.

"Don't ever read the damn thing. Promise me that."

"No," she said. "I will not promise you that."

She'd already been thinking about Kate's autographed copy of James's book. It was a heavy tome; nevertheless she'd been contemplating taking it up to her room and reading a portion each night before she went to sleep.

"So, then," James said, sounding faintly disappointed, "your curiosity has been aroused after all."

"What do you mean?"

"Like thousands of other people, you've wondered what sort of information something called *A Personal Sex Bible* could possibly contain."

"No," she said.

"What, then?"

Stacy looked him right in the eye. "I'm thinking about reading your book because I'd like to find out what made a man like you decide to write it in the first place," she said, and was satisfied when James Ashley-Sinclair couldn't give her a quick reply.

Stacy called Colleen Reynolds later that morning, and they agreed to meet for dinner that evening. Colleen said she planned to work at the shop until at least six. Stacy suggested she pick her up there.

The phone call completed, she looked over Kate's cupboards, fridge and freezer again and made a list of things she wanted to get at the supermarket. James was out walking the beach when she left the house to go uptown. She was gone over an hour. It was nearly noon when she got back, and she found him pacing the floor.

"Where the hell have you been?" he demanded as she came in, staggering under a load of grocery bags. He relieved her of one of the bags and set it down on the kitchen table. "Well?" he asked.

"Where does it look like I've been?" she retorted.

"You could have said you were going shopping."

"You were out communing with the Atlantic."

They faced each other, Stacy having to tilt her head back so that she could look straight into his face. She knew he was angry with her—at least it seemed so—and she couldn't understand why.

"You could have left a note," he said, biting off the words.

"James, for heaven's sake, I only went uptown to the supermarket."

"I thought you might have gone for good," he blurted.

She was astonished. She reared back on her heels so suddenly that she nearly lost her balance. Once again James's arm shot out to steady her, and he didn't let her go. She heard him mutter something she couldn't quite make out, but it sounded like another one of those expletives that were so surprising coming from him. Then he drew her close to him and, in another second, he meshed his mouth with hers.

This was an entirely different kiss than he'd given her at the foot of the beach steps yesterday. This kiss was laden with a kind of energy she suspected James had long been restraining, and now he was venting it—and considerable passion with it—on her.

His tongue pried her lips open. She felt the tantalizing fire of his invasion, and there was no question about either letting herself go or not letting herself go. She *went*. Everything that had been building up inside her tumbled out in her response to him. She wound her arms around him and pressed closer. Being in his embrace was even more wonderful than she had thought it would be. They kissed until they both had to stop to regain their breath and, even then, that breathing was ragged.

James began fondling her hair, brushing his lips across her forehead, her nose, her cheeks, before meeting her lips again. And Stacy decided not only was she clutching him like a drowning woman trying to cling to her lease on life, but they were both becoming aroused to a pitch that could very well go beyond the treacherous point of no return.

It took every ounce of her inner strength to slowly but firmly push away from him, and then she felt so shaky she wasn't sure she was going to be able to stand upright on her own two feet. She saw James heave a deep sigh, saw the glazed expression in his eyes and the bewilderment on his face and was sure she must look very much the same way.

They'd both just thrown each other curves, because Stacy was sure he hadn't intended to let anything like this happen between them any more than she had. They were both rational adults, after all, forced into this proximity by a set of unusual circumstances. In the ordinary course of things their paths never, possibly, would have crossed....

She saw James straighten and take another deep breath. She sensed the second that he was back in control of himself and envied him his ability to recover so quickly. She was returning to reality at a much slower rate, despite the fact that she'd been the one to end their embrace.

James ran his hand over his thick autumn-leaf-colored hair, and Stacy watched that British aplomb that was such an integral part of him fall into place. But she wasn't prepared at all when he asked politely, as if he were inviting her to have the next dance with him, "By any chance, Stacy, do you know how to type?"

Chapter Six

Stacy stared at James, still so emotionally shaken she didn't see for a moment what he was getting at.

Then he smiled, a quirky smile that tugged at his lips but didn't reach the rest of his face. "I'm sorry. That was really out of line."

"No, no," she said quickly, "I wasn't sure I heard you right, that's all."

"I don't blame you."

"You were asking me if I can *type*?"

"Stacy, please..."

"Well, that's what you were asking me, isn't it, James? Yes, I can type. I'm not the world's greatest, but I'm adequate. Why..." she began, and suddenly no longer needed to ask the question. "Are you suggesting," she asked him instead, "that *I* take your dictation?"

"It was a crazy, absolutely insane thing to ask of you," James said. "Forget it, please. I said I was out of line, and I was."

"James..."

"Please, Stacy. No more."

The haughtiness was there again, that certain aloofness. It would have been easy to become intimidated by him. But a new thought was forming in Stacy's mind. James's request might provide her with just the kind of solution she needed to her problem with Colleen Reynolds.

"Yes, I'll be glad to take your dictation for you," Stacy said, "and to type up your notes. My shorthand is somewhat self-invented, but if you don't go too fast, I think we can make out all right. I may not be able to stay around till you get all the way through your book, but at least I can get you started. Anyway, by the time I have to leave, your finger may have healed up enough so that you'll be able to handle whatever's left by yourself."

James had walked over to the kitchen window and was looking out at the tangled undergrowth studded with spindly pines and cedars that spread beyond Kate's narrow side yard. He swung around and said, both swiftly and imperiously, "Don't be ridiculous."

"It was your idea, remember?"

"I've already said it was an utterly stupid idea," he snapped.

She pulled out one of the kitchen chairs and sat down at the table. "What are you planning to do, then?" she asked him. "I'm presuming this is the book that was referred to in that television program I saw you on in London a year ago. So you must be way, way overdue with it."

"I've already said I'm overdue with it," James retorted. "Way overdue, if you prefer."

"Well, what do you plan to do about it?" she persisted, trying to exhibit a patience she didn't feel. James, she was discovering, could be incredibly stubborn. In fact, downright obstinate.

"I shall simply have to ask the publisher for a further extension and go back to England and see what can be done once I get there," he told her.

Go back to England. Stacy was discovering the last thing in the world she wanted him to do was go back to England, even though his doing so might be the best thing that could possibly happen to her. It would be a great deal harder when the time came for him to leave if she had got to know him much better in the meantime. She conceded that. Even so... there was always some element of risk to life, damn it, and right now she was willing to risk some of that personal peace she'd been cultivating so carefully if it meant having James Ashley-Sinclair around a little longer.

"I suppose," she said acidly, the words springing out of an inner well she hadn't even known she possessed, "your competent secretary can solve all your problems if you go back to London?"

"Iris?" he asked, frowning. "Iris couldn't solve my problems about the book when I was there, so what makes you think she could now?"

"You said she farms things out?"

"She sees to it that my material is typed up efficiently, without my having to contact the individuals involved," James stated.

"Do you run *that* scared of women, James?"

He glared at her. "What the hell is that supposed to mean?"

"Well, is it really necessary to isolate yourself so that you won't have to face up to the admiration of some wistful young girls who might be enthralled by being asked to do your typing for you?"

"There are moments when I'd like to isolate myself from humanity," James said bitterly. "I guess you can't understand that, can you? And if you think I enjoy being a sex symbol of sorts to a population of females who don't even know me—well, I don't. I suppose that may sound tremendously conceited on my part, but that's the way it is."

"No," Stacy said slowly, "it doesn't sound conceited. I saw the way those women were looking at you at the Ritz."

"It's not women alone, Stacy," James informed her. "I have a fair proportion of men among my followers. It's just that the women are more..."

"More?"

"Direct," he said. He turned his back on her and stared out the window again.

"James," she suggested after a moment, "why don't you pour us out some of that brandy we had last night?"

He glanced at his watch. "The sun is hardly over the yardarm," he observed. "That's always Kate's expression for determining the proper drinking hour."

"The sun's over the yardarm in London," Stacy said.

To her relief, he smiled. "So it is," he agreed, and set about taking down the snifters and getting out the brandy.

When he had joined her at the table, Stacy swirled her brandy around in the snifter, then set it aside. Until she'd gotten her points across to James in the conversation that was about to ensue, she needed to keep her wits about her. She also needed to ask him another question before she started telling him why, after all, she should help him out with his book. "How old is Iris?"

James seemed totally abstracted, as if he'd become preoccupied about something else entirely. He shook his head slightly, focused on her, then asked, "What was that?"

"Never mind," Stacy said hastily, already regretting the question. It had been a stupid one, designed only to satisfy a nagging curiosity on her part. After all, what difference did it make if his London secretary was eighteen or eighty?

"No, no," James said. "You were asking about Iris?"

"James, never mind."

"You were asking me how old Iris is. That was it, wasn't it?"

"Let's not play twenty questions," Stacy said testily.

James laughed, and it was almost worth her embarrassment to see the spark of amusement in his clear gray eyes. "Iris is fifty-eight and a genuine love. Still married to the same man she married when she was twenty. Three children, six grandchildren. As for physical statistics, I've never been good at guessing people's weight, but Iris is, shall we say, on the plump side. She has blue eyes that are almost as beautiful as yours, and snowy white hair, and I hope she never, ever, decides she wants to retire."

He was enjoying this, every moment of it, Stacy saw, and her own sense of humor suddenly bubbled to the surface. "It's nice to hear that kind of endorsement." Impishly she added, "I hope that's the way Kate feels about me."

"It would be foolish of Kate to feel that way about you," James said, his face still reflecting that nice touch of amusement.

"Why do you say that?"

"Because one of these days, inevitably, someone will come along who will convince you that there are greener pastures than Kate's Klosets, estimable though they may be."

"It would take a great deal to make me even think of making a career switch," Stacy said. "What I do with Kate suits me very well."

"I wasn't talking about a career switch, Stacy. How old are you? Twenty-eight?"

"Almost twenty-nine."

"You can't seriously imagine you're going to stay single for the rest of your life, can you? One of these days a man is going to walk into your world who will be able to convince you that you should share your life with him. When that happens, I wouldn't place any wagers on Kate's being able to keep you around."

"If you're speaking of someone sweeping me off my feet and convincing me I should marry him, there's no way," Stacy informed him. "Never," she added, a shade more vehemently than she'd intended.

"Stacy," James said quietly, "certainly you're not going to say that one unfortunate experience has turned you off men for all time?"

"No," Stacy replied honestly. "I like men. I enjoy their company, their companionship. I'm not saying that I'll never again have a relationship with a man. Maybe—very possibly—with more than one man," she added recklessly. "But I never again want a serious involvement, James, and marriage is a very serious involvement. Once was enough."

"He hurt you that badly?"

"Yes, he hurt me that badly." The words came out before she could draw them back in, and immediately she wished she hadn't said them. She suddenly became aware that she had been on the verge of discussing her private life with the world's foremost, contemporary sex expert. And she had no intention of permitting James Ashley-Sinclair's professional eye to zero in on her. She was damned if she'd ever, ever, let herself become one of his case histories.

"Was your husband a lot older than you, Stacy?"

"I don't want to talk about my husband, James," Stacy said flatly. "My ex-husband, that is. I don't want to talk about marriage." She reached for the brandy snifter and tested its contents.

"It's not always good to hold things in, Stacy," James admonished gently.

"Please," she said tartly, "I'm not your client—that's what you call the people who come to consult you, isn't it? Nor do I want to be your client, even if you'd consider taking me on. So let's get off the subject, shall we?"

For a couple of seconds James had to fight for composure. He didn't know whether to laugh or to be insulted. He did know that Stacy MacKenzie was a woman very much in a class by herself, at least where he was concerned. She'd just rebuffed him, and it was quite a novelty to be rebuffed in such a fashion.

He decided that, perhaps, in some future article he might do a bit about times when psychologists overstep and get egg on their faces. It wasn't wise, after all, to go where one wasn't invited. And Stacy, most definitely, gave no indication of inviting him into that innermost realm of her private self, her private thoughts.

She was glancing at her wristwatch, James saw, and he wondered if she was about to dismiss him, like a teacher who was tired of a recalcitrant student she'd kept after school long enough. He could picture himself slinking out of the kitchen, abashed, conscious of Stacy's stern gaze following him, and the vision was a pretty funny one.

He was forced from fantasy into the here and now by Stacy's next comment. "Look, James, I'm quite serious about wanting to work on your book with you," she said abruptly. "And before you start shaking your head, you should know I have an ulterior motive."

"Oh?" James queried, intrigued.

"Do you know why I came to Devon?"

"On a mission for Kate, right?"

"Yes. There've been telltale signs of problems at Kate's Cape Cod Kloset, which is managed by a woman named Colleen Reynolds. I went to see Mrs. Reynolds yesterday—that's where I'd been before I came back here to find you... dripping blood." Stacy shuddered at the memory, then glanced at James's bandaged hand. "Does it hurt much?" she asked, the memory of yesterday and her concern for him taking over.

"Throbs a bit," he admitted.

"I have the painkillers the doctor gave me," Stacy said. Contrite, she added, "I should have given you a pill when you went to bed last night."

He shook his head. "I slept well, regardless."

"Do you want a pill now?"

"What is this, Stacy?" James asked, sounding somewhat exasperated yet not displeased. "No, I don't want a pill. Now, what about Colleen Reynolds?"

"When I visited the shop yesterday and saw her—we'd met previously in New York a few months back—there was no doubt in my mind that she's having problems. Kate does have an instinct for that sort of thing. I thought she might be overreacting because the sales figures at the Cape Cod Kloset weren't as good this past summer as they were the previous year. But she was right, Mrs. Reynolds is in some kind of trouble. So..."

"So?"

"So it becomes my job to find out what's going on. But, as Kate pointed out on the phone last night, I don't want to tip my hand. I told Mrs. Reynolds yesterday that I'd been in Boston on business and took the opportunity to come down here for a couple of days relaxation. That would mean, to most people, that I'll head for New York at the end of the weekend. . . in other words, that I'll only spend a couple of more days in Devon. *My* problem is that I doubt I can solve the shop problem that quickly. Kate insisted that I take my time on this, because Mrs. Reynolds has been valuable to us until recently. But she's certainly going to be suspicious if I stay on for no good reason."

James waited.

"Well," Stacy said, "you make a good reason."

James leaned back and surveyed her, and this time his smile was a full-fledged one. "Do I, now?" he teased.

"James, you can see, can't you, that if I tell Colleen Reynolds I'm helping you with your book—something she can even verify for herself if she feels so inclined—then she won't wonder about why I'm poking around Devon?"

"Yes, I can see that," James admitted, sobering. "But there's another aspect to this, Stacy."

"What?"

"I'm not saying that I'm here on Cape Cod incognito, but surely you can see that I prefer to keep a low profile," he told her. "That's why I gave the clinic only part of my name yesterday. If you tell Mrs. Reynolds what you're contemplating telling her, I might as well make a public announcement of my presence, if I'm correct about the way small towns function. Certainly I know how news spreads in a small town in England. I doubt the American counterparts are that different."

"No," Stacy admitted. "No, they're not." She stared at James unhappily. "I admit," she said finally, "it wouldn't be fair to you—to chance broadcasting your presence in

Devon, that is. You'd have no peace at all once people found out you were here."

It was beginning to occur to her that being a celebrity—on the level on which James was a celebrity—did have its drawbacks and pitfalls. She'd heard movie stars and other prominent persons gripe about celebrity status when interviewed on TV, but she'd always put that down to a kind of public relations puff job. Protesting all the attention one received automatically made one seem important, desirable.

James Ashley-Sinclair didn't need to be made to feel important, she thought wryly. He had a quiet confidence, a self-assurance, a built-in coolness of manner when he wanted it, that spoke for itself. As for being desirable...

Stacy took another swig of brandy and nearly choked. Seated across the kitchen table from her, wearing stonewashed jeans and a dark green knit shirt, he was undoubtedly the most desirable man she'd ever seen.

"Possibly, in this instance, there's a way of burning the candle at both ends," James said suddenly.

"What do you mean?"

"My alias worked yesterday. No one recognized me. Thus far I haven't had as much exposure on American television as I've had on British television. I've been on *Today* and a couple of your other major programs, but that was several months back. The lecture I gave in Boston this week was my first in the New England area. Thus, my face isn't as well-known as my name in this part of your country, and it would seem that a slight change of name might do the trick. It worked yesterday."

"You think if I said you were Kate's cousin, James Ashley, Colleen Reynolds wouldn't realize who you are?"

"Perhaps something a bit more different than that," James said. "Jim Sinclair, maybe. You could say that I'm a struggling novelist, that I write mysteries or horror fiction."

"Horror fiction," Stacy decided, and James didn't know quite how to take that.

He didn't know how to take Stacy at all, he decided a bit later as he struck out for a walk along the beach. He'd invited her to accompany him, but she told him she had a few odds and ends to attend to, then informed him that at six o'clock she'd be picking Colleen Reynolds up at the Cape Cod Kloset and the two of them were going to dinner together.

The afternoon was overcast. The ocean was pewter, the sky milky white. The surf wasn't as strong as it had been yesterday, and the tide line was littered with an assortment of debris washed up by the ever-churning sea. James saw a soggy baseball, an equally soggy grapefruit, a broken picture frame, a single red plastic shoe, and a child's bright blue sand pail, among other miscellaneous items.

There was a mystery to the sea that had an eternal fascination, and he could think of no place where one could view it in more of its majesty than here on Cape Cod's famous Nauset Beach. But, he discovered, he wanted to view it with someone. Specifically with Stacy.

Stacy was presenting him with a new and different kind of challenge where a woman was concerned. For one thing, she stood up to him...and, especially since his sudden fame, so few women did. He also sensed a lively intellectual curiosity about her, and he liked that. It would be interesting to have her work with him on his book. He wondered how she'd accept his ideas, how she'd feel about his dissertations on current relationships and their values, or lack thereof.

He had a lot to say on the subject. He had learned a great deal since the publication of *A Personal Sex Bible*.

Life, in his opinion, had to be a constant learning process, or an individual—regardless of his place or prominence—became static. He, certainly, hadn't been content to rest on his laurels simply because his book had become an unexpected international bestseller and his reputation as a psychologist thus assured for all time. He'd continued to observe, to study, to contemplate, to speculate. He had a lot he wanted to say in his new book, and he wondered whether or not Stacy would agree with him.

She'd shown, in a variety of ways that might not have been as discernible to someone less trained, that she had an inquisitive mind, keen intelligence and, God knows, plenty of spunk. Beyond that...

James paused, gazing out at the vast ocean that separated this country from his, his face suddenly pensive. She had a way of getting to you, Stacy did. It was a particularly powerful way, because she was so totally unaware of her effectiveness as a woman. That seemed odd because—at nearly twenty-nine—she was in her way a prototype of the sophisticated, successful, American career woman. Yet James was willing to swear that no man had yet ever taught Stacy all there was to know about what there *could* be between man and woman. No man, he felt sure, had ever fully aroused Stacy as he knew very damn well she was capable of being aroused. He'd had a touch of her fire today. She'd responded to him that time, by God. But he knew it was only a token of what there could be between them.

James turned abruptly and increased his pace as he walked along the beach, his footsteps leaving patches in the glistening sand.

"I bought a locally made chicken pie at the supermarket today," Stacy told James. "It should be good. When you feel yourself getting hungry, preheat the oven to four-hundred degrees, then pop the pie in for about forty-five minutes. Also, there's some carrot salad from the deli in the fridge and some rolls you can heat up. Plus, I bought a chocolate cake at the bakery."

"Wait a minute," James protested. "What are you trying to do, fatten me up?"

"Well," she said, "you could do with a few extra pounds."

That was true and not true. James had lost some weight during his recent American lecture tour—the schedule had been hectic, and he'd never been much for airline meals—but he was anything but thin. He felt like flexing a few muscles just to show Stacy that he was stronger than he perhaps looked at the moment. He could imagine her expression were he to do so, and had to laugh at himself. He was reacting to her like a schoolboy trying to prove he was macho.

Stacy slipped on a royal blue wool coat. Like most of her clothes, the coat looked as if it had come out of a chic boutique and, James was sure, it was almost certainly a product of a Kate's Kloset. Stacy, he mused, made a good model—and consequently a good advertisement—for his cousin's wares.

"Do you want one of the painkillers before I leave, James?" Stacy asked, picking up gray leather gloves and a gray leather handbag.

He was sitting in an armchair in the living room, thumbing through a copy of *National Geographic*. He stood, then slowly walked toward Stacy, pausing just in front of her.

"I appreciate your concern," he told her, "but it's really unnecessary, Stacy. I don't need a painkiller. Also, when I feel hungry, I'll have the sense to prepare something to eat. So stop worrying, will you?"

He saw Stacy draw back, and wished he'd phrased that small speech in another way. As it was, he'd sounded so damn ungrateful and... stuffy.

"Look," he began, wanting to leave her with a different impression. "I honestly do appreciate your concern..."

"But you're a big boy, right?" Stacy finished for him, a rather nasty edge to her tone. She nodded. "Okay, James, I'll leave you on your own, and I'm sure you'll do just fine."

James was tempted to reach out and grab her, take her in his arms and show her, by actions rather than words, what he seemed to be fumbling so badly at saying. But he'd done a great deal of heavy thinking as he'd paced along the beach a while earlier, and he knew that if they were going to work together, he was going to need to keep a tight control on the impulses that surged all too easily when he was with her.

Stacy already had been hurt by one man. He didn't want to do anything to add to that hurt. Though, in his opinion, she needed a man in her life, he wasn't that man. Though she attracted him, tempted him, though he yearned to go to bed with her, he was determined not to have an affair with her because it could only lead to disastrous conclusions.

He was too old for her, for one thing—thirty-eight to her almost twenty-nine. A difference of almost ten years... which, he had to admit as he thought about it, might not be insurmountable. But there were other factors that *were* insurmountable. Their lives were so totally different. Stacy, he already felt sure, was quite a private person. Maybe she'd always been that way, maybe life had made her that way, but the result was essentially the same.

He, too, was inherently a very private person, but he'd had his privacy blasted to hell, and he feared there was no way he could ever fully get it back again. Stacy would hate the kind of life he was leading these days. She'd hate being in a constant spotlight. Furthermore, she'd made it plain to him that she'd *made* her life and she liked it the way it was. She had her career with Kate, she lived in the exciting city of New York most of the time, she undoubtedly had a circle of interesting friends and all the "dates" she might ever wish for. Though he was sure it was true—as he'd thought earlier—that she'd never known life as she was capable of knowing it, that was certain to be rectified. An American would walk into her life, recognize her wonderful value and—unless there was absolutely no justice at all—he would teach her what it really meant to love and be loved....

James felt a pang of hot jealousy toward a man who, so far as he knew, might not even exist.

He became aware that Stacy was watching him closely. He also became aware that he'd been standing in front of her like a robot, staring down at her and saying absolutely nothing.

Stacy, looking faintly alarmed, asked, "What *is* it, James?"

"Nothing," the author of *A Personal Sex Bible* said huskily. "You'd best go on," he added quickly, "or you'll be late for your rendezvous with Kate's store manager."

Chapter Seven

The wonderful aroma of freshly brewed coffee awakened Stacy the next morning. She slipped on a robe and went downstairs, unable to resist having a cup of coffee before she dressed and made plans for the day. Plans, she knew, that were certain to revolve around James.

Was he going to decide to start working on his book today, or had he changed his mind about letting her take dictation for him? They'd parted on a rather ragged note yesterday when she'd left to keep her dinner date with Colleen Reynolds, and James had already gone to bed when she returned.

She found James in the kitchen, sipping from a mug of coffee as, again, he scanned the *National Geographic*. He was wearing a cranberry-colored shirt that did great things for his coloring, and he looked well rested and at peace with the world. She knew there was no logical reason why that should annoy her, but it did. She, for her part, had done considerable tossing and turning last night because of him. She'd been disappointed when she'd gotten back from her dinner engagement to find he'd gone upstairs. She'd hoped they could talk for a little while and maybe get back on a smoother footing again.

Now James was acting as if nothing had ever happened between them to raise either of their temperatures. He greeted her pleasantly, put the magazine aside, then nodded at it. "There are still a few places in the world where a person might be able to get away from it all. Problem is that in most of them one would be apt to either freeze to death or quickly become roasted to a crisp."

Stacy, in the process of filling a mug with coffee, chuckled. "Are you thinking of becoming a hermit?"

"Sometimes it's tempting."

He waited till she came over and sat down at the table before continuing. "Being here in the Hideaway for even this brief time has given me a heady sense of what it can mean to just drop out of sight for a while." He swiftly changed the subject. "Would you like me to make you an omelet? I'm rather good at whipping up omelets."

"May I take a rain check?" Stacy asked him. "I'm never especially hungry when I first get up."

"Anytime," James said, nodding.

He was being so pleasant, so agreeable, that it was making her suspicious. She had the dire feeling maybe he'd decided to scrap trying to finish his book at the Hideaway and was going to go back to England after all and work on it there. Just now he'd spoken of being at the Hideaway almost as if the interval was already past tense. Was he that ready to put these few days behind him? How long, Stacy wondered dismally, would it take him to forget all about her once he got back on his home turf?

She would never be able to forget about him. That realization struck her, and her hand trembled. Some hot, black coffee spilled over the edge of her white china mug.

"What's troubling you, Stacy?" James asked as she quickly wiped up the spill.

That was a question she definitely couldn't answer.

Fortunately he gave her an out by posing a second question. "Didn't your dinner meeting last night go well?"

"Not very," Stacy admitted which, unfortunately, was true. James had been only three-quarters responsible for her restless sleep last night. She placed the blame for the remaining quarter on Colleen Reynolds.

"Want to talk about it?" James invited.

He was coming on as a friend rather than a psychologist in the way he made that suggestion. Stacy responded wearily. "There's really not that much to tell. If I had to describe what happened in a few precise words, I could only say it was a dull session. I was bored. I suspect Colleen was, too. Somehow we just couldn't seem to communicate, and so it was all surface politeness."

"You got no clue to the problems you've spoken of?"

"No, and of course the bad part is that I have no concrete evidence as to what the problems really are. I only know that whatever's happening with Colleen Reynolds is affecting the way she runs Kate's shop, and thus the profit margin. Our customers expect special care and consideration. That's why people keep coming back to us. Obviously that didn't happen at the Cape Cod Kloset this last summer—as I can see now that I've really analyzed the situation—because our sales volume was way down. That meant that either people from the previous year didn't come back to us, or came back and didn't like what they saw, or the way they were treated, and so didn't buy."

"Mrs. Reynolds would offer the same kind of clothes one would find in Kate's other Klosets, wouldn't she?" James asked.

"Yes. But the way she displays them is...atrocious. It's astonishing what bad, or indifferent, display can do to clothes and accessories. When I went to the shop the other morning, she'd opened late, for one thing, and if I'd had to describe the entire ambience in a single word, I would have said *dowdy*." Stacy paused. "A Kate's Kloset is never dowdy," she told James seriously. "But there was absolutely no verve to the atmosphere in the Kloset here the other morning. In fact, I got a sense of lethargy, hopelessness, that was actually depressing. I had the impression no one cared how things looked, that no one cared especially about pleasing customers and making sales. There was a general feeling of defeat." Stacy paused again, then said, "Maybe I'm dramatizing things."

"Maybe not," James said. "One's gut feelings count for a great deal if one is basically intuitive—as I am sure you are. That is to say, I imagine the impulses you received from the shop were quite valid. Yet this woman has not only the same merchandise to deal with as the other Klosets have, but the same promotional backup and support from headquarters, I would imagine?"

"Yes."

"The store has a good location?"

"An excellent location. James, this has been a very successful operation until this past season, and Kate's had the Cape Cod Kloset open for five years. Colleen Reynolds has been manager for two of those five years, and her first year she did just great."

"Then the problem almost certainly must be with her directly," James said.

Stacy looked at him as he said that and saw that he was frowning slightly, as if absorbed in deep concentration. It came to her that James was giving this matter of Colleen Reynolds and the Cape Cod Kloset his full attention and consideration. He hadn't merely been listening to her spout off to be polite.

Also, she was impressed with the *way* he had listened to her. He'd given her grave, courteous attention, and she had the feeling nothing else had infringed upon his mind, in his thought processes, as he heard her out.

He cared. That was the thing that surfaced as she continued to observe him. He genuinely cared about people and their problems. Stacy took it a step farther. She imagined that James must actually shoulder the problems of many of his clients, for a time anyway, and she could imagine the enormous strain that must put on him.

She began to feel slightly ashamed of herself as she realized that, so far, she'd taken James's profession, and his enormous success with his book, rather lightly. She'd found it amusing that a person so renowned in his field could have such problems keeping women at bay that he didn't even want to hire a temporary secretary when he needed one.

Now she could see that most women, in addition to being attracted to James—and if one had any red blood in her veins, how could one help being attracted to James?—probably unloaded on him just as she had been unloading on him. Normally, she was sure, he dealt with much heavier stuff than the problems of a resort area boutique. She could imagine the dark side of human relationships that must so frequently come his way. Serious issues, life-and-death issues, sometimes. She could picture James considering each in turn, weighing and evaluating the problems even as he was now weighing and evaluating the much lesser problem she'd presented him with.

She made a quick decision. "Enough," she said.

James looked up, "Enough what?"

"Enough of Colleen Reynolds and Kate's Cape Cod Kloset," Stacy said, trying to sound light about it. "Now..."

He held up an admonishing hand. "Wait a minute."

"No," Stacy said, "I really mean it. This is my problem, and one way or another I'll solve it. So let's go on to something else."

James pushed back his chair, leaned back and surveyed her. "Just like that, eh?" he said.

Stacy noted that his gray eyes suddenly looked stormy. "We really have talked enough about Kate's shop, James," she said, puzzled.

"Have we?" James surveyed her in silence, then asked, "Don't you ever share a problem, Stacy?"

"No, not usually. There isn't any need. I talk the situation over with Kate, of course, but I try to spare her as much as possible in having to deal with what's become my area in her business."

"That's not what I mean."

"What did you mean, then?"

"Do you always feel you have to handle everything in your life on your own? I'm not referring only to the work you do for my cousin. Haven't you ever learned that it usually helps, sometimes helps very much, to talk out what's bothering you with someone else?"

He was hitting too close to home, and Stacy began to search for ways to avoid this particular issue. The fact was, she long ago had been accustomed to keeping her problems to herself. She'd become accustomed to keeping almost everything to herself. Paul hadn't been interested in the small details—he'd considered them small, anyway—that arose during the course of her day. She'd found that out very soon after they'd married when he'd made no effort to hide his boredom as she poured out the day's events to him once he got home. He hadn't been interested in hearing about her accomplishments, her triumphs, either—all of which also had seemed on the small side to him. So she'd learned to keep things to herself, and the habit had become so ingrained it was now second nature to her.

"Well?" James asked.

"I don't like to bore people, or to bother people," Stacy said feebly.

"You neither bore me nor bother me, Stacy," James informed her. "I doubt you bore or bother most people you meet." He nearly added that he supposed this was yet another repercussion of her marriage, but before he blurted out that supposition, his professionalism came to the rescue. This wasn't the moment to find out more about Stacy's marriage—though that moment would come, James promised himself grimly. By God, he'd make it come!

He began more gently. "You've told me you had a dull evening with Mrs. Reynolds, but I'm sure there was more to it than that, and I'd honestly like to hear the rest of it." He smiled. "Maybe I'm just naturally nosy," he suggested.

James saw the skeptical look Stacy gave him, but he did get a response from her. "Well, I avoided getting into details about the store," she said. "I tried to act as someone would who really was here on vacation for a couple of days."

"And?"

"Colleen suggested a few things I might enjoy doing. Since this is my first trip to the Cape, she told me to be sure to drive out to Provincetown and wander around. She suggested a little restaurant out there called Napi's as an interesting place to have lunch. She mentioned taking a day trip out to Nantucket on the boat from Hyannis as something else she thought I'd enjoy."

"She said nothing about the store?"

"Very little. I think she was waiting for me to question her and wasn't about to impart any more than she had to. She's a smart woman, James. She knows what's happened, what's continuing to happen. Maybe, just maybe, my looming up on the scene will alert her sufficiently so that nothing more will have to be done. She'll spruce up and get down to business as she should."

"Do you really think that?"

"I'd like to think it," Stacy admitted. "But such simple solutions seldom happen." She finished her coffee, then said, "I did tell her about you. That is, I said you were Kate's cousin, Jim Sinclair, who was writing a novel in the horror genre and came up here to finish it. I told her you'd cut your hand, and since you were right at your deadline I was going to stay on a few days and do your typing for you."

"Did she accept that story?"

"Yes, I think so." Stacy hesitated, then volunteered, "There was one thing more."

"What?"

"I drove Colleen home—she doesn't live far from the shop—and as I pulled up in front of her house the front door opened. There was a man standing in the doorway—I could see him only in silhouette, since the light was at his back—but he was a big, burly man, and when she saw him Colleen really scampered out of the car. Regardless, he started giving it to her before she was halfway up the walk."

"What do you mean, he started 'giving it' to her?"

"He was very unpleasant," Stacy said. "He started bellowing at her. I mean he was quite loud. He asked her where the hell she'd been, among other things, and then said something about someone named Cissy. They went inside, and he slammed the door behind them, so that's all I heard. But..."

"But what?"

"I'm sure it was Al Reynolds, the man who delivered that emergency oil supply to us," Stacy said. "I recognized the voice and... the shape was the same. He seems to be a very unpleasant man, James. I wonder if he's the root of Colleen's problem."

At midmorning James decided to go for a walk on the beach and asked Stacy if she would accompany him. This time she did.

Again the day was overcast, with dark clouds to the west. "Looks as if we may be in for some more rain," James said.

He'd been walking at quite a clip, and Stacy had been struggling to keep up with him. His legs were so much longer than hers. He suddenly became aware of her struggle and stopped short. "Why didn't you say something?" he demanded.

Stacy, gasping slightly, managed, "About what?"

"About letting me put you out of breath like that. Don't you ever speak up for yourself, Stacy?"

Stung, she retorted, "Yes, I speak up for myself. You make me sound like a wimp, and I am not a wimp. Get that very straight, James Ashley-Sinclair. I am not a wimp."

James smiled, and Stacy caught her breath for an entirely different reason. When he smiled like that, he was mesmerizing. There was a gleam in his gray eyes as he held out his arms to her and said, "Prove it."

As if drawn by an invisible magnet, Stacy moved closer to him. She stood on her toes and flung her arms around his neck and—even as she wondered what in the name of God was motivating her to behave like this—she kissed him, all the fire and passion inherent in her coming to the surface as her lips met his.

Briefly James was staggered. He's been teasing her, true, and he'd hoped for some response from her, but he'd never dreamed she would rise to his bait in this way. He felt as if she were branding him with her lips and, the crazy thing was, he was welcoming the branding. He wanted Stacy's imprint on him. He couldn't imagine any other woman in the world ever being able to match up to this kiss of Stacy's.

He knew he should put firm hands on her shoulders, set her back on her feet—for she was standing on tiptoe and then bring rationality back into the picture by gently, teasingly, saying, "Hey, there, little girl. Hold up!"

But he did no such thing.

Instead, he drew her even closer to him, his left hand moving to tangle itself in her dark hair, his right hand yearning to follow with the same action but unable to do so because of the stiff bandages.

Rain began to spatter down, but Stacy and James continued to cling, to kiss, until finally he became aware that they were both getting soaked. "We'd better make a run for it," he said, clasping her shoulder.

Stacy looked at him, her eyes dazed. He had the feeling she was temporarily out of touch with reality. But then she let him take her hand and they scampered back down the beach—James matching his steps to hers this time—to the sanctuary of Kate's Hideaway.

They changed into dry clothes, Stacy made hot chocolate while James got a fire going in the living room, and then they sat on the floor in front of the fire sipping the hot chocolate and saying very little until they were warm again.

"You might as well tell me, James," Stacy said finally.

"Tell you what?" he asked lazily.

"Have you decided to bag the book and go back to England?"

"In this case, 'bag,' I suppose, means to give up on something?"

"Yes."

"What makes you think I'd want to give up on the book, Stacy? I owe it. I've been paid a hefty advance for it. I'm way overdue. Rather than bagging it, it's imperative that I get on with it and finish it as quickly as possible."

"But you spoke about going back to England?"

"That was before you offered to help me. I would have gone back to England at this point only if it had become mandatory to do so."

"So—" her pulse was pounding as she asked the question "—you still want me to work with you?"

Instead of answering that, James scowled and asked his own question. "Have you changed your mind, Stacy?"

"No," she said quickly. "No, of course not."

"Then why—"

"I just thought maybe you'd changed your mind, James."

"Perhaps you're the one of us whose mind has changed, Stacy," James said. "If that's the case, please say so. I can understand that you may have made your offer impulsively and subsequently regretted it."

Stacy was getting the impression she'd just hurt his feelings. He was assuming that she didn't want to work with him, and the mere thought of that assumption made her want to laugh aloud. Working with James would mean having the chance to stay with him a little while longer....

She stopped short, appalled at the direction her thoughts were taking her.

"I should see about renting a typewriter," she said, forcing herself to become practical. "If I can get a good electronic typewriter with a sufficient memory bank and all, I think it might be a better choice than a word processor. With a word processor we'd also require a printer...."

"I'll leave that up to you."

"Then I'd better look into things after lunch. I'll go through the classified section, make a few phone calls. James, when do you want to get started?"

"I don't know," he confessed glumly.

"You don't know?" she echoed in surprise. "Is there something holding you up?"

"Only me."

"You?"

He nodded. "I don't have it together, Stacy," he confessed. "Oh, yes, I have lots of material already typed up, scads of notes, but... I still don't have it all together. The problem is, I've been forced to interrupt the writing of this book so many times because of other commitments. The lecture tour took such a large block of my time and, during the course of it, there was no chance to even think of the book. It's almost as if I'm starting all over again, and that causes its own confusion because I'm not starting all over again. I'm going to have to pick up where I left off, which is infinitely harder. Does that make sense to you?"

"Yes. I can see the difficulty."

"It's rather like saying goodbye to someone you think you're going to see again the next day, and then months pass before you see them again," James said. "In the interim a great deal has happened, and so there's so much to catch up on. If you're very close to the person, the catch-up can be accomplished with astonishing speed. If you're not—or if a variety of things have come between you during the enforced absence—then sometimes gaps remain that can never be filled satisfactorily. Does that make sense to you?"

"Yes."

"Nothing more than 'yes,' Stacy?"

"I've the feeling you're trying to chicken out, James," Stacy told him.

"What?"

"I have the feeling you're trying to talk yourself out of finishing the book, at least for now, because you've lost enthusiasm for it or, maybe, you can't get yourself into the right mind-set."

"The second's the truest," James admitted. "I haven't lost enthusiasm for this project and I have a lot I want to say. But I admit I'm not ready, as far as getting back to work is concerned. Perhaps that's due to laziness on my part, but I don't really think so. I think I'm rather afraid of failure, Stacy."

That was such an astonishing admission coming from James Ashley-Sinclair that Stacy gaped at him. Rallying, she asked, "How can you think such a thing?"

"It's not easy to follow one's own act when the act's had the success of my first book, Stacy," James said quietly. "Though it's quite true that I've disliked all the fuss and furor made over *A Personal Sex Bible*, I suppose I've learned to live with the results better than I realized.

"Now, with a second book, I'm putting out into uncharted waters, and at this stage I can't help but wonder how it will be if the book is a total flop. I can learn to live with that, too, I'm sure, if it happens—but it would be far more of a disaster than it would have been if my first opus hadn't been quite so successful."

Stacy was astonished. She'd felt, till now, that James was so extremely self-confident that not much, if anything, could daunt him. Now he surprised her.

"My first book has come to mean quite a lot to a lot of people, and that one aspect of its success is gratifying. Now, I should hate to let those people down with something that didn't offer them nearly as much."

Listening to James say that, Stacy saw it as yet another example of his caring. But he was also showing her a vulnerability that touched her very much.

She reached over and clasped his hand. "Stop worrying, James. You've got nothing to worry about," she advised, and she'd never meant anything more. "Your new book, as I'm sure the critics will be saying in London, is certain to be smashing."

That night, after she was sure James was asleep, Stacy sneaked back downstairs and cautiously made her way across Kate's living room. She took the autographed copy of *A Personal Sex Bible* up to her room with her and closed her bedroom door. Only then did she switch on her bedside lamp.

She settled down, tucking the sheets and blankets up around her, and started to read. An hour later she was still reading. And now she could see why James Ashley-Sinclair's book had become such a success.

James spoke to people in simple terms. Reading his words, one had the effect of sitting in the same room with him, listening to him talk. He got down to basics in his philosophy, and there was no posturing about him. He wrote clearly, succinctly, addressing problems that were, indeed, universal in their impact. He lightened what he said with a rare humor that shone through just when it needed to. He was brilliant, Stacy realized, really brilliant.

Finally she closed the book and set it aside till she could get back to it the next night. She turned out the light and lay in the darkness, marveling how she'd ever had the nerve to throw her arms around James on the beach earlier that day and kiss him as she had. How she'd had the gall, at moments, to chide him and chastise him and to argue with him . . .

He was looming as a larger-than-life figure to her, after reading only the first portion of his book, and she wondered how she could possibly face him across the breakfast table in the morning as if he were an ordinary man.

Chapter Eight

When Kate called from Miami the next day, Stacy asked her if the large drop-leaf table in the living room was an antique.

"Yes, I guess so," Kate replied indifferently. "Why?"

"I wouldn't want to put a typewriter on it if that might damage it," Stacy said.

"The reason it's antique is because it has endured," Kate said. "Go ahead and use it."

Stacy and James moved the table to the far end of the living room, placing it in front of the picture window. When fully opened, the table was large enough so that Stacy could use half of it for her work space, and James could use half of it for his.

It was Saturday. The typewriter rental agency was open till noon, and it was slightly after noon when Stacy got back to the Hideaway with the machine she'd chosen, a supply of typing paper, some other writing supplies and a couple of bags of groceries.

Once she and James had finished setting up their work space, Stacy made sandwiches and coffee, and they paused for lunch. Lunch over, she suggested to James that perhaps they could get started on the book.

James evaded her. "Let's go for a walk on the beach first," he said.

"You went for a walk while I was uptown doing the errands," she reminded him.

"Yes, I know," he said. He shrugged. "Well," he admitted sheepishly, "I can't put it off forever, can I? It will take me a good hour, though, to get my notes organized. Probably more like two hours. I have a lot to go through. So perhaps you'd like to take a walk on the beach yourself."

"No," Stacy said, "but I will take advantage of the time to go over to the Kloset."

She deliberately hadn't gone near the shop yesterday and hadn't really intended to make a return visit until Monday. But on Monday, she reasoned, she might be deep into her work with James. This seemed the better time.

As she drove across town, Stacy hoped that maybe just knowing she was around might have inspired Colleen Reynolds to start sprucing up, perhaps beginning by doing the front window display over.

But that hadn't come to pass, she saw quickly as she parked across the street from Kate's Kloset and then sat in her car for a few minutes, studying the front of the shop. The bushes on either side of the entrance weren't only straggly, they looked as if they were dying. The window display hadn't been changed. There was even some paint chipping over the front door.

Stacy felt depressed as she got out of the car and slowly crossed the street. She even began to wish she'd delayed this visit till the first of the week. It was going to be difficult to deal with Colleen Reynolds under these circumstances without giving anything away, and she still felt she shouldn't bring about a real confrontation until she'd garnered a little more information.

The store was empty when she walked into it. No customers, no salespeople. She'd made up her mind she was going to tell Colleen she'd come to pick up a couple of sweaters, since the weather was getting cool. She knew the Klosets had contracted for some especially stunning sweaters for fall. As a matter of fact, she already owned a couple of them but had left them back in her New York apartment when making the trek to Boston and the Cape. After all, this was supposed to have been a brief stay.

The light was on in the manager's office, so she was sure Colleen—or someone—must be on the premises. She was tempted to head straight for the office if only to see what Colleen was doing. Then she decided that discretion was still the better course right now, so she browsed.

There were some stacks of sweaters, but they weren't the new stock Stacy had been thinking about. Possibly, she conceded, the new sweaters had gone over so well that Colleen had already sold out on them. But somehow she doubted it.

Finally she edged close to the office door and coughed. The cough sounded as contrived as it was, but at least it worked. Colleen appeared in the doorway. "I'm sorry. I didn't realize anyone had come in."

She came closer, recognized Stacy and stood rooted to the spot, obviously disconcerted. Stacy couldn't help feeling sorry for her. She was such a potentially attractive woman, but right now she looked pathetic.

"Stacy," she said, finally moving forward and forcing a smile. "What can I do for you?"

"I thought I might pick up a couple of sweaters," Stacy said, returning the smile.

"Sweaters? Right over there," Colleen led the way toward the sweaters Stacy already had been looking at.

"I was thinking of the new line," Stacy said as she followed her. "The Clarisse originals. If I'm remembering right, they come in some gorgeous fall colors."

Colleen paused. Her back was ramrod straight. The woman was a bundle of nerves. "I'm not sure we've been sent any of the Clarisse originals, Stacy," she said, her voice low and taut. "If we have been, they must be with some of the merchandise in the storeroom that hasn't been unpacked yet."

Stacy was glad Colleen's back was still turned to her as she heard that. She'd seen an excellent display of the sweaters in question at the Boston Kloset, and the manager there had pointed them out to her enthusiastically, stating, "Those are one of our hottest-selling items at the moment."

Colleen certainly must have received her fall merchandise about the same time the Boston store had. Stacy tried to hide her shock. She needed nothing more to convince her that Colleen was letting the business slip through her fingers.

She could imagine Kate's reaction, were she to call her in Miami and tell her that Colleen hadn't even unpacked some of the best of the new fall clothing. Kate was patient to a point, but then she could be very unyielding. It wouldn't take much more to cause Kate to replace Colleen Reynolds and, despite the apparent evidence, Stacy still wasn't sure that was the right thing to do. Thankfully she was reprieved by a couple of customers coming into the shop, and she took the opportunity to slip away.

Colleen was obviously short of help, Stacy mused as she went back to her car. There had been another saleswoman in the store the last time she'd visited. Maybe now that saleswoman was out having a late lunch. But an effectively run Kloset needed more than a manager and a single salesperson.

The first of the week, Stacy resolved, she'd have to sit down and have a straight-from-the-shoulder talk with Colleen and then report back to Kate. For better or worse.

James was sitting at the worktable surrounded by a sea of papers. Stacy, looking at him, felt as if she were gazing at the embodiment of chaos. She didn't see how he could possibly hope to make any sense out of the mess that spread out on all sides of him.

She sat down on her side of the table and surveyed him. He looked miserable. Also, he'd poured himself some Scotch and, as she watched, he took a hefty sip of it. Maybe he could drink and work. She couldn't. Even a little alcohol made her too fuzzy to think clearly when she had a job to do.

Funny...last night, brooding about James's book as she'd lain in the dark, Stacy would have sworn she could never again dare to be half as impertinent to him as she'd been ever since they'd met. She was too impressed by the brilliance she'd discovered and the fame, which she really hadn't taken all that seriously until then. But now, in the bright light of day, she saw James as James, and she began to get annoyed with him.

"Do you call this the way to get started?" she said, her voice laced with considerable asperity. "It seems to me we should begin with an elemental filing system for your material, so you'll know what you have and what you don't have."

James mumbled something under his breath, then admitted, "I'm not good at organizing things like filing systems. Anyway. . . this is what comes of staying away from something you should be doing for as long as I've stayed away from this." He pointed his bandaged hand accusingly at the miscellaneous heaps and clusters of papers.

"I just happened to buy a box of file folders," Stacy said, ignoring his complaint. "So suppose we get to it?"

He gave her a wry smile. "No excuses with you, I take it?"

"No excuses," she said firmly.

For the next hour they worked steadily in surprising harmony, even though James grumbled constantly about what they were doing. By late afternoon, though, he had to admit that he had a much better idea of where he was going with the book.

"Thanks to you," he told Stacy.

"Maybe I'm a natural-born file clerk," she muttered.

"The devil you are," he retorted. "There's certainly nothing wrong with being a file clerk, but I wouldn't say that's your true forte, even though you're extremely good at getting things organized."

"What would you think was my true forte, James?"

The moment Stacy voiced the question, she deplored asking such a leading one of him. But he considered it quite seriously—at least he pretended to consider it quite seriously—until he could no longer restrain a smile that spread across his face and set silvery lights dancing in his gray eyes.

"Someday I'll tell you," he promised. "But not now." He pushed back his chair and announced, "That's it for today."

Stacy shook her head. "We should put in another hour or two," she told him. "Then we might reach the point where you could actually pick up the threads and begin dictating tomorrow."

"No," he said. "For one thing, this isn't a marathon I'm running. I want to get the book done, yes, but I don't intend to break my neck over it. For another thing, I've been thinking..."

Stacy couldn't resist impishly retorting, "Dangerous sport."

James chuckled. "You don't know how dangerous." He met her eyes, and she felt a funny little shiver crawl up and down her spine. His wonderfully mellow voice, with that disarming British accent to spice his words, could be so suggestive. She felt as if he were verbally caressing her, and she began to wish he'd translate tones into action. She shivered anew as she imagined what it would be like to be undressed by James, to be made love to by James, and she wouldn't have believed that just *thinking* about something like that could actually make her feel giddy.

"Ms. MacKenzie," James said suddenly, "may I have the pleasure of your company at dinner?"

Stacy had become so absorbed in her work with him that she'd forgotten all about dinner. Now she frowned and said, "I meant to buy a steak, damn it, and I didn't. Well, how about some excellent chicken chow mein, courtesy of a very large can? I can embellish it with... something or other."

"No," James said, "I was thinking of our going out to Provincetown. Why don't I call the restaurant you mentioned—Napi's, wasn't it—and see if I can reserve a table at eight? If they serve luncheons, one would surely think they'd also serve dinners."

He had a good memory. A very good memory. Stacy wasn't sure she could have recalled the name of the restaurant Colleen had mentioned.

"I've heard a great deal about Provincetown," James added, "and obviously, since this is my first trip to Cape Cod, I've never been there. So let's both do a little exploring and enjoy dinner in the course of it."

"I don't know," Stacy said. The memories of her feelings in the middle of the night were beginning to surge again. Nothing could have made her more aware that they traveled in very separate leagues—had she been about to forget it—than reading his book, even reading the blurbs on the back cover about it, those written before he'd gained his present fame. Those blurbs had concentrated on his professional expertise, which was considerable.

James smiled and asked drily, "Now don't tell me you don't have anything to wear?"

"No, it's not that," she answered honestly. "Colleen said Provincetown's pretty informal. That is, you can dress up if you want to, but you don't have to."

"Good," James said. "I don't want to."

"James..."

"All right," James said with a mocking smile. "Tell me one reason why you shouldn't go out to Provincetown for dinner with me."

She had to laugh at him, then said, "You know, it may sound clichéd, but it really isn't such a great idea to mix pleasure with business."

This time James laughed. "Oh, come on, Stacy," he chided. "That surely doesn't apply in our case. Mixing pleasure with business, indeed. Look, you're not my employee, you know. You're working with me, not for me. You're doing me a great favor, as a matter of fact. So let's scratch that one. What next?"

"James, I don't know what Kate would think of our..."

At that, James looked exasperated. "Are you saying you don't know what Kate would think of my taking you out to dinner?" he queried, the haughtiness surfacing again. "Stacy, I should think Kate would expect me to take you out to dinner. She'd consider me an idiot if I didn't."

Stacy, clutching at straws, discovered what was probably the best reason of all why he shouldn't go out to Provincetown for dinner himself, let alone take her. "You might be recognized," she said.

To her surprise, James was undaunted. "I thought of that," he admitted. "Frankly, I think it unlikely, unless the restaurant turns spotlights on its patrons. But, even if I were recognized, it wouldn't be the end of the world. I doubt we'd be followed back here, don't you, Stacy?"

He was being generous with the sarcasm. Miffed, Stacy said, "I wish you'd stop making fun of me."

The request sounded childish to her as soon as it left her lips. Now all she needed to do was pout, she thought ruefully. It wasn't her style to behave this way, but James *had* just annoyed her. She'd only been trying to protect him, after all—hadn't she?

She admitted the truth. She wasn't trying to protect James right now; she was trying to protect herself. She was afraid to take risks where he was concerned. For the sake of her own self-preservation she couldn't chance much more with him than going through their daily working sessions together. There, at least, she could keep their relationship reasonably professional. Even sharing meals here in the Hideaway, or relaxing in front of the fireplace, she could remain objective, she tried to tell herself, then admitted that that just wasn't so. She was vulnerable around James whether sitting at a typewriter, sipping coffee across the kitchen table from him, walking along the beach with him or simply being in the same room with him.

"I wasn't aware I tend to make fun of you, Stacy," James said. "We both tend to poke a bit of fun at each other now and then, and I'd say we both find that enjoyable. But right now all I want is to take you out for a change of pace and scene. So how about it?"

Stacy tried to appear indifferent. "All right, if you're sure," she said, shrugging. But she was sure James was well aware that the assumed indifference was a camouflage for several other feelings that were playing havoc with her nerves and emotions.

Actually, James was tempted to throttle her. He hadn't expected so much reaction from a simple dinner invitation. As Stacy tried to toss a series of obstacles in the path of their spending a single evening together in Provincetown, he tried to figure out why she was doing so, and it wasn't too difficult to reach an answer.

Stacy was running scared where he was concerned. Very scared. If he hadn't known better, he would have said she actually was afraid of him—which made no sense at all.

"We could always toss a coin for the shower, of course," he said rather shortly. "But I'll be gallant about it. You go first."

While Stacy showered, James went outside and strolled around the house. He didn't go down to the beach. Instead, he stood at the foot of the steps for a while and stared out to sea.

He was trying to erase the image of Stacy taking a shower from his mind. He wanted to go back inside and get into the shower with her, a big cake of soap in his hand. He wanted to soap her all over, and after that . . .

He gazed down at his bandaged hand and had to smile. The doctor had warned him against getting the bandages wet. When taking a shower so far, he'd simply held his hand out of the shower stall while the water splashed down on the rest of him. But the job he wanted to do on Stacy would require total ambidexterity.

James offered to drive, but Stacy declined. "I think I'd better. It might be difficult for you."

He was quite certain it wouldn't be difficult for him at all, but he didn't say anything further. Once they started out, though, he stole a sideways glance at her and wondered if it would have been better to settle for her chicken chow mein after all. She looked absolutely beautiful... but much too tense.

He knew she hadn't brought many clothes to the Cape with her, yet she'd appeared in a deep red creation that was absolutely gorgeous on her. She explained that she'd taken one dressy dress to Boston to wear when dining with the manager of Kate's shop there, and James was happy to discover the manager was a woman. Any man would have coveted Stacy looking as she did tonight.

James, who would have sworn he didn't have a jealous bone in his body, was again surprised at himself. This wasn't the first time he'd realized how easily he could be jealous of Stacy. He hadn't even liked the looks the young doctor had given her in the clinic the other day. He'd wanted to growl, "Back off, man, she's mine," and that sort of caveman thinking was *very* out of character.

In any event, she wasn't his, James reminded himself. She was a free person; she'd made that abundantly clear. She'd also made it clear she intended to remain a free person....

"Do you want me to turn the heater up?" Stacy asked.

James was tempted to tell her that he didn't need the heater, since he had plenty of personal heat firing up inside himself just thinking about her. Instead, he asked politely, "Are you cold?"

"No. I thought you might be."

"No. Don't you know we English aren't even accustomed to central heating—and generally prefer it that way?"

"So I've heard," Stacy said.

"Did you like England, Stacy?"

"Yes. I loved England. I just didn't see enough of it, that's all. I think I already told you I missed the trip to Stratford because I had a rotten cold."

"And that's when you saw me on the telly?"

"Yes."

"I rather wish you'd never seen me on the telly."

She cast a curious glance his way. "Why do you say that?"

"Because I think maybe watching that interview gave you some preconceived ideas about me I'd much prefer you didn't have."

"I don't understand."

"Don't you? I didn't think I came off too well."

"Really? I thought you bested your interviewer beautifully, especially when he pretty much accused you of trying to hold out information on your second book so that you could assure its sale."

"Well," James said, "he was certainly wrong on that score, wasn't he? I'm sure people who were watching have forgotten all about whatever it was I said concerning the book. And God knows when the book will ever get out, anyway. I'm wondering if I'm going to be able to finish it."

"You'll finish it," Stacy promised.

"You make that sound like a threat."

"You have to get with it, James," Stacy said.

She sounded like a strict schoolteacher chastising a child who hadn't been doing as well as he should, and James chuckled, leaned back and relaxed. The atmosphere had softened between them, for which he was thankful. Stacy's lips were curved in a slight smile. He caught a whiff of her perfume and decided it had to be the sexiest perfume a woman had ever used. He thought about every place in the world he'd ever been—and he'd been a great many places—and knew he'd never been happier than he was right now, driving out to a little town at the tip of Cape Cod with Stacy.

He wanted to snatch that happiness and preserve it, even though he knew the futility of trying to clutch happiness. It was much too elusive.

They parked on the large public wharf built out over Provincetown Harbor, then strolled toward Commercial Street and along Standish Street toward Napi's.

The lights were dim in the restaurant. They were ushered to a small corner table and, as they sat down, James smiled at Stacy and observed, "Well, so far I'm incognito."

"Shush," she said, glancing around.

"Stacy, love, you'd make a hell of a spy," he teased. "You'd give the whole show away with reactions like that."

"All right, all right," she conceded. "I admit I'm not much good at camouflage, but..."

"Stay the way you are," James said softly, and their eyes met across the candle-lit space between them.

Stacy was wearing faux ruby and diamond earrings that glittered in the soft light. Her lips were slightly parted, and her cheeks were flushed. As he watched her, feeling a surge of tenderness toward her, James saw her beautiful blue eyes fill with tears, and he reached across the table and gripped her hand.

"What is it, love?" he asked anxiously, heard the word he'd just said, and recognized its truth. She was his love. The last thing in the world he'd intended to let happen was happening. He was falling in love with Stacy MacKenzie. He *was* in love with Stacy MacKenzie.

"Excuse me a minute, will you?" Stacy asked, and bolted for the rest room. James sat back, stunned both by the discovery he'd just made about his own feelings and by the effect he knew just a little solicitousness on his part could have on Stacy.

Hadn't anyone ever been kind to her? How could people *not* have been kind to anyone as caring, as giving, as Stacy was?

A waitress came with menus, and James recklessly ordered a bottle of very fine champagne. Tonight, he decided, was going to be special. He was going to toast Stacy as she should be toasted. He was going to pay attention to her as she should be paid attention to, and when they got back to the Hideaway, he hoped she would let him make love to her as she should have been made love to long ago.

Stacy looked pale when she came back to the table, and finally, after his persistent questioning, she admitted to James that she felt slightly queasy. She barely touched the champagne and did less than scant justice to the excellent dinner he ordered. Though the atmosphere in the restaurant was intimate and romantic—and James felt both—Stacy seemed preoccupied and ill at ease. James decided to skip dessert. He called for the check and they left.

"I'm sorry, James," Stacy said in a very small voice as they were walking back to the wharf.

"There's nothing to be sorry about," he said. "It's not your fault that you don't feel well. I'm sorry about that."

They reached her car, and before Stacy knew what James was about to do, he reached out a hand and placed it first on her forehead, then touched each cheek with it. "No fever," he diagnosed.

"What made you think I might have a fever?"

"I thought you might be coming down with something. When did you start to feel ill, Stacy?"

"Believe me, I wouldn't have left Devon with you if I'd felt ill, James," Stacy said quickly. "Something just came over me in the restaurant, that's all."

"To do with me?"

"What do you mean?"

"I want to know if whatever came over you in the restaurant had to do with me, Stacy."

Stacy stared at him, distressed. How could she possibly answer that question honestly?

She'd suddenly felt so overcome by him in the restaurant. He'd sat there looking so handsome, so absolutely wonderful, and so totally self-assured. That aristocratic air he wore so easily came naturally to him, she knew, but it still set him apart from most people in an indefinable yet very distinct way.

She'd thought of his book, and she'd become aware that this was *James Ashley-Sinclair* she was sitting with. It was the first time they'd shared a purely social situation, and she'd begun to feel more and more uncomfortable.

Then she'd met James's eyes and found that he was looking at her as if she were the most alluring, intriguing person in the world. Suddenly she'd gone cold all over. She'd begun to feel sick because she'd been sure she couldn't measure up to James now or ever. That certainty had become overwhelming, and suddenly she'd been unable to stay at the table with him for even another second....

Now she felt James's fingers touch her chin, cup it and force her to look up at him. "You don't have to tell me now what happened back there, Stacy," he said softly. "But you will, sometime."

Before she could answer him, he bent his head and kissed her. It was a long kiss, a sweet kiss, a totally loving kiss.

Stacy's senses were still reeling when James commanded, "Give me the car keys, will you, please? I'm going to drive us home."

Chapter Nine

James was already at work when Stacy went downstairs Sunday morning. He looked up as she approached their worktable, and frowned. "I'd expected you to sleep in late this morning," he told her.

"Why?" she asked, taken aback by the frown.

"Because obviously you were exhausted last night."

It was true that she'd fallen asleep in the car on the way back from Provincetown last night. James had put some soft music on the radio, and under its—and his—spell she'd relaxed more than she would have believed possible. He'd woken her when they reached the house, and he'd insisted that she go directly to bed. There had been a ragged edge to his voice as he'd said, "Go up *now*, Stacy," as if her scuttling under the covers immediately was somehow imperative.

She'd caught the ragged note, seen that James had looked flustered, or unhappy, or a combination of both, and had been tempted to stay down with him for a while if only to try to make amends for her behavior in the restaurant. But it was true—she had been exhausted. Emotionally exhausted, though, not physically. As a result, her night's sleep hadn't been all that great.

Now she responded rather testily. "I'm fine, James. Why didn't you wake me? It's after nine. We should have been at work by now."

"I've been at work for the past hour and a half, Stacy," he informed her loftily. "I'm still going over my notes. I doubt if I'll be ready to start dictating anything to you today. Anyway, it's Sunday. Sunday is supposed to be a day of rest."

"I don't need a day of rest, James. I'd like to get started," Stacy informed him.

"I just told you," he said, the haughtiness creeping in. "I doubt I'll be ready to work with you today."

She faced him, shoulders set, her chin tilted defiantly. "Why are you stalling?" she demanded.

James put down the papers he'd been holding. "What makes you think I'm stalling?" he countered.

"Because you are. When we finished yesterday we had things in good order. You said yourself we could start work this morning."

"I forgot it would be Sunday."

"Come off it, James," she snapped.

James scowled at the papers he'd just put down and pushed them away. "All right," he admitted irritably. "I just can't get down to it, that's all."

"Why not?"

"My God, do I have to spell everything out for you?"

He was glaring at her, a picture of righteous, aristocratic indignation, and Stacy nearly backed off. Then her own indignation surfaced. "You know," she pointed out coldly, "I can't stay up here forever with you. Kate's your cousin, and she thinks the world of you, but she's not going to indulge you forever, either."

"*Indulge* me?" James's voice was icy.

"Precisely. Kate seemed pleased that I was going to be able to help you out, but once I straighten out the mess with Colleen Reynolds, I'm going to have to head back to New York. Kate will have other work for me to do."

"Such loyalty," James scoffed.

Stacy bristled. "Yes, such loyalty. Don't you rate loyalty fairly high on your list of necessary ingredients for a good relationship? If not, maybe you should think about revising the list."

James was incensing her with his superior attitude. Right now she didn't give a damn what she said to him. She was speaking the truth, and that was what counted. Maybe he needed to hear more of the truth. Maybe too many people deferred to the great James Ashley-Sinclair, a suspicion that made her all the more determined not to become one of them.

Anger was heightening her color. Her eyes were sparking, and she looked young and healthy and vital and so absolutely marvelous that James was sure his heart actually flipped over.

The stern lines in his face softened. He picked up a pencil and toyed with it. "All right, you've called my bluff," he said slowly.

"What's that supposed to mean?"

"I do have cold feet when it comes to the book, Stacy."

She stared at him. She couldn't believe that James Ashley-Sinclair could develop cold feet over anything.

He stood up, moved closer to the window and looked out at the sea, a serene, beautiful blue today, deep and clear, close to the color of Stacy's eyes. "I'm sure the problem is that I've put it aside for too long and so I'm finding it very difficult to get back in the right tempo. Also, there are moments when one . . . wonders."

"Wonders what?"

"When *I* wonder just what the hell right I have to preach to people."

She was dumbfounded. "I don't see why you feel you're preaching to people," she said, puzzled. "Certainly you weren't preaching in your first book."

His eyebrows lifted. "I thought you hadn't read my first book."

"I hadn't when I said I hadn't. But the other night . . ." Stacy glanced guiltily toward the coffee table where the book usually lay.

James followed her glance and saw that the coffee table was bare where his book had been. He had a sudden vision of Stacy sitting up in bed, late at night, reading what he'd written, and he didn't know how he felt about that. On the one hand, he was flattered she'd decided to read his book. On the other hand, the book—in his mind—was still a professional treatise, and he was becoming far more interested in presenting his personal rather than his professional side to Stacy.

He wanted to ask her what she thought of the book—as much of it as she had read—then decided that would be a stupid question. Suppose she didn't like it? She'd be polite enough not to say so, but then he might sense she didn't like it, and where would that leave them?

James ran an agitated hand through his smooth golden hair, thus loosening up some of the natural wave he usually tried to keep suppressed. The result made him look younger and even sexier, and it became Stacy's turn to feel as if her heart was behaving strangely.

"I'm pleased that you decided to read my book, Stacy," he said hastily, as if trying to dispose of the subject. "Now, about my second book . . ."

"Yes?"

"Maybe if I just talked through some thoughts with you, without our putting anything down for the moment, it would help me get going again."

She nodded. "All right."

"Suppose you make a fresh pot of coffee, and I'll build a fire. It's rather cool in here, even though the sun's out. . . ."

"All right."

A few minutes later James was seated in the armchair by the fireplace, and Stacy was curled up in a corner of the couch. Stacy waited for him to start talking and, when he didn't, she prodded. "Maybe you should tell me just what it is you plan to write about, James."

"Well, when I said on that television program last year that I'd changed some of my earlier conclusions, that wasn't entirely accurate. Later I wished I could have rephrased those particular statements. It isn't so much that I've changed my earlier conclusions, you see, as that I've altered my thinking about what one should do, knowing those conclusions. The more I've learned about relationships, the more I've realized how much more there is to learn. . . ." He paused again. "Am I boring the hell out of you?" he asked abruptly.

"No," Stacy said. "Of course you're not boring the hell out of me."

James looked at her rather skeptically, but after a moment he continued. "Well, you see, I think that what I've come to realize more and more is that relationships—all kinds of relationships—require work, a lot of work, on the part of the individuals involved. But instead of working, once we've achieved a friendship, or a romance, or a marriage, or a liaison of any kind, we tend to sit back and rest on the laurels we think we've already gathered. That's where things fail.

"The involvements and interactions between individuals are conditioned by so many different things. But I think what I've discovered since the publication of my book—and, thus, meeting and dealing with so many more people than I ever would have ordinarily—is that you can't take your relationship with any other individual for granted, or chances are it will eventually go down the drain."

Stacy didn't say anything.

"What I'm saying essentially," James went on, "is that there are no one-way streets in dealing with other people. There has to be a two-way street, give-and-take, for real communication with anyone else on a significant level."

"In other words," Stacy said, "each person in a relationship has to consciously give as well as take. That's what you're saying, isn't it?"

"Yes. If only one person does all the giving—or all the taking—whether it's a marriage or a friendship or whatever, it's going to come to a dead end."

"Suppose one person wants to give, but the other person doesn't want to take?"

James could have bitten his tongue off the moment he spoke, but the words escaped before he could stop them. "Is that what happened in your marriage, Stacy?"

Stacy was ominously quiet for a long moment. Then she said slowly, "There's something I must tell you, James."

"What?"

"I refuse to become one of your case histories."

He stared at her, appalled. "What the hell makes you think I have any intention of using you as a case history?" he demanded.

"Why else would you be curious about my marriage? This isn't the first time, either."

For as long as he could remember, James had always been able to maintain control of a dialogue between himself and anyone else he was dealing with, whether an individual or an cntire audience in a lecture hall. Now he felt that control fraying. "The reason I'm curious about your marriage is that I'm curious about you, damn it," he said hotly. "How could you possibly think that I would *use* you?"

"I imagine you're accustomed to taking mental—if not actual—notes on everyone you meet, James. That's how you build up material, isn't it?"

"I can't believe I'm hearing this," James said flatly. "Do you think a surgeon automatically starts to sharpen his scalpel every time he goes out socially?"

"That's a poor analogy."

Stung, he admitted, "Well, maybe it is. But, damn it, Stacy, I would think you'd know that I certainly don't consider you a client, and I would never tolerate myself or anyone else exploiting you."

Stacy was surprised at his vehemence. Also, at the impression she was getting that he thought she'd actually insulted him. "James, look . . . I overreacted," she said.

"Do tell," he said scathingly.

"I am sorry," she persisted. "I'm honestly sorry."

"You should very damn well be sorry!"

"All right, I *am* sorry."

Stacy spoke with a certain vehemence of her own, and James, looking across at her, began to relax.

Silence came between them for a while, but it wasn't a particularly strained silence, and finally Stacy broke it. "I admit I don't do much talking about my marriage. It was a dismal failure, and no one particularly likes playing up their failures. Ours was a one-way street relationship all right, Paul's and mine. From the beginning."

"Paul MacKenzie?" James asked.

"No. Paul Delacorte."

James sat up a bit straighter. He recognized the name immediately. Still there could be two Paul Delacortes. "Is your husband a journalist by chance?" he asked cautiously.

"Yes."

"He interviewed me earlier this fall for a magazine article. It isn't out yet. He's quite well-known, Stacy."

"Yes."

James conjured up his memory of Paul Delacorte. He was a tall, slender, dark-haired man, handsome but with a restless kind of energy. Somehow James couldn't picture Delacorte and Stacy together.

"How did you meet him?" he asked.

"In college. I was the editor of a magazine we published quarterly," Stacy said. "Paul Delacorte came to speak as part of a lecture series. After, there was a dinner in his honor and, because I was the magazine's editor, I was seated next to him. We talked quite a bit during the course of that dinner. He managed, rather surreptitiously, to ask me to slip away with him later and have a drink. I did. He fascinated me. He was extremely suave, sophisticated, even somewhat famous...."

Though not a quarter as famous as you are, Stacy thought silently.

"Anyway," she continued, "he asked me to give him a call the next time I was in New York. I'd been planning to go to New York on my next break to visit my sister, who was living there then, and so I did...."

"And?"

"Well, I called Paul, and it...sort of took off after that. We were married the day after I graduated from college." Stacy sighed. "I was such a babe in the woods, James. My father had died long before then. My mother had remarried. My sister was already involved with the man whom she later married, and with whom she moved to Alaska. There was really just me, so you can imagine how—well, how overwhelmed I was by Paul. He was considerably older than I was, and so very sophisticated."

"How much older?" James asked sharply.

"Close to ten years. I wasn't quite twenty-two when we married. He was thirty-two."

James winced, and hoped he hadn't spoken the "Ouch" he was feeling aloud.

"The thing is," Stacy went on, "women are like toys to Paul. I mean that literally. He soon tires of one and wants another...and that appears to be an endless process with him. Also, he's a master at the put-down, so you can imagine the position I found myself in, being so much younger and—in the beginning—so incredibly naive. On the other hand, it suited his image to be married, to have a wife who could act as hostess when he wanted to entertain. So we just kept on going...for over six very long years, James. Meantime, if you can understand this, I sort of...shrank into myself."

"Yes, I can understand that."

"I lived from day to day," Stacy said. "Don't they say a lot of people lead lives of quiet desperation? I guess that would be an accurate description of mine. Paul, from almost the beginning, went his way. Finally I couldn't stand not having something of my own to do and that's when I answered a want ad and went to work for Kate. I regard that as the real changing point in my life.

"Then, by last fall when I was in London, I came to realize that I wasn't really living, being married to Paul. I was just marking time. All the advantages of our being married were on his side. He could fool around as much as he liked, and then always be able to tell the woman in question the truth, which was that he was married. I kept a home he could come to when he wanted to. I was there to entertain when he wanted a hostess. I was such an absolute idiot for so long, James."

"Did Kate make you see the light?"

"No. Kate was there when I needed her, for which I'll always be profoundly grateful. But she knew the decision had to be my own. I think she often wondered at the long time it was taking me to make what *was* the only viable decision. But I made it, I went down to the Virgin Islands over the winter, and the feeling of freedom when I flew back to New York after a time was pretty heady. Kate had helped me find a place of my own, and it was wonderful to be surrounded by my own things, my books, my records, and to be able to do what I wanted to do anytime I wanted to do it. Actually, I know now that I'd thrown off the shackles long before I made that flight to the Virgin Islands. That decision was simply the culmination of a lot of thinking, a lot of soul-searching. And, finally, finding myself, my own identity..." Stacy looked at him and smiled faintly. "Is that enough?"

James's gray eyes were unhappy as he said, "Yes. It's enough. More than enough. I wasn't trying to subject you to an inquisition, Stacy."

"You asked only a few questions," she reminded him. "I gave all the answers voluntarily. Now..."

"Yes?"

"Do you suppose we could get to work?"

They got to work late that Sunday morning, and it was midafternoon before they even thought about stopping for lunch. It was only then, as they took a breather, that James realized how tense he'd been about the book and how Stacy had managed to loosen that tension for him so that now, once again, his ideas were flowing freely.

But the real reason for plunging so deeply into his work today had been to defer thinking about what she'd told him about her marriage. She'd left great gaps, he could see that, but it didn't take much expertise to fill them in. She'd married an arrogant, self-centered bastard who had used her, James thought bitterly. He knew Paul Delacorte's type. Women married to that type of man had been among some of his earliest clients when he'd first started in as a practicing psychologist.

He suggested, when they both decided it was time for a break, that they go find a drive-in, get some food and take it over to a beach where they could picnic in the car.

Stacy fell in with that suggestion and, once they'd found a drive-in that was open, was amused when James ordered a hot dog with every possible embellishment from sauerkraut to tomato relish piled on top of it.

They chose a beach on the bay side of the Cape and, after finishing their picnic lunch, went for a long walk. It was milder here than over on the ocean side, despite the fact that only a couple of miles separated the two locales—the Cape was narrow at this point. James found a quarter in the sand, turned nearly purple by the action of saltwater, and that started a treasure hunt. By the time they went back to the car they'd each amassed a few nickels, dimes and pennies—though James's was the only quarter to be uncovered—and were acting as if they'd just come upon a pirate's buried treasure chest.

Back at the house, Stacy suggested they put in some more work time and, in the interest of his own sanity, James agreed. He wasn't sure how much more proximity to Stacy he could stand—except at those times when work managed to keep both mind and hands occupied—before he gave way to his overriding desire to make love to her.

Later, still needing to keep busy, he became insistent about making omelets for their supper, and he felt ridiculously pleased when Stacy insisted his was the best omelet she'd ever eaten. After dinner they played Scrabble. Still later, James made another fire in the living room, and they stretched out in front of it with some of Kate's brandy.

Their mood had turned mellow. James, trying not to be clinical about it, nevertheless did suspect that maybe Stacy's telling him even as much as she had about her marriage had had a therapeutic effect on her. At least she seemed more relaxed around him.

"You never did get to finish what you started to tell me about your mother the other night," Stacy suddenly said.

"What was that?" James asked lazily.

"You said something about your mother's greatest goal in life being to get you married off."

James turned and regarded her. "I said that?"

"Essentially, yes."

"Well, I guess it's true enough," he admitted, smiling as he spoke. "My mother really should have gone into politics. She's in her mid-seventies—I'm the youngest of her brood by several years—but she has the energy of a woman half her age. Maybe two women half her age," he reflected.

"Also, I inherited my father's title, and it bothers her that I'm not about to play the role in the House of Lords that he did. So, at the least, she wants to see me married with the hope that maybe I'll then have a son who will grow up to take *his* rightful place in the House of Lords."

"Well," Stacy said, "there is something to all that heritage, wouldn't you say?"

"My heritage tripped me up very badly once," James said. "So, no, I wouldn't say."

"What do you mean, your heritage tripped you up?"

"It wrecked my one and only marriage," James told her.

Stacy sat up very straight and regarded him through widened eyes. "You've been *married*?"

"A long, long time ago, back when I was at Oxford," he said. "It lasted for a very short time. The marriage was annulled—by the wishes of her family as well as mine."

"Why did her family object to your marriage?" Stacy asked. Her thoughts were whirling.

"We came from entirely different classes," James said simply. "And, believe me, one doesn't necessarily have to be of the nobility to have a very fierce class consciousness and to want to protect what's innately one's own," he finished.

"I'm not sure I understand that."

"I suppose what I'm saying is that someone from an alleged lower class can be just as snobbish in his way as someone from an alleged higher class."

"Where does your ex-wife fit in all of this?"

He grimaced slightly. "It sounds strange to hear Cora referred to as my wife, though she was for a few days. I also suppose I have to admit that marrying her was a kind of rebellion on my part. She worked in a pub in Oxford where I used to go with friends whenever we could escape the classrooms. She was very pretty. I was nineteen years old at the time, and I became hopelessly enamored with her. As it happened, she was only sixteen. Underage, so an annullment—when our mutual parents became insistent that the marriage be terminated—was quite simple to arrange. Especially," he finished bitterly, "with my father's connections."

"Didn't you have anything to say about whether or not your marriage was terminated?" Stacy demanded.

"I might have had . . . if Cora had wished to stay married to me," James answered. "As it happened, my father was willing to settle a liberal sum of money on her—to become hers when she reached maturity—if she would agree to the annullment. Once she thought about *that*, it didn't take Cora long to decide she wanted out. She made quite a scene when I tried to talk her out of leaving me, and I have to admit I quickly saw a side of her I might not have come to see for a long time otherwise.

"I was," James said slowly, "so damn disillusioned. My devoted little blonde was actually quite an opportunist. A short while later the whole thing was over. Cora's father saw to it that she got out of Oxford and went to live with relatives in York until I was finished at the university. I heard later that she married, in York. By now I imagine she has a healthy brood of children. In fact—that was almost twenty years ago—she could even be a grandmother by now. An astonishing thought."

"You never saw her again after she left Oxford?"

"No."

"You must have wanted to leave Oxford yourself at that point."

"Yes, I did. But my father convinced me to stay on and finish. What he couldn't convince me of was to follow him into the legal profession."

"Was it because of Cora that you decided to become a psychologist, James?"

James thought about that for a moment, then said, "Yes, I guess you could say so. She had disillusioned me so completely. Like you, when you entered into your marriage, I was naive. She wasn't naive. She was far more—advanced, shall we say—than I was, despite a three-year gap in our ages. The thing is, I was willing to try to stay married and make a success of that marriage despite our families' intervention. But she quickly saw that she'd have the devil of a time getting very far with my family, which meant that the tangible goods and other rewards she had been looking forward to would, in large measure, be denied her. So she took the practical course.

"I found all of that incredibly difficult to understand... because I was in love with her. It became a part of the healing process with me to try to figure out why Cora was the way she was, why my father was the way he was, why my mother was the way she was, why I, for that matter, was the way I was. That need to know caused me to begin an investigation that has never really stopped. Learning about people becomes an endless procedure, Stacy."

Stacy digested that for a moment. "I've read a few things about you, James, especially since I found out you're Kate's cousin. How is it your marriage is never mentioned?"

"The annullment was accomplished very discreetly. The marriage and the annullment were subsequently hushed up very thoroughly. My father had a lot of influence."

"And now your mother still wants to marry you off?"

He smiled. "She'd like to have a bride of her choosing, this time from what she'd call the right kind of background. I've lost count of the number of daughters of friends and acquaintances she's arranged to introduce me to. My mother's wonderful, Stacy. Don't misunderstand me. She's a real character in her own right, and I love her very much. She's a natural-born matriarch, that's all. And I'm afraid at heart I'm a maverick. Also—as far as marrying me off—I can assure you she doesn't have the proverbial snowball's chance in hell."

Chapter Ten

The telephone rang, and James went to answer it. Stacy watched him walk out of the living room toward the kitchen, and she felt a stir of conflicting emotions.

What James had just told her had made her begin to see him in still a different light. She'd assumed he'd had a relatively easy life, despite the fact that he'd indicated in one of their early conversations that there had been bitterness between his father and himself. Now she could imagine the trauma of having had his marriage "wrecked," as he himself had put it, by both his parents and his bride's parents. Then, learning that Cora had actually accepted money for her part in the affair...

What a greedy little person Cora must have been.

James was as strong as steel in most ways. Stacy had already discovered that. But he was also a deeply sensitive man. She could imagine how terribly hurt he must have been at age nineteen to discover that the girl he loved wasn't willing to stand by him. True, because she was underage maybe the parents could have forced the annullment, anyway. But at least she would have shown that she cared for James with a love that went beyond a silly infatuation for a rich, handsome young Oxonian.

Stacy heard her name being called and roused herself to say, "Yes?"

James was standing in the living room doorway. "The call is for you," he said. "Colleen Reynolds."

"Are you sure?" Stacy asked. She'd been so certain that the next move in the Kloset situation was going to have to be hers.

"That's how she identified herself," James said rather shortly.

Colleen Reynolds began their conversation with an apology. "I'm sorry to bother you."

"That's quite all right," Stacy assured her.

"Ms. MacKenzie...I know why you're really in Devon," Colleen said. "I checked this afternoon with a friend in New York who also works for Kate's Klosets. I wanted to determine exactly what your position with the company is, and she told me. She called you Kate Clarendon's troubleshooter."

Stacy drew a long breath, then said, "You could have spared yourself a long-distance phone call and asked me that question directly, Mrs. Reynolds. I would have answered you."

"Would you? It seems to me you've been pretending to wear a hat you haven't really been wearing at all, Ms. MacKenzie."

"Perhaps you'd better tell me what you mean by that," Stacy suggested.

"Kate Clarendon doesn't have a cousin named Jim Sinclair."

"Well, your contact—that's where you got your information, I presume—certainly is wrong there," Stacy said, though she hated to fib. "Kate's cousin Jim is in the other room at this very instant. You just spoke to him, as a matter of fact. Perhaps you'd like me to call him to the phone and let him verify his identity for himself."

"I'm sorry," Colleen Reynolds said. "I didn't mean to sound so accusatory. It's simply that I'm alone in the house right now, so I took the opportunity to call you up. I saw the look on your face when you walked into the store the other morning. And again when I told you I still hadn't unpacked the fall stock. I don't blame you for the way you must feel, but I—"

"Mrs. Reynolds," Stacy cut in crisply, "this really isn't something we can talk about over the phone. I suggest we meet."

There was a long pause. Then Colleen Reynolds spoke. "I'd like to ask you to come to my house but, frankly, I can't. It's late and my husband will be home any minute. My daughter should be coming in before long, too. It wouldn't do for you to be here."

"Then why don't we meet at the shop in the morning?" Stacy suggested. "Before your opening hour, say, eight o'clock?"

"I feel that's imposing on you."

"No," Stacy said. "In any event, it seems the best alternative."

After a few more words, she hung up. Turning, she saw James watching her from the kitchen doorway.

"All right, I was eavesdropping," he confessed before she could say anything. "I'm puzzled, though. Why didn't you ask her to come here?"

"Tonight?"

"I was thinking of tomorrow morning, though tonight would have been all right, too," he said.

"This place isn't that big," Stacy muttered.

"Stacy, if you didn't want me to meet Mrs. Reynolds, I could have gone upstairs," James pointed out.

"I didn't want to ask that of you. And, no, I didn't want her to meet you. She's already been told by some friends of hers who works for Kate that Kate doesn't have a cousin named Jim Sinclair. It wouldn't take much more of her to figure out who you really are. Anyway..."

"Anyway?"

"Tomorrow morning at the shop will be soon enough," Stacy said rather dourly, and James let it go at that.

Morning came too soon as far as Stacy was concerned. She left the house at a quarter to eight—having seen no sign of James since coming downstairs—and drove over to Kate's Kloset. But, as she pulled up in front of the store, she knew this was no place for the kind of talk she and Colleen Reynolds needed to have.

She wished she could consider taking the store manager back to the Hideaway, but she couldn't. Though James might not agree, she didn't want to run the risk of having him recognized. In a town such as Devon everyone would be beating a path to his door if it were discovered that he was in residence, and he'd never be able to find enough peace and quiet in which to finish his book.

Also...she didn't want to share him with a potentially adoring public. Inevitably, one of these days—probably much too soon—she and James were going to have to part company.

This is a time of togetherness I'm going to have to make do with for the rest of my life, she told herself as she walked up to the shop entrance.

The door, she discovered was locked, but before she could rap on it Colleen Reynolds opened it. Colleen had at least made a little effort with herself this morning. She was wearing one of Kate's dresses in a becoming shade of deep green, and the dress fit her well. She'd arranged her hair in a chignon and had put on a little makeup. But the transformation didn't extend to her eyes. Her expression gave her away. She looked like a weary, frightened woman.

Stacy took one look at her and said, "Let's go somewhere." When Colleen looked confused, she added, "Let's go get breakfast somewhere."

"I'd rather not if you don't mind," Colleen said. "I'd run into people I know anywhere we went around here. People I'd just as soon not see right now."

"Then I'll get some coffee and Danish at the supermarket and we can go over to the beach," Stacy decided, remembering her "picnic" with James. "We can turn the heater on in the car if it gets chilly."

She chose the same beach where she and James had walked together and found their small treasure trove. She felt as if every grain of sand, every shell or pebble, every blade of beach grass, was reminding her of him, and it was difficult to force her concentration on the problem at Kate's Kloset.

It was a relief when Colleen made the opening gambit. "I never intended to let things get into this state, believe me. I love my job...though I admit you'd never know that to look at the shop the way it is right now. But my personal life's become such a mixed-up mess that it's reflecting on everything I do." Colleen stared at Stacy unhappily. "That's not your problem I know," she said. "And I don't blame you if you recommend to Kate Clarendon that she fire me. I'd have it coming."

"Let's not get so far ahead of ourselves," Stacy cautioned. "Look, Colleen, your performance, to a point, was superb. Then the decline at the shop here was very gradual. It was only when the summer season figures came in that Kate began to realize something must be seriously wrong."

"I'm what's seriously wrong," Colleen said unhappily.

"Taking that tack won't help either of us," Stacy reproved. "I'm not here to condemn you, Colleen. I'm here to help if I possibly can. If your problem is personal, you're going to have to have a certain amount of confidence in me. I mean, you're going to have to level with me. And my telling you that you can trust me doesn't really mean that much when you don't even know me. But . . . I don't carry a guillotine around in my pocket. As I say, I'm here to help."

Colleen looked at Stacy, and her eyes suddenly misted. "I believe you," she said brokenly. "So here goes . . ."

As she drove back to the Hideaway, Stacy could begin to appreciate what a toll James's work must sometimes take on him, now that she'd heard Colleen Reynolds's problems in full. It was difficult, very difficult, to attempt to shoulder another person's burdens and then try to help that person to deal with those burdens.

James was in the living room going over some notes when she got back. He looked up and smiled when he saw her, and for a moment Stacy stood very still. She wanted to hold in her mind forever this picture of him sitting in front of the big picture window in Kate's house, with the sky and the ocean as a backdrop.

She realized he was scanning her closely, and he asked quietly, "How did it go?"

"I'm not sure," Stacy said wearily.

"Come over and sit down and tell me about it," James invited. "First, though, I have something I want to give you."

He produced two white pebbles that were almost identical, and each was close to being perfectly circular. "I started hunting for stones on the beach today, and I finally matched up these two. I was reading one of Kate's books about the Cape earlier. These stones are glacial rubble—left when the glaciers pushed across this part of your country many, many years ago.

"These pebbles," he went on, putting the white stones on the palm of one hand and studying them intently, "are aeons old...and have endured a great, great deal. So, one is to be yours, and one is to be mine. As a sort of bond between us. Forever and ever."

He held one of the pebbles out to Stacy as he said that and, when she took it, closed his fingers over her hand. "Forever," he said solemnly, and she found herself repeating the same word while tears, inevitably, stung her eyes.

His small ritual finished, James leaned back and asked, "Coffee, first? Or do you want to talk first?"

"We're both going to become a jangled mass of caffeine nerves if we keep on drinking so much coffee," Stacy said, her voice trembling slightly. She was still deeply touched over his small, unexpected gift and the way he'd presented it to her.

"All right, then, tell me about Mrs. Reynolds."

"Are you sure you want to hear this, James?" Stacy protested. "We should be getting down to your work, you know."

"It can wait fifteen minutes more, Stacy."

"Well, then..." She paused, trying to decide exactly how to begin. "The fact is," she started, "Colleen Reynolds has been through quite a bit of hell over the better part of this past year. She has a sixteen-year-old daughter named Cissy who has been a real problem. She's in her second year of high school. I guess she's extremely pretty and very attractive to the boys. Unfortunately Cissy became interested in a boy of whom her family strongly disapproved. This was right after Christmas vacation last year. This boy was new in town, new at the high school. He came here to live with an uncle and help out in that uncle's business.

"Colleen's husband is, indeed, Al Reynolds, the man who delivered the oil the other day. Al, Colleen says, was a successful builder until everything seemed to fall apart for him a year or so ago. A couple of contracts that would have been lucrative fell through. Then it became just one thing after the other. Al started drinking heavily. Finally he closed up shop, as far as his own business was concerned, and got a job with the oil company. It's not much more than a part-time job. The financial pinch on the family has been rather hard.

"Meantime...Cissy became pregnant. Colleen began to suspect what was wrong, and finally Cissy broke down and told her. The child was scared to death and begged Colleen not to tell Al. But this was news Colleen couldn't see how she could keep from her husband for very long, and so she went against Cissy's wishes. Al was furious and all set to force a marriage for the sake of his daughter's reputation when Cissy took matters out of her family's hands and went to Boston, lied about her age and had an abortion. Colleen was crushed. Al was furious, and he hasn't spoken to Cissy since, though they live in the same house. The boy in question turned his back on Cissy and left town once he knew she was in trouble. Evidently he went back to wherever he came from originally.

"Meanwhile, Colleen was working under tremendous emotional pressure as it was. But when the financial pressure became acute, she—well, she didn't dip into the till, James. What she did was to try to cut corners in the store by doing things herself. She paid herself the money for those things that would ordinarily have gone to other employees. That's why the shop is so short-staffed. Colleen's been trying to do the work of three salespeople, and obviously that's impossible. She's been so exhausted she started opening the store late. She's even tried to attend to the stocking herself—which is why the fall merchandise isn't on display yet. She's been running herself ragged in absolute desperation, because the way Al's been acting she's afraid he may be fired from his job with the oil company. Meantime there's Cissy, who's in school right now. But Colleen's afraid she may drop out and that would be the end of the road for her. She dotes on her daughter. She feels she's been a failure with Cissy, or Cissy would never have gotten involved with the kind of boy she did...."

Stacy came to a sudden stop, then said, "It's a mess."

"Yes," James agreed. "Yes, it most certainly is. What are you going to recommend to Kate, Stacy?"

"I don't know," Stacy said unhappily. "I've told Colleen that the first thing she has to do is to get the merchandise out in the shop, spruce up the displays, get the boards over the front door painted and do something about those awful-looking bushes outside and..." She paused, aware once again of what a good listener James was. "Why am I getting into all of this with you?" she demanded suddenly, beginning to feel that she was taking advantage of him in spilling out all of Colleen's—and her own—difficulties to him. "It's not your problem."

"You're getting into it with me because I invited you to," James said gently. "And it's no longer your problem, either. I would say that at this point the thing to do is to make a report to Kate, and let her take it from there."

"I can't do that, James."

"You've done what Kate pays you to do, haven't you, Stacy?" James persisted. "You've done your trouble-shooting, found out what's wrong. It isn't also up to you to correct all the wrongs, is it?"

"I try to do what I can," she muttered.

"Well, I would say you've done all you can. You can't take on the problems of the world, Stacy. So report back to Kate and move on."

"Are you saying I should go back to New York?" she asked him.

"No," he said. "No, I'm damned well not saying you should go back to New York. I'm saying you should wash your hands of the Reynolds matter at this point, let Kate take over and then go on helping with my book until we get through with the damn thing."

She regarded him levelly. "James," she pointed out, "I work for your cousin, not for you."

"So?"

"So it's Kate who pays my salary."

"Well, we could rearrange that," James said. "I can borrow you from Kate and then, as long as you're working with me, I could pay your salary."

"You already pointed out that you're not my employer."

"True. But that, too, could change."

"I don't want you as an employer, James," Stacy told him. "And I also like to think that Kate wouldn't give me up quite that easily."

"Who's saying anything about Kate giving you up? This would be just a temporary arrangement, Stacy."

"Until you'd gotten what you wanted out of it, right?"

James stood up, came around the edge of the table and faced her angrily. "Suppose you explain what you meant by that," he challenged.

"You're so used to getting your own way, that's all," Stacy sputtered.

"*I'm* used to getting my own way," James retorted indignantly. "Lady, I'll have you know there have been damn few times in my entire life when I've gotten what you might consider my own way. Your agreeing to stay here and help me out with the book is one of the very few of them...."

His words trailed off. He looked at Stacy and saw the weariness on her lovely face and felt ashamed of himself for switching the situation around as he had. Naturally she'd feel a responsibility to Colleen Reynolds. Stacy was that kind of a person, and he wouldn't have had her otherwise. On the other hand, he did wish he could spare her what continuing to shoulder Colleen Reynolds's problems might entail. On that score he could speak from experience. God knows how many problems he'd shouldered that rightfully belonged to others, since he'd started in the practice of psychology. "We shouldn't quarrel," he finally said.

Stacy smiled at that, a wobbly little smile. "Why not?" she asked. "We can't go around wearing happy faces all the time."

"I like your face...no matter what it's wearing," James said thickly. He couldn't possibly have kept himself from spanning the distance between them and taking her into his arms.

She felt so soft to him, and so wonderful and so vulnerable. He was conscious of an odd sort of responsibility toward Stacy as he brushed her hair away from her face and then gently kissed her forehead, her eyelids, her cheeks.

Maybe he could have lived up to that sense of responsibility if Stacy hadn't responded with a low moan, and then suddenly she was clinging to him, her mouth seeking his, and James—noted for his self-control—began to spin out of control entirely.

Their hands moved, searching in unison, exploring, pausing, then beginning their voyages all over again, and James's bandages weren't that much of a handicap.

They moved to the couch, taking long, slow steps in a dance of their own invention, their pace sensual and almost languid at first. With his unbandaged hand, James eased Stacy's sweater over her head, then loosened the fastener on her skirt. She unbuttoned his shirt, her fingers fumbling on each button, and they were fumbling even more as she finally gained the courage to reach for his belt buckle.

Finally she stood before him, wearing only peach satin and lace briefs and a wisp of a bra. And he stood before her in tightly sculpted dark blue shorts. And desire swept over them with the lazy heat of a hot summer afternoon so that they moved in a kind of adagio tempo as they slowly sank down onto the couch.

Stacy and James got rid of the rest of their clothes and lay next to each other, skin touching, bodies touching, contours molding in the way they'd been meant to be molded since the first man and first woman made love. James's lips nuzzled all her secret places . . . the hollows behind Stacy's ears, the soft indentation in her throat where he felt as if his tongue were touching her pulse beat. Then he rained kisses upon her until he came to the most secret place of all and—even bemused by passion though he was—he had the sudden, deep conviction that no one had ever done this to Stacy before.

That knowledge, in itself, was enough to slow the tempo of his own response because he wanted this to be her time. He wanted as much for her from it as there possibly could be. But, inevitably, it also became his time, and when finally they culminated what they had begun, it was with a mutual blending that was, in itself, a miracle.

There were embers in the fireplace, left over from a fire James had built earlier that morning. Stacy stirred slowly and saw the glowing embers, and it seemed to her they symbolized the feeling deep down inside her. She was glowing in the wake of James's lovemaking. Nothing in her life before had ever paralleled what he had just given her.

She clutched that thought to her, knowing that what had happened between them this morning could never be taken away.

Stacy and James went for a walk on the beach, after a time, and then they tried to get down to some work on his book. But it wasn't easy. They were so conscious of each other that it was difficult to be objective about much of anything.

Once again they opted for a drive-in lunch, and getting out of the house for a time helped put things into perspective. They settled in at the worktable when they got back, and James finally decided to start his dictation, making the effort to pick up his text where he had left off with it months before.

He invited Stacy to comment as they progressed, but at first she didn't take the suggestion seriously. He, after all, was the expert here. What, she asked herself, could she possibly have to offer?

When, after a while, he did say something about which she had thoughts of her own, she felt too shy for a few minutes to interrupt him. But then she couldn't hold back any longer. He was touching upon areas in which she'd had experience and about which she had ideas. She wouldn't have believed she could express herself so freely to a professional of James's caliber. And she suddenly broke off "I'm sorry. I didn't intend to stand up on a soap box and start orating."

"No, no," James said quickly. "I find what you said very interesting."

Stacy waited for him to resume dictating, but he didn't. Rather, after a few minutes, he asked, "Would you mind if we go back a few paragraphs? I'd rather like to rephrase some of the things I was saying."

They worked until the world outside their window became a blend of blue and amethyst shadows with the sun gone over the horizon and dusk descending. Then Stacy went around and switched on all the lights and was about to sit down at the table again when James said, "I think we've done enough for one day, don't you?"

"I could keep right on going," she said honestly. She was fascinated with James's work, with his straightforward way of cutting to the heart of an issue.

"I could do with a drink," he said. "Join me?"

"All right."

"Want to go out to dinner somewhere after a while?"

"James..."

"If I were recognized," he said, "and the press coupled my name with yours, I wouldn't mind in the least. How about you?"

She had no answer for that.

James insisted on doing the driving that evening. Stacy soon found that he had a yen for exploration. He drove around a series of back roads, and became so fascinated with these Cape byways that he decided they were going to have to take some time off and retrace the route so that they could see everything in the daylight.

Finally they discovered a small Italian restaurant and stopped for dinner. During dinner they concentrated on what James laughingly called "catch-up talk." He wanted to know about the things Stacy had liked best as a child. He wanted to hear anecdotes from her childhood, and when she told him that turnabout was fair play—after she'd surprised herself by recalling all sorts of things—he painted a word picture for her about what it had been like to grow up as the only son of an English lord.

"I think," he said after a time, "that you had a lot more fun than I did."

"Maybe," she conceded. "But there's something very glamorous about having grown up in those impressive mansions, with servants to cater to your every want, and actually meeting the queen and her husband, and..."

"You make it sound like living in a fairy tale," James said. "It wasn't."

"Were you lonely?"

"Yes."

She couldn't imagine what prompted her to ask the follow-up question. "Are you still lonely?"

"I've been too much so," he admitted, then smiled directly into her eyes. "But no longer," he said.

Once again Stacy lost her voice. And by the time she found it, James had gone on to something else.

It was late when they got back to the Hideaway. And there was something very intimate about unlocking the front door, going into the house and turning the lights on, as if this were their own place and the two of them really belonged here.

Stacy, after a few minutes, said she thought she'd go on up to bed. James said he thought he'd stay down and read for a while. But then she paused in the living room doorway and looked back at him. She saw that he was standing, book in hand, staring after her.

Her love for him overflowed, and there was no possible way she could have contained it just then. She took a tentative step back into the room. Their eyes met, and James flung the book down on a chair and covered the distance between them in a couple of strides.

"I want you," he said, his voice ragged. "God, I want you! I can't bear the thought of walls separating us tonight."

"Neither can I," Stacy told him softly.

Chapter Eleven

For the next couple of days life fell into a pattern for Stacy and James. They shared the same bedroom, so that waking up brought a new kind of pleasure. Stacy usually awakened first, maybe because of the inner excitement that possessed her at the thought of having James so near. She would look across at the tousled autumn-gold head on the pillow next to hers, and there would initially be such a sense of unreality that she'd have to reach over and touch him to make sure he was really there. That would cause him to open his eyes slowly, to stare at her sleepily, and then to smile, reach for her and take her into his arms.

Eventually they would go downstairs, have breakfast and then set to work. James couldn't remember when thought upon thought had come to him quite so clearly. He gave the credit for that to Stacy. She brought out the best in him. They had reached a stage where she didn't hesitate to speak up, and she spoke up often. He was surprised at how astute she was. She didn't hesitate to criticize him—that, in itself, he found refreshing—and her criticisms almost always were valid. It came to the point where he began to tease her about which of them was the professional psychologist.

Stacy was at first taken aback by the teasing. Her initial response was to assume James was making fun of her and that his comments were a kind of warning to shut up and keep her opinions to herself. For a while she didn't say much. When she'd been silent for quite sometime, James slanted a glance at her and asked, "Cat got your tongue?" After that, she recognized his teasing for what it was: good-natured raillery.

She got back at him when his secretary called from London one morning. This wasn't the first call James had received from Iris, but this time Stacy overheard him say, "No, don't give her my number. For God's sake, Iris, don't give any of them my number." Stacy couldn't help chuckling.

"You know, I've been thinking, James," she said during their lunch break, "about writing an article about you myself."

"About me?" he said, startled. "What in the world would possess you to do anything like that?"

"Well," Stacy said, "I thought of a rather interesting angle that I doubt has ever been presented about you."

His eyes narrowed. "What?" he demanded suspiciously.

"The story of the sex expert who runs scared of women," Stacy teased.

James stood up and leaned across the kitchen table where they'd been sharing lunch. "Exactly what makes you think I run scared of women?"

"Everything," she said. "The way you try to escape from your fans. The way you don't want your phone number given out to adoring females . . ."

He rounded the table, grabbed her shoulders and drew her to her feet. "Shall I show you how 'scared' I am of women?" he threatened.

Stacy grinned. "I'm not 'women,' James. I'm just one woman."

"Just one woman, eh?" His lips descended upon hers, choking off any answer she might have made. He raised his head briefly to say, "I think I really do need to teach you a lesson, Stacy."

She smiled. "I'm a very willing pupil," she murmured.

On Thursday morning Stacy drove James over to the clinic so that he could have the stitches taken out of his hand. Some of the leaves were beginning to turn, she noted, and the cranberry bogs were becoming a deep, rich garnet. Nature was about to put on her most spectacular burst of color as the year wound toward its close. Beyond, would be winter's bleakness. Stacy shuddered when she thought about that, because long before winter James would be back in England and she would be back in New York and this idyll would be over.

She was determined not to view this relationship that had blossomed between James and herself as anything other than an "idyll." She told herself that facing the truth would lessen the hurt when the time came to say goodbye. She had no illusions about their being able to go on to "live happily ever after." The usual courses of their lives followed paths that were so entirely different that it was impossible to think they could ever reach the crossroads James frequently referred to when dictating to her, from which point they could follow the same road together.

She had come to know James Ashley-Sinclair on a very personal level. But beyond the charming man with whom she'd been spending her days and nights, there still stood the renowned scientist, the expert in his field, the world-famous authority. That aspect of James she simply couldn't cope with.

She waited for him in the car while he went into the clinic. It was sunny, and she didn't even have to turn the heater on in the car to be comfortable. As she sat, lost in thought, she saw two sea gulls swoop in to perch atop the clinic's roof. There was always that nautical touch to Cape Cod, that tang of salt in the air, that sense of proximity to the sea, and she loved it. But she wondered if she could ever bear to come back to the Cape once she'd left it. Everything, *everything*, would remind her of James, and it would be a long time before the wound healed sufficiently for her to deal with that.

James's wound had healed quite nicely, she found, once he'd rejoined her. The bandage had been removed, but Stacy was appalled at the length of the scar. She knew the cut had been deep; it had also been more extensive than she'd thought. She marveled that he hadn't made more of a fuss about it. At first, anyway, it must have hurt him quite a bit.

"No need to come back, according to the doctor," he said. "He warned the finger will be sensitive for a while. Unfortunately, as you can see, the damn cut went right to the top. Which rather knocks out my doing any typing for myself."

Had he been thinking about typing for himself? Stacy's face gave her away, and James said, "Every now and then I realize I'm imposing on you, Stacy. But I'm afraid I'm going to have to impose a while longer if I'm to get the book finished."

"Unless you'd like to hire some pretty, young secretary," she teased.

"Witch," he muttered, but the look he gave her was as warm as summer sunshine.

Perhaps it was because she'd done so much thinking while she'd waited for James at the clinic, forcing herself to realize the inevitability of what was bound to happen between the two of them. Whatever it was, Stacy felt irritable even before they started work that afternoon and, as they progressed, her irritability surfaced more than once.

Her mood had its influence on James, and they began to disagree about some very small things they ordinarily wouldn't have bothered with. Finally he glared at her and asked explosively, "What the hell happened to put you in such a snit, Stacy?"

"I'm not in a snit," she snapped.

"The devil you're not. I appreciate your sharing your thoughts with me. I have all along. But you're being ridiculous this afternoon, and you seem to forget that I do have some degree of knowledge about the subjects I'm covering." It was a definite reproof, and it didn't help when James pushed his chair back, stood up and said, "I'm going for a walk."

It was the first time she could remember that he hadn't invited her to go along with him. Obviously she had overstepped. She realized as much when she gathered up notepads, pens, pencils and papers and put everything in order so that they could resume work in the morning. Although it wasn't that late, she was sure there wasn't going to be any more work accomplished today. Certainly she wasn't in the mood for it, and James wasn't either, unless she was badly mistaken.

But she wasn't. James stayed out for over an hour, and when he came back he went upstairs and slammed the bedroom door. His bedroom, Stacy realized, not the room they'd shared these past few nights.

The silence in the house was oppressive. She thought about putting on a coat and going for a walk on the beach herself, but the idea didn't appeal to her. She thought about driving over to Hyannis and going to a movie. She'd seen the movie notices in a local paper a couple of days ago, and there were several films playing that she wanted to see. She vetoed the movie idea, though, and thought about just driving around. But driving around the Cape would only remind her of the small explorations she and James had shared.

Finally she rummaged through last Sunday's papers, still stacked on a chair in the kitchen, and found a large crossword puzzle in the *Boston Globe*'s magazine section. She made herself a drink and headed for the living room with her glass and the puzzle.

It was dusk, and with the sun gone the house was getting chilly. Stacy set about making a fire in the living room fireplace, but—as she had their first night on the Cape—she once again forgot to open the damper. Smoke belched into the room.

"Well, history does sometimes repeat itself, doesn't it?" she heard a quiet voice observe. James knelt down and quickly set things to rights, and in a moment the wood on the hearth was crackling merrily. He sat back on his heels and looked at her. "I'm sorry," he told her.

"No," Stacy protested, "I'm the one who's sorry. I've been acting bitchy. . . ."

"Indeed you have," he agreed, but he was smiling as he said it. He reached over and touched her face. "You've got soot on your cheek."

"I guess I'm just not good at getting fires going," Stacy said, her voice wavering slightly as she spoke.

"Too much of a city girl."

"I guess so."

"I think you may be the first native New Yorker I've ever met."

"We're a rare breed," she said shakily.

"A rare breed, indeed."

"James..."

"Yes?"

"I really am sorry about today," she said, trying to get control of her uncertain voice. "I have no right to ever say anything to you about your work."

She glanced at him and saw that his gray eyes were fixed squarely on her face, and she felt as if he were impaling her with that steady gaze of his.

"What brought that on?" he asked.

"Sometimes I... well, I tend to forget who you are," Stacy confessed, her voice still shaky. "I mean, I doubt if many peers in your field would consider quibbling with you, so who am I—"

"You are you," James said, "and you have every right to quibble with me, my love...."

The telephone rang.

James groaned. "I suppose I'd better answer the blasted thing."

He set about doing so while Stacy stayed huddled in front of the fireplace, watching the flames, those two words he'd just spoken repeating themselves over and over again, deep inside her.

My love...

James appeared in the doorway, and the tone of his voice made Stacy sit bolt upright.

"It's Colleen Reynolds again," he said. "But she's so distraught I can scarcely make out what she's saying."

Colleen was, indeed, distraught. She mumbled apologies for calling, then explained her situation. "I couldn't wait any longer, Stacy. I had to call you. Cissy didn't come home last night. She didn't go to school today. God knows where she is. You're the only one outside of the family who knows about my problems. I've been so embarrassed. And now Al's walked out...."

"Have you called the police about Cissy?"

"No. I'm afraid to call the police, Stacy. Something else has happened."

"What?"

"When I went to work this morning, someone had gotten into the office safe. I intended to make my bank deposit for the week this afternoon. There wasn't that much money—sales haven't been all that good, as you know—but there was still a considerable amount. A few hundred dollars."

"Who else knows the combination to the safe, Colleen?"

"I'm not sure," Colleen said. "But I think maybe Al might. Cissy, too. They've both been with me in the office when I've put money into the safe. It never occurred to me that they'd watch and—"

"Never mind," Stacy said. She was trying to put herself in Colleen Reynolds's place, trying to decide where *she'd* stand if she were Colleen Reynolds right now. "Colleen, I'm coming over to your house."

James had gone back into the living room, and as Stacy approached him he grimaced and said, "What is it with that woman now?"

"Serious trouble I'm afraid," Stacy said briefly. "I'm going to have to go over to her house." She hesitated, then asked, "James, would you consider coming with me?"

"Are you sure you want me to do that?"

"Yes, oh, yes," Stacy said, and had never felt more sure of anything.

The Reynoldses lived in a fairly small Cape Cod-style house. It could have been charming, but it wasn't. There was a drabness to the worn furniture, a lack of sparkle to everything. Colleen, Stacy thought, had been letting things go on the home front as well as on the business front. Yet she couldn't blame her. A combination of constant worries—domestic and financial problems—was more than enough to keep anyone down, and Colleen looked like a woman who'd been kept down for a long time.

Her eyes were red-rimmed and swollen. Obviously she'd been weeping. Stacy introduced her to James—as Kate Clarendon's cousin Jim Sinclair—and for a second Colleen looked apprehensive. But then she politely extended her hand and greeted him. "You do look so familiar, Mr. Sinclair," she said once they were seated in her living room.

James smiled. "I've been told I'm rather typically British," he said, and Colleen—to Stacy's relief—let it go at that.

It was a wonder that Colleen didn't begin to suspect that she had a bit more than a typical Briton in her living room as James began to question her, very skillfully, about her husband and daughter. To Stacy, anyway, his expertise was showing—and she had to admit that he was very good at what he did.

Colleen gradually revealed a story of frustrations, misunderstandings and small impasses that could have been corrected at the outset but grew instead into major obstacles or major chasms, as the case might be. It was a scenario that poignantly showed the importance of the techniques of relating that James was writing about in his new book, and how singularly bereft the Reynolds family had been of any of them.

"When did you first realize your daughter hadn't come home last night, Colleen?" James asked, finally getting around to the current situation. By then they were all on a first-name basis.

"She never stops for breakfast anymore before she goes off to school," Colleen said. "So I didn't think much about it when she didn't show up in the kitchen. I assumed she'd gone on to catch the school bus. Then, when I went to leave for work myself and was getting my coat, I saw Cissy's jacket—she has one of those lined, stonewashed denim jackets—still hanging in the closet. But her good wool coat was missing. I went up to her room at that point, and her bed hadn't been slept in. All her schoolbooks were stacked on the small desk she uses for homework."

"When did you last see her?" James asked.

"Last night. It was Al's poker night, so Cissy came downstairs and watched some TV with me. When Al's in the house, she stays up in her own room. As I've told you, Jim, they haven't spoken to each other for months."

It sounds so strange to Stacy to hear James Ashley-Sinclair being called "Jim."

"I've tried to talk to Al, but he's such a bitter man," Colleen went on. "Ever since his business failed, he hasn't been himself."

"Perhaps he blames himself for not having been able to help Cissy more than he did, and for not having been able to provide for both of you as he might want to," James suggested.

"I don't know," Colleen said wearily. "I just don't know anymore."

"Colleen, when Al stamped out of here a while ago, where do you think he might have gone?"

"Probably to a bar," she said in a low voice.

"Does he have a bar he favors?"

Colleen's mouth twisted into a sad semblance of a smile. "I'd say he patronizes every bar around from time to time. Most of the time, though, I think he goes to the Port and Starboard. I'm not certain of that, Jim. I know that often I find match folders from the Port and Starboard when I'm washing his clothes. Other than that..."

"I'll start there," James decided.

Alarmed, Stacy asked, "Just what are you planning to do?"

"See if I can find Al," James said calmly.

"But..."

She wanted to tell him that if he started going around to all the area bars he'd definitely be recognized. But she bit back the words. James knew what he was doing, after all. If he was willing to risk giving up his privacy...

"May I take the car?" he asked her. "You'll wait here with Colleen?"

"Yes, of course," she said.

James, having gotten directions from Colleen, found the Port and Starboard without difficulty. It was past the cocktail hour and early for the regulars who came in each evening, so the place was fairly empty.

Even if it had been crowded, though, James was sure he would have quickly spotted Al Reynolds from the description Stacy had given of the man. Reynolds was sitting on a stool at the far corner of the bar, hunched over a large glass mug of beer.

James ordered a Scotch and took a sip of it before he turned toward Colleen's husband. "Mr. Reynolds?" he asked.

There was no friendliness in Al Reynolds's face and even less in his voice as he grunted, "Yeah?"

"Could we go over to a table and sit down?" James suggested. "I'd like to talk to you."

"What about?" Reynolds queried suspiciously.

"I don't want to broadcast what I have to say," James said quietly.

Reynolds's glance was appraising. "Who are you? I don't recall seeing you around town before. Yet...you look kind of familiar."

James sidestepped that particular issue. "I want to talk to you about your wife...and about your daughter," he said.

Reynolds's scowl deepened. "Don't know that my family is any of your business," he stated bluntly.

"Then why don't we go sit down at a table so you can find out?" James said softly.

James led the way, hoping Reynolds would follow him. He did. They sat down at a table in the far corner of the tavern, and James ordered another beer for Reynolds and another drink for himself.

Then he began to talk.

An hour and a half after James had left Colleen and Stacy, he returned. With Al Reynolds a few steps behind him, he walked into the living room.

Stacy got to her feet, searching James's face anxiously. She wasn't quite sure what she was searching for. She did know that she needed reassurance from him. Sitting here with Colleen Reynolds while they both waited to find out whether or not he'd been able to find Al had been pretty unnerving.

"Al and I have been talking things over," James said, "and we both still wonder whether or not we should call the police in on this. Maybe we should. Cissy may be in danger. But her father doesn't think so, not yet, anyway, and frankly... neither do I."

James was sitting down in one of Colleen's worn, old armchairs as he spoke. Al Reynolds sat on a straight-backed chair nearby. The scowl had faded from his face. He looked worried, thoughtful, and now and then he cast rather apprehensive glances toward his wife.

Finally he spoke, his voice rough, heavy. "Colleen," he said, "you ought to know I don't want anything to happen to Cissy any more than you do."

Colleen faced him, showing the first trace of defiance Stacy had seen in her. "I don't know what you want anymore, Al," she admitted.

Al Reynolds said gruffly, "I want the three of us to get together...stay together...like we used to be." He sighed heavily. "I guess maybe we can never be like we used to be... but if we can get Cissy back without her coming to any harm, we can go on from here."

Stacy glanced at James admiringly. What a transformation he had wrought in an amazingly short space of time.

"Seems to me one of Cissy's friends must be hiding her," Al said. "Question is, which one? Unless she's left the Cape and gone to Benny Hubert."

"She'd never go to Benny," Colleen said quickly. "He walked out on her when she needed him the most. She'd have too much pride."

"Okay, I'll buy that," Al agreed. "Which means she's probably holed up on the Cape somewhere until she decides what to do next. How much money do you think she got out of your safe, Colleen?"

"Four hundred and seventy-six dollars and fifty-eight cents," Colleen said with a precision that surprised Stacy. "Then it wasn't you?" she added, her voice low and questioning.

Al Reynolds looked her directly in the eye. "No," he said. "I've done a lot to you I shouldn't have done, Colleen, but I wouldn't stoop that low. Cissy, though... she must have felt an awful need to get away from here. She must have memorized the combination to the safe when she was in the office with you. I bet her plan was to pay you back every cent as soon as she could get somewhere and find herself a job."

Al was sticking up for his daughter, despite the fact he'd refused to speak to her for months.

James was right, Stacy thought, remembering some of the things he'd said to her at their work sessions. People were forever unpredictable.

"Colleen... you know who Cissy's friends are," James said. "Try to think of the people—the girls, I'd say—she's closest to." He paused. "Try to concentrate on girls whose families may own a second property. Maybe a cottage they rent summers. Even an old shack on their properties. Someplace where Cissy could hole up. I doubt very much she'd take refuge in anyone's home if their parents were around."

Colleen and Al worked together on drawing up a list of all the girls they could remember who Cissy knew well. Then they worked on the list, narrowing it down to those whose parents owned either a rental cottage or, as James had suggested, even an unoccupied shack on their own property.

Later, much later, James and Al set out together. And it was after midnight when they returned, bringing Cissy Reynolds with them.

Cissy was a slight blonde who looked very much like her mother, except for her coloring, which had obviously come from Al. She looked like such a child, Stacy thought, as she watched the girl sink down onto the shabby living room couch and burst into tears.

After a time, James beckoned Stacy to come into the kitchen. "I think it's time for us to cut out," he said when she had joined him. "Colleen and Al have to work things out with Cissy from this point on...and something tells me they're going to manage to do so. Al's been a pent-up mass of frustrations, but I think this has proven to him that he's got to stand up and be counted as the man of his family. I think he can do it, too. I think he'll shortly come to realize that Colleen and Cissy need *him* more than they do the income he was bringing in when he was a successful builder."

"Thanks to you," Stacy said softly.

James didn't answer that. Instead, he went to the door and beckoned to Colleen. She looked up and met his eyes, then left her husband and daughter, who were in deep conversation with each other, to come out to the kitchen.

"We're leaving," James told her.

Colleen's dark eyes swept the two of them. "I don't know what to say," she said. "Stacy, just for the record, Cissy hadn't spent a cent of that money, and she'd made up her mind not to. After she'd had time to think it over, she realized what her having taken the money would do to my reputation, and all she could think of was trying to sneak into the shop later and put it back.

"I'm glad she didn't try it, though," Colleen said wryly. "We do have a pretty foolproof security system in the store, and she would have walked right into it. As it is, she took the money the day before yesterday when she stopped in the store to see me after school and I was busy with customers. I can't expect you to keep any of this from Kate Clarendon, Stacy. In fact, I don't want you to. She deserves to know. But I honestly believe Cissy has learned her lesson. And, I think, so has Al." Then she turned to James. "How can I ever thank you?"

James smiled. "By getting this family act of yours together, Colleen. And I think you're already well on the way to doing that."

James let Stacy take the wheel as they started back toward the Hideaway. She glanced at him and saw that he was leaning back against the headrest, his eyes closed. He looked very tired, and she didn't wonder. The emotions he'd dealt with over the past few hours were enough to tire anyone out.

"James," she said softly.

He stirred and answered, "Yes?"

"You did a number of very wonderful things tonight."

"No," he said. "No. Tonight you only saw an example of what I do, Stacy. There was nothing miraculous about it."

"So you think," Stacy said, and he didn't answer her.

They drove down the lane to the Hideaway, pulled up at the rose-covered wall and then both of them stared disbelievingly at the Hideaway itself. The small house blazed with lights.

James frowned. "I did leave a light on in the living room and one in the kitchen, just so we wouldn't trip over ourselves. But . . ."

"Maybe we're the ones who should call the police," Stacy muttered.

Then they saw the front door open, and light blazed out onto the narrow flagstoned walk. Against the light the figure of a rather short and fairly stocky woman was silhouetted.

"Well, you two," they were greeted cheerfully. "About time you came home."

Stacy recognized the voice of her employer, Kate Clarendon, and suddenly had the dire premonition that the idyllic time through which she'd been living was about to come to an end.

Chapter Twelve

"Darlings, do you know you went off and left the front door unlocked?" Kate said.

"That's only because we didn't have a key, dear cousin," James retorted. "That's a detail you neglected to provide."

The three of them were sitting at the kitchen table. James had already poured drinks. He and Kate had greeted each other with an affection that made Stacy suspect the two of them were even closer than she'd realized. Suddenly she felt like an outsider.

Kate was in her forties. She was short, pleasingly plump, redheaded and had enormous, expressive green eyes. Though she could be serious enough when the occasion warranted it—and also, on occasion, pensive and moody—she generally was a delightful extrovert, enthusiastic over just about everything. She and James, Stacy thought, glancing surreptitiously at her employer as she bantered with her English cousin, were totally different in both looks and personality. Yet there was an underlying rapport between the two of them that shone through.

"I gather," Kate said teasingly, addressing both James and Stacy, "that the two of you have found some interesting nighttime action here on the Cape. You'll have to initiate me."

James had been smiling as he joked with Kate, but now he sobered. "We weren't exactly indulging in fun and games tonight," he told her.

She glanced from one to the other of them. "Stacy, you look exhausted. Why didn't I notice that before? I was so glad to see both of you. Once I got back to New York from Miami, I couldn't wait to get up here. That's why I decided to simply pack things in this afternoon, get in my car, and come along. Miami was wonderful, but Carlos is one canny businessman. It took a lot of negotiating before we arrived at a contract satisfactory to both of us. Anyway..." Kate leaned back and surveyed her favorite cousin and her favorite employee. "What's been going on?" she asked.

Stacy sighed. She'd hoped maybe they wouldn't have to get into the Colleen Reynolds story tonight. She wasn't sure she was up to it. Also, she wanted to be in good enough form to try to present Colleen's side of the case so that Kate might have some sympathy for her.

James spoke, and she felt as if he'd been able to read her mind. "It can keep till morning, Kate," he said.

"I think I'd rather hear it tonight," Kate decided, her eyes zeroing in on Stacy.

"Look," James said, "Stacy has rather had it. She's had a lot to handle, a lot of tension."

"Why don't you let Stacy speak for herself, James?" Kate suggested.

"If Stacy's to speak for herself, I think we'd better wait until morning," Stacy stated firmly. "I've got a throbbing headache. I'm done in. In short, if you'll excuse me, Kate, I'm going to bed."

Kate, evidently on the verge of saying something, paused. "I'll excuse you, Stacy," she said. "Try to get a good rest. If there's anything you need, just call out."

James watched Stacy walk out of the kitchen, those erect shoulders of hers held high, and he was proud of her.

He knew his cousin Kate. Not too many people could stand up to her. Stacy had just proved that she not only could, but also that she had no compunction about stating her own case when necessary.

James would have made a bet this wasn't the first time Stacy had stood up for herself before Kate. And, knowing his cousin as he did, he was sure that was one reason why Kate admired her troubleshooter so much.

"She's a terrific young woman," Kate said, once they'd heard Stacy's bedroom door thud shut.

"Yes," James said, and poured himself another Scotch.

Kate's eyebrows rose. She knew her cousin. He was usually very cautious about his drinking, and this was his third Scotch since they'd come to sit down at the kitchen table.

"I take it," she said, "that you and Stacy have been getting along well."

James smiled wryly. "Stacy's a perpetual challenge," he admitted.

"You've always liked challenges, James."

"So I have, I suppose."

"That sounds rather evasive. You do get on with Stacy, don't you?"

"Yes," James said rather shortly.

"I take it you went with her tonight to straighten out whatever the mess it is that involves Colleen Reynolds?"

"Yes."

"I thought you were trying to preserve your anonymity while here on the Cape."

"I'm not exactly a household word," James said drily.

"Enough of one. How's the book coming, James?"

"A bit too well," James said.

Kate frowned. "What?"

"It's going along very smoothly, at quite a rate," James said. "Stacy has been an enormous help to me. Sometimes I think she must have a degree in psychology she hasn't told me about."

"How can a book go too well?" Kate asked him.

"We're apt to get through before...well, before I really want to get through," James admitted.

Kate stared at him. "Are you saying what I think you're saying?" she asked.

"Hell, Kate," James exploded. "Must you always prod?"

Kate smiled. "I can't quite believe this," she said. "You know very well I'm a matchmaker at heart, James, and I would dearly have loved to try to arrange a match between you and Stacy. But, frankly, I wouldn't have had the nerve to attempt it. The two of you are such blatant individuals. To tell you the truth, I was very much afraid you'd clash on sight."

"In some ways we did."

"I thought that aristocratic British manner of yours might put Stacy's back up," Kate admitted.

"Come off it, Kate," her cousin growled.

"You can be very much the lofty lord of the manor, James," Kate informed him. "That, plus all this sudden fame of yours..."

James glared at her. "You're enjoying this, aren't you, Kate?" he accused.

Kate smiled complacently. "Yes, darling," she said. "I know how you've hated all the notoriety," she added gently. "I know how you've become absolutely gun-shy where women are concerned, and I can't blame you... though it's rather funny, in a way."

James's glare deepened.

"Stacy isn't too easily impressed," she said, "so I doubted if all the glitter that's come your way would overwhelm her. But, I admit, I was afraid you yourself might. Don't look like that, James," Kate cautioned. "I was merely worried that there might be a chance if Stacy became too interested in you that she could wind up being hurt, and she's been hurt enough. On the other hand, you and Stacy are my two favorite people in the entire world. I can't think of anything more marvelous than that the two of you should fall in love with each other."

"I know you don't want to get into this, Stacy," Kate said. "I can fully understand your sympathy for Colleen Reynolds. Who knows? By the time I hear the whole story, maybe I'll share it. But you do need to tell me the facts, my dear."

Stacy and Kate were sitting on either side of the worktable in the living room. James had escaped to go for a walk on the beach. Stacy was looking out the window, trying to get a glimpse of his tall figure.

"He's pretty terrific, isn't he?" Kate said, following her gaze.

Startled, Stacy said, "Yes."

"I'm pleased the two of you have been getting along so well. Now that this Reynolds matter is about to come to an end, one way or another, I have a favor to ask of you, Stacy."

Stacy regarded her employer suspiciously. "What?" she asked bluntly.

"Stay on and help James until he's finished the book, will you? It's doubtful from the looks of that finger of his that he'd be able to type for another month, which brings us to November. Early in November James has his lecture in New York, after which he'll be returning to England. I think it's extremely important that he get the manuscript to his publisher before he leaves the States...which means before he leaves Cape Cod. And there's no way he can do it without you, Stacy. He'd never hire temporary secretarial help, I'm sure he's already told you that."

"Yes, he's told me that," Stacy said rather sourly.

"You will stay on here with him then, won't you?" Kate asked.

"No," Stacy said.

Kate looked perplexed. "Why in the world not?" she asked.

"Because I have a job to do for you, Kate, and being a safe factotum for your celebrated cousin isn't a part of it."

"Just now, aside from this episode at the Kloset here, things have been amazingly tranquil," Kate said. "As long as that condition continues, I'd be able to spare you."

"You know perfectly well there are a thousand things I should be doing in New York, Kate," Stacy said. "My job isn't one hundred percent on the road."

"Are you saying you don't want to stay here? Is that it?" Kate asked.

"It's not a question of wanting..." Stacy began, and then suddenly shut her mouth and became determined not to say anything more. Anything she might say might also hang her. Kate was sharp, very sharp. It wouldn't take much to make her aware that her right-hand woman had fallen hopelessly in love with her English cousin.

Stacy saw James heading back toward the steps and was glad to have a reason to avoid further probing by Kate. "Since the subject of our discussion is approaching, let's leave this in abeyance, shall we? What you wanted to know about was the Reynolds situation, so suppose I start filling you in."

As she told Kate about Colleen Reynolds and her problems, Stacy tried to soften the facts with the telling as much as possible. Still, facts were facts, and she knew that no matter how she tried to camouflage them she wouldn't be fooling Kate.

By the time she'd finished the story, James, freshly showered and looking terrific in jeans and a plaid shirt, had joined them. When, finally, Stacy said, "That's about it," she tried not to be too obvious about studying Kate's face to gauge her reaction to all of this. But it was clear that Kate was deeply troubled.

"I don't see how we can keep her on, Stacy," Kate said, finally. "I know you're sympathetic toward her, and I might very well be myself had I been through as much with her as you have. But . . . let's face it, she's let the shop run down so that it's really a disgrace to the company at this point. In a way, she's stolen from us as well, by taking the money for doubling at jobs she should have been employing others to do. Obviously she hasn't been able to handle her personal problems with her husband, and attend to business, too—and that's not a good recommendation, as you well know. Then her own daughter dipped into the till. I would say that it was careless of Mrs. Reynolds to let her daughter learn the combination to the safe."

"Oh, for heaven's sake, Kate," Stacy burst out. "How can you say that. How could Colleen possibly have imagined that her daughter would have been desperate enough to do what she did?"

"Her daughter presents a real problem," Kate said, "but she's not our problem, Stacy. She's the Reynolds's problem, and I would say they haven't been able to deal with it very well."

"Damn it, Kate, don't be so smug," James said quietly.

Kate turned toward him, her expressive face reflecting curiosity more than anything else. "You, too, Brutus, eh?" she observed.

"No one's trying to stab you in the back, Kate. You might be a little more human about this, that's all."

"So," Kate said, sitting back and regarding her cousin speculatively. "Just what would you recommend, Dr. Ashley-Sinclair?"

"I would recommend that you get off your high horse and listen to what Stacy's been telling you," James said flatly. "The woman deserves another chance."

Kate sat back and whistled softly. "Well," she said, and repeated herself. "Well."

"Some people learn lessons, and some people don't," James went on. "What might seem to be a display of damaging weakness on the part of many people wasn't, in the case of Colleen Reynolds—at least that's my opinion. She had too many things coming from her in too many directions, dating back to when her husband's business failed. She coped admirably for a time—you've said yourself that that she'd done very well in the Kloset here until this past season. So, stop to think that she was dealing with her husband's problems and then with problems concerning her daughter, as well, during that period. It was only when *all* the problems zeroed in on her—and one of the most trying was the rift between Al and Cissy, with both of them living right there in the same house with Colleen—that she began to fray. Even then she was *trying* to keep up, which was causing her own health to suffer, so that was yet something else to handle.

"I could be wrong," James conceded. "And I would say a careful eye should be kept on Mrs. Reynolds until it's been proven that she's standing strong on her own two feet again. I presume that Stacy could take care of the 'careful eye' detail. She's gained the woman's confidence. But... this isn't the time when you should dismiss Colleen Reynolds, Kate."

Kate was staring at James. "I think that's the longest speech I've ever heard you make, except when you've been on a lecture platform."

Stacy was staring at him, too, but for a different reason. She'd heard him make longer "speeches" in the course of his dictation to her, so she was well aware of how he could put his thoughts together. What was surprising her now was that she had more than half suspected he'd be in favor of letting Colleen Reynolds go, that he would have thought her too weak a person psychologically, to pull things together as they should be pulled together. And yet here he was staunchly championing her.

James was showing that in his analyses of people he was surely anything but judgmental. In fact, he was even more compassionate than she would have believed him to be.

"You've surprised me, James," Kate said.

"Have I?" her cousin inquired lazily.

"Yes. If I didn't value your opinion so tremendously, I'd say that you're being downright soft about this. But I know you. I know you know people. You have a rare understanding of the human psyche, I'm not about to negate that. So—" Kate spread out her hands and smiled at both of them "—the two of you win."

Stacy couldn't believe her own ears. "Are you saying Colleen can stay on as manager at the Kloset?" she demanded.

"With certain provisos," Kate said.

Stacy was sure that the provisos involved her, and she was right.

"For the next two weeks," Kate said, "I'd like you to spend mornings at the Kloset with Mrs. Reynolds, Stacy. James, don't look like that. If Stacy is so inclined, she can go on helping you with your book in the afternoon. Stacy, what I want you to do is to help Mrs. Reynolds get her act together again in the most effective way possible.

"I would say that some definite decorative changes are needed in the shop," Kate went on, warming to the subject. "I'm going to suggest that Mrs. Reynolds hold a super sale of the merchandise she has in the store now . . . really slash prices . . . and the sale should be advertised extensively, beginning right now. I would suggest, naturally, that the present stock be displayed effectively for the sale. And you'll want to see to it that plenty of extra help is hired. Check the stock with Mrs. Reynolds tomorrow, Stacy, and if she doesn't have enough out to hold a really worthwhile sale, then let her go into the new fall merchandise she hasn't unpacked. She can use that, too."

"That could mean losing some profits, Kate," Stacy warned.

"Yes, I know. But luring people back to the Kloset via the sale would be worth any loss we might incur. This sale must be very colorful, Stacy. Get a motif—maybe an autumn leaf motif—and splash colors all over the place. If you hire enough people and Mrs. Reynolds puts her heart into it, you should be able to hold the sale next week—let's say a three-day sale, Thursday, Friday and Saturday."

Stacy issued another warning. "Next week would be pushing it."

"Then push it, my dear," Kate said, not unkindly. "In the meantime Colleen is to line up people who can give the Kloset a complete new look. I think her husband could be helpful there. He could direct you and Colleen to competent people who could take care of any exterior repairs. You'll also want to repaint the interior, get new wall-to-wall carpeting. A brand-new color scheme, Stacy, with a Cape Cod motif. Sand and sea—tones of beige and aqua and deep pinks and corals and touches of vivid blue. You picture what I mean, don't you?"

"Yes," Stacy admitted reluctantly.

"Aim to have a grand opening on Halloween," Kate said. "Champagne punch and delectable little canapés and a gift for each customer." Kate beamed. "I have it. In addition to his designs, Carlos has come up with a fabulous perfume. He's been searching for a name for it, and we can call it 'Haunting.' I'll see to it that an adequate supply is air-shipped from Spain so that we can package it appropriately in New York and get it up to you in time for the grand opening. . . ."

Stacy could see that as far as Kate was concerned the renovation of the Cape Kloset and the Halloween grand opening was already faits accomplis. "Suppose," she said carefully, "Colleen Reynolds doesn't go along with all of this? Suppose she feels she's just not up to handling it?"

"From what I read between those eloquent lines James spoke a few minutes ago, I think Colleen will welcome this opportunity to prove herself," Kate said. And that was that.

Kate left early Monday morning to drive back to New York. When James was carrying his cousin's suitcases out to her car, Stacy found a moment to pull her employer aside. "Kate, you mentioned my staying up here for two weeks to monitor the store. I'm presuming that's the time schedule you want me to stick to."

"No," Kate said promptly. "I hadn't thought things through when I said that, Stacy. I hadn't come up with the thought of the sale and the renovation and the Halloween grand opening. Definitely you'll need to be here through that. The whole thing could fall through if, despite James's predictions, Colleen Reynolds can't follow through after all. In that case, I'm going to want you to call in Marcia Smith, who is assistant manager at the Kloset in Boston. Or, rather, tell me and I'll see to it that Marcia is ready to come down here and take over as manager, at least temporarily. I admit I'm not as sure about Colleen as James is. It makes sense to take the precautions of having a backup, just in case."

Stacy slowly shook her head. "I can't, Kate," she said.

"What can't you do, Stacy?"

"You're asking me to stay here for the better part of a month, and I can't do that."

"Because of James—is that what you're saying?"

"Yes."

"I should think the timing might be rather good," Kate said. "If you spend the afternoon hours working with him on the book from now till Halloween, he should have it ready to send off, from what he's told me. He has to be in New York in early November. He has that last lecture to give before he goes back to England. So, all in all, I don't see how the timing could be better, Stacy."

Stacy wondered if Kate could possible be as obtuse as she was pretending to be. It had been one thing just going along with James from day to day, helping him out with his book. It had been like living in a dream, and at the back of her mind there had been the protective knowledge that all dreams end, and so would this one.

Now Kate was setting a boundary on her time with James, a finite number of days after which they'd part. And that was somehow infinitely harder, as far as Stacy was concerned, than taking their relationship a day at a time and not thinking too much about tomorrow, except when such thoughts were forced upon her.

She couldn't bear to start counting the days and the hours, and then the minutes, until she and James would be saying goodbye. Each day spent with him would make that time of parting—of leaving and losing him—all the more difficult. She was going to be bereft enough as it was once he went back to England. Having another month with him would only make things infinitely worse. Because, by then, she'd love him even more than she did now . . . and she already loved him far too much for her own good.

Couldn't Kate see what she was doing?

"Stacy, I really don't understand the problem," Kate said impatiently. "This is where I want you to be, where I'd want you to be regardless of James. This is where I need you the most right now, and your job had always involved being in the places where you're the most needed. You and James obviously enjoy each other's company, so I would think that his presence would be an added plus."

Stacy had liked Kate Clarendon from the moment she'd met her, and she'd been deeply fond of her employer for a long time. But, right then, she could have throttled her. It seemed to her that Kate was showing an astonishing lack of understanding.

"Kate," she said thickly. "I can't stay. I simply can't stay here in your Hideaway with James. Will you please understand that?"

She saw the warning expression in Kate's green eyes and knew without turning around that James had come into the room. Had he heard what she'd just said? If so, what sort of an interpretation would he put on it? She didn't know, but she did know that she'd just spoken the truth.

"I think Colleen's going to have to put everything she has into this effort, Stacy," Kate said. "We had a long talk on the phone last night, and she'll be ready to get started this morning. I told her you'd be along around nine-thirty. About everything else... I'll phone you tonight, and we'll have a talk, all right?"

It had to be all right... which was maddening. Stacy stood with James, watching Kate start off down the bumpy lane, aware that probably now the next thing on her plate before she went off to the Kloset would be a confrontation of some kind with James. She'd stolen a few glances at him. She was sure he'd heard what she'd said to Kate, and from the stormy expression on his face she knew he hadn't liked it.

When she turned to speak to him, though, she found that he'd silently vanished. Evidently, while she was waving goodbye to Kate, he'd silently slipped around the side of the house, because had he gone in the front door she would have heard it thud as it closed.

She walked around the side of the house herself and over to the top of the steps that led down to the beach. James was already striding across the sand, she saw, walking at a pace she couldn't possibly catch up with. So there was little point in trying to follow him.

He still hadn't come back to the Hideaway by the time Stacy was ready to go to the Kloset. She left reluctantly—she would rather have had this out with him before the issue had time to age and thus possibly fester. On the other hand, she didn't want to be late for this particular appointment with Colleen.

Colleen was dressed becomingly that Monday morning in a cinnamon-colored wool dress, augmented with striking gold-toned accessories. She looked as if she'd had a good night's sleep. Her eyes were clear, her smile genuine.

She and Stacy set about planning the steps to be taken in carrying out Kate's wishes, one at a time, and by the time Stacy left the shop at noon she was actually beginning to believe that they were going to accomplish the sale, the renovation and the Halloween grand opening, something she'd seriously doubted until then.

When she got back to the Hideaway, she found James hunched over the typewriter on their worktable, laboriously putting words on paper, using a hunt-and-peck system.

She glanced apprehensively at his injured finger and saw that he had covered it with what looked like a small cast. "Where in the world did you get that?" she asked, pointing at the cast.

James sat back and surveyed her expressionlessly. "It's a finger guard," he said. "I'd heard of such things and thought they might have one in the local pharmacy. As you can see, they did."

"How did you get to the pharmacy?"

"I walked."

"Why in the world..." Stacy began, then stopped and pulled herself together. "You could have called me at the Kloset. I could have picked that up for you."

"There was no need," James said flatly. "It's not that long a walk to the center of town."

"Didn't they recognize you in the pharmacy?"

"I don't think so. I found an old cap in Kate's coat closet that fitted, and since it's a sunny day I was able to wear dark glasses without attracting undue attention."

"You should have let me get it," Stacy said unhappily.

"Stacy, I've let you do more than enough for me," James said. "I'm deeply appreciative, but it's occurred to me that you shouldn't be asked to divide your time between the Kloset, and all that's to be done there, and helping with the book. I don't think Kate realized how much was entailed when she made that suggestion."

"James..."

"No, please, hear me out," James said with a definite touch of that haughtiness that always made her feel as if a barricade had been thrown up between the two of them. "My progress may be slow, typing for myself, but thanks to your excellent organization everything is in very good order, and we've come a long way. I find it rather valuable, to tell you the truth, to put my own thoughts directly on paper just now...."

Without my sometimes quibbling with you. Stacy thought bleakly. *What a fool I was anyway to venture my opinions when you're the world-famous expert in your field.*

"I am not ungrateful," James went on, the haughtiness persisting. "But I do think I need to do this by myself from here on in. I plan to start airmailing portions of the manuscript to Iris in London. She can have it prepared in final form there. I will need to stay on the Cape until it's finished, Stacy. I hope you'll accept that. But—"

"You heard what I said to Kate, didn't you?" Stacy blurted.

"Yes."

"James, you took it entirely the wrong way."

"I don't think so," James said levelly. "I think the problem is that we were thrown together here and, for a variety of reasons, too much happened too soon. We found each other attractive. That chemistry, which can be so insidious, flowed a bit too freely between us, and we yielded to its spell. . . ."

"You're speaking as if we're one of your case histories," Stacy accused him hotly.

"I don't mean to. But it's really not so different from one of them. I suppose it can be said that nothing's really new. . . ."

Why was he doing this? Stacy looked at James and saw that he was staring at a point somewhere over her shoulder rather than meeting her eyes. Certainly he didn't look happy. Yet he was still so damn much in command of himself.

"Well, if that's the way you want it," she said, so hurt she marveled she could speak at all.

James didn't answer her.

"Perhaps you'd rather I moved into a motel for the duration of my time here?" she suggested.

"No," he said quickly. "Kate would be very upset were that to happen, and I can see no way we could keep it from her. As you know, she calls at all sorts of odd hours, and she's certain to want to keep a check on your progress at the shop. Anyway, I see no reason why we should bother each other, Stacy." He smiled at her, and it was the most infuriating smile she had ever seen. "You have your work to do," he told her, "and I have mine."

Chapter Thirteen

Stacy became so busy with the Cape Kloset's affairs that she didn't see how she could have possibly done her job for Kate and also have helped James out, even if he'd still wanted her to work with him.

She left the Hideaway by eight-thirty each morning that early October week after Kate went back to New York, and it was at least twelve hours later before she returned. She wasn't trying to stay away deliberately; there was that much to do. And each hour of her day was so busy that she was able to go for reasonably long periods of time without thinking about James.

Maybe, she conceded, she was doing more than she really had to do. On the other hand, Colleen Reynolds needed all the help she could get. Not because she was incapable of attending to the things that needed to be done, but simply because there was so much to cover.

The immediate task was to get effective advertising for the upcoming sale into all the area papers. This meant asking the advertising directors of a couple of the weekly papers to bend their deadlines slightly. At first they insisted that was impossible. But when they heard of the extensive plans being set in progress at Kate's Kloset and the advertising budget the company was prepared to put out right through the entire fall-winter season, rules were set aside.

Colleen asked Stacy to take a major hand in the advertising, and introduced her to a woman in town who'd worked a few years back for a major New York agency. They huddled together and in record time came up with stunning layout designs and scintillating copy, and once all of their material had been turned over to the newspapers, Stacy knew there was no going back. They *had* to be ready for the big sale come Thursday.

Al Reynolds, to Stacy's surprise and pleasure, was proving to be a real treasure. He latched on to a couple of men he knew who agreed to drop everything else and make some temporary exterior repairs to the shop. As a result, by the day of the sale Kate's Kloset had been so beautifully camouflaged that Stacy was beginning to wonder if the extensive job Kate had contemplated was really necessary.

She worked with Colleen most of Wednesday arranging the displays in the shop and made the decision that they should go all the way and put some of the new fall merchandise on sale, too, on a first-come basis. Among the items were the Clarisse sweaters that had been selling so well.

The effect that some simple rearranging made was astonishing. Stacy placed a rather reckless order with a local florist to further enhance the interior decor, and baskets and bouquets of flowers were delivered late Wednesday afternoon. By the time this final bit of transformation had effected its magic, Colleen, looking around, said, "This is hard to believe." Her eyes misted. "How can I ever thank you, Stacy? I'm certain that but for you Kate Clarendon would never have given me another chance."

"No," Stacy said honestly, "that's not so. Her cousin really went to bat for you."

"Jim Sinclair?"

"Yes," Stacy said, wishing she could tell Colleen who Kate's cousin really was. But she wasn't about to tangle with the issue of James's privacy.

Colleen had found several local women to come in for the sales days, some of whom had worked in the shop before. But when Thursday came the response was so overwhelming that Stacy, too, was pressed into service. She'd had very little sales experience, so this was a challenge. On the other hand, Kate's beautiful things pretty much sold themselves when presented properly—especially at the sale prices.

By six o'clock Saturday night there wasn't much left in the shop, and Stacy and Colleen, having said good-night to the last of the sales force, collapsed in Colleen's office.

A moment later Al Reynolds appeared in the doorway, his face wreathed in smiles. Al was carrying a bottle of champagne and some plastic cups and, as he put the bottle down on Colleen's desk, he looked around. "Thought you might have asked Jim to come over and celebrate with us," he said.

It took a moment for Stacy to realize that Al was referring to James. Obviously James had made a deep impression on Al during that conversation they'd had at the Port and Starboard.

"I should have asked him," Stacy said which, of course, was true.

As she let herself into the Hideaway an hour or so later, she was feeling slightly guilty about having failed to include James in a celebration for a cause with which he'd had a lot to do. She felt even guiltier as she sniffed something cooking that smelled wonderful and then, going to the living room doorway, saw that James had a fire crackling on the hearth.

During the week Stacy had subsisted on whatever she could put her hands on in the way of food, and she knew that James had lived mostly on the TV dinners with which she'd stocked the freezer. Now he'd evidently decided he wanted something better and so must have walked to the supermarket and gotten the makings for whatever this was he had on the stove.

She was standing in front of the fireplace, warming her hands, when James came into the room. He was wearing one of Kate's aprons, a red-and-white check with a ruffled edge. Only James, Stacy thought, could possibly have managed to wear something like that and still look dignified.

"I'm baking a steak and kidney pie," he said without preamble. "I found a cookbook of Kate's with some English recipes, and I thought it might be amusing to try doing something like that."

"It smells fantastic," Stacy said.

She was trying not to meet his eyes as she spoke because just being near him was enough to badly dent her self-control. But she felt as if he were compelling her to look at him, and when finally she did, she wished she hadn't. James seemed as self-assured as ever, and he was smiling—a rather diffident smile—but the expression in his eyes was so bleak that it hurt to see it.

"How about a cold drink while we're waiting for the pie to finish cooking?" he asked.

"A ginger ale would be great. I can get it," she volunteered.

He shook his head. "Sit down, Stacy. You've had quite a week, and I should imagine you need to get off your feet. Two ginger ales coming up."

When he came back, he had divested himself of the frilly apron. Stacy was curled up in the corner of the couch and, after handing her drink to her, James sat down at the other end of the couch, keeping a careful distance between them.

"I imagine this should really be champagne," he said, glancing at the ginger ale.

"Al brought a bottle of champagne in after we closed," Stacy had to admit. She hesitated. "I should add that he limited his own imbibing to a single glass. Also, he thought you should have been there to help celebrate, as of course you should have. I didn't realize he'd do something like that, or I would have suggested you come over."

"Was the sale successful?" James asked, sidestepping the issue.

"The sale was sensational. I can't believe it went over as well as it did. Kate was absolutely right in her prescription for the Kloset."

"Good," James said, but his tone lacked enthusiasm.

Stacy stole a glance at him. He looked tired and preoccupied. "How's the book going?" she ventured to ask.

"It's going."

"Is that all you can say?"

"What do you expect me to say? I thought I had it all in hand, but I've had a, well, I guess you could call it a touch of writer's block, these past couple of days. The words aren't coming out as I'd hoped they would." He shrugged. "Tell me more about the shop," he suggested.

"Tell me more about the book," Stacy countered.

"There's no need for me to bore you about the book, Stacy."

Stacy's mouth tightened. "How can you say something like that to me?" she demanded after a tense moment. "You know how interested I am in that book, James."

James was staring moodily at the leaping flames.

"James," she repeated, her need to communicate with him overriding her need for caution, "why are you being like this?"

"Why am I being like what?"

"You know what I'm talking about. Does it have to be like this between us, all because you leaped to a stupid conclusion?"

"I leaped to a stupid conclusion?"

"Yes, damn it, you did." Stacy's eyes were sparking. "You overheard me tell Kate I couldn't stay in the house with you for another month, and you completely misinterpreted what I meant. That's what comes of... of eavesdropping."

"I wasn't eavesdropping, Stacy," James said coldly. "I'd carried Kate's luggage out to her car and put it in the boot. I didn't realize I was perhaps supposed to stay out there."

"Of course you weren't supposed to stay out there."

"Very well, then. I came back into the house, and I overheard what I overheard through no fault whatsoever of my own. But I'm glad I did."

"What do you mean?"

"Hearing what you said to Kate put things in proper perspective," James said. "I've already told you that it's been a case of too much too soon with us, as I think you realized even before I did. I think you were very aware of that when you said what you did to Kate, and the more I thought about it, the more I concurred."

Stacy stared at him helplessly. He seemed to be determined in a very perverse sort of way, to take off on an entirely wrong tack.

She was about to tell him what she'd *really* meant in those remarks to Kate, and came close to the edge of doing so. Then caution surfaced. My God, she'd be blabbing to James that the reasons she hadn't wanted to stay on in the house with him was because she knew she'd only come to love him so much with each passing day that it would be all the more unbearable when he left her....

It was going to be unbearable anyway when he left her.

Stacy felt hot tears sting her eyes, and she blinked hastily. James, fortunately, didn't notice. "I'd better go check the oven," he said, getting to his feet.

James's steak and kidney pie was a culinary triumph, much to his surprise, but he didn't appreciate it, and he doubted Stacy did, either. He might as well have been eating sawdust.

He was feeling miffed, for one thing, because she hadn't asked him to come over to the shop and share in a glass of champagne. She could have phoned him, damn it.

Furthermore, the deep hurt he'd felt on hearing her tell Kate she couldn't stay in the house with him still stung unbearably. Maybe they'd rushed things, he conceded that, but his feeling for her had been so deep and so genuine that the passion that had flowered between them had seemed as natural and wonderful as breathing.

It had been more than passion, James thought darkly. Passion too often was transitory. What he'd felt for Stacy—what he still felt for her—far transcended a purely sexual expression, no matter how ecstatic that sexual expression might have been.

Also, in addition to those golden moments they'd shared in bed with each other, just being with her had been so... wonderful. He'd never in his life felt as close to anyone as he'd come to feel to Stacy, in an admittedly short time. Walking on the beach together, sitting in front of the fireplace together, just being here together in Kate's Hideaway had made him begin to realize as he never had before how much was lacking in his life.

His days and hours ordinarily were so full he didn't have that much time to think about himself and, if anything, he needed to compress even more into them. There was no limit to the social life he could lead if he wanted to. He could surround himself with people if he were so inclined. But the rapport he'd achieved with Stacy on all levels—intellectual as well as physical and emotional—was something so special that James felt in his bones this was a once-in-a-lifetime thing and, as a psychologist, he'd never quite believed in once-in-a-lifetime relationships.

He'd reacted defensively to that statement of Stacy's to Kate, and that surprised him, too, because he thought he had better control of himself. To react defensively automatically put a person in a weakened position, and that he didn't want.

He'd decided it was for the best when Stacy became so absorbed in her work at Kate's shop that he'd scarcely seen her all week. Then that, too, had boomeranged. He'd discovered that he couldn't work without her. He'd grown so accustomed to having her there across the worktable from him that he'd felt a real void when she was away. He'd gotten used to bouncing his ideas off her, and he'd become increasingly enthusiastic about hearing the contributions she made from time to time. She'd caused him to consider a different viewpoint on many issues, something he'd needed to do.

These past couple of days, as far as ideas were concerned, he'd been as sterile as a blank piece of paper, James thought ruefully.

The phone rang at a moment when James was about to blurt out to Stacy that they needed to clear a lot of cobwebs between the two of them, and this time the jangling, intrusive sound was a reprieve. It was Kate, calling primarily for Stacy. She'd already spoken to Colleen Reynolds and was jubilant about the success of the sale.

By the time Stacy finished talking to Kate, James had gotten a new grip on himself. They cleaned up after dinner pretty much in silence, then James opted to stay downstairs and read for a while, and Stacy went up to bed.

The next week was as busy as the previous one for Stacy, though in a different way. She and Colleen worked for the most part out of Colleen's house while the shop was being redecorated. They went through back paperwork, brought accounts up to date and phoned orders in to the company headquarters in New York for exciting new merchandise to be rushed to Devon in time for the Halloween grand opening.

Al Reynolds, meantime, took some vacation time that was coming to him from the oil company, and appointed himself foreman of the works at the shop. He looked after everything, kept tabs of the workmen and the material they were using, saw to it that the men kept to their schedule so that there would be no lags that would interfere with the completion date. Stacy had to admit that she didn't see how they could have done the job a quarter as effectively without him.

Working out of Colleen's home, Stacy also began to get to know Cissy Reynolds better. The girl was coming home promptly from school each afternoon, and had taken upon herself the job of preparing supper for her family each night.

Cissy, Stacy reflected, had been through a great deal for a person her age. But she seemed to be learning from what could have become such a severe personal tragedy that she might never have recovered from it. Cissy began to warm up the more she got to know Stacy, finally revealing that she had a delightful sense of humor when she relaxed and was herself. One day she confessed shyly that what she really wanted to do was to become a fashion designer. She showed Stacy a couple of ideas for dresses she'd sketched, and Stacy, impressed, made a mental note to speak to Kate about this. It would be a good publicity move for Kate's Klosets to initiate a scholarship fund for promising young American designers, and Stacy could see Cissy being one of the first recipients.

Stacy was always invited to stay for supper with the Reynoldses, and sometimes she accepted, both because it pleased the family and because it kept her from having to share a stilted meal with James. But she wondered what would happen when the weekend rolled around again.

The previous Sunday—after James's steak and kidney pie dinner—she'd driven over to Hyannis and gone to a movie. James had decided to work, and so it had made sense to leave him alone.

This Sunday, though, she awakened to a gorgeous autumn day, with the sun sparkling and the air like dry wine. Looking out her window, she realized that she'd left James without a car each day, and although he seemed to have become accustomed to walking to town to get whatever he wanted, it seemed to her he might be feeling somewhat stir-crazy about now.

He always made a pot of coffee first thing in the morning. When Stacy went down to get a cup, she found him sitting at the kitchen table, glancing through yesterday's newspapers. "Would you like to take my car today?" she asked. "I thought you might want to drive around for a while. It's so beautiful out."

James surveyed her gravely. "I would like to get out and drive around," he admitted. "But I'd also rather like to have company." When Stacy didn't answer, he expressed exasperation. "Would it really be so impossible for the two of us to go off for the day, Stacy? I know we haven't exactly been getting along of late, but I should think we could tolerate each other's company enough for an outing where we might get a glimpse of some of New England's famous fall foliage and perhaps stop for dinner somewhere."

He made it sound so simple . . . and so innocuous. Stacy knew that being with James all day would be neither. On the other hand, she wanted to be with him so much . . .

"Where would you like to go?" she asked abruptly.

"I thought of Plymouth," James said. "I've been hearing the foliage reports on the telly. The foliage is pretty much done with farther north. But in southern New England it should be at its most vivid about now. Also, I'd rather like to see the job they've done at the Plymouth Plantation. It's a replica village of the kind of setting the Pilgrims lived in. And, you know," he added with a slight smile, "your Founding Fathers *were* English."

Normally Stacy would have come back with an answering quip over something like that. But her sense of humor seemed to have deserted her.

When they started out, though, with James at the wheel, the sheer beauty of the day and the scenery did begin to get to her. In Plymouth they went aboard the *Mayflower II* and marveled at how such a cramped little ship had ever carried so many people across the Atlantic. Then they drove to Plimoth Plantation and spent nearly three hours wandering through the recreated village.

James, at that point, said he was starving, and so they found a restaurant on the waterfront where they feasted on steamed clams and lobster. And Stacy, who'd made the resolution when they left the Cape that she was going to put everything else aside and enjoy this day with him, felt the sweet stab of happiness that came only when she was with James.

She looked at him, her eyes shining with her love for him, and James intercepted her glance. He'd been about to say something to her, but he totally forgot what it was as he felt himself drowning in the beauty of her deep blue eyes.

Stacy saw his expression change suddenly. He looked at her with such longing that she caught her breath. She felt her heart respond so that her pulse was like a small drum punishing her body. But, painful or not, she was alive, every inch of her was vibrantly alive, and no matter what happened no one could ever take away the memory of this particular moment.

"Stacy..." James said huskily.

Stacy couldn't speak.

"Stacy," he persisted, "I... suspect I've been a fool."

Stacy still couldn't speak.

James wasn't doing such a good job of communicating himself. He reached across the table and took her hand in his. Her fingers were trembling, and his were none too steady.

"I wish," he said, "we could go back to just before Kate came and start all over again."

Stacy found her voice. "People can't go back, James," she said sadly.

"I know. I still wish . . ."

He wrested his eyes away from her, wishing for many things, most of which he knew to be impossible. He wished he'd never written *A Personal Sex Bible*. He wished he'd met Stacy under simple, ordinary circumstances, maybe when paying Kate a visit in New York. He wished they could have come to know each other without that backdrop of fame and fortune forever looming on the horizon. Because then—if any of that fame and fortune had come later—she would already have known *him*, and she would have been able to better cope with the outward trappings of his success.

As it was, he was aware that at moments Stacy had been intimidated by the notoriety that had become such a part of his public image. He'd sensed that reading his damn book had only further intimidated her, and thus far she'd known only the tip of the iceberg. She'd only seen him once in a professional setting—at the Ritz after his lecture was over and a sizable segment of the audience had already gone home. That was nothing to what she'd see if she were to accompany him into his usual mileu, and—knowing Stacy as he did—he was sure that she'd detest all the trappings that went with his success.

He didn't attempt to elaborate aloud on all that he was wishing.

James made an impromptu trip to New York toward the end of the next week and stayed through the weekend. The reason for the trip, he told Stacy vaguely, had to do with his upcoming lecture in the city in November. And there was some truth to that, though he could have attended to the details by phone, if need be. Actually, he'd simply had to get away. He knew he couldn't possibly stay another night in the Hideaway without humbling himself, going to Stacy's room in the middle of the night and telling her that he loved her so damn much nothing else mattered.

He stayed with Kate in New York in her roomy Fifth Avenue apartment. He was moody and withdrawn and not very easy to get along with, and Kate was remarkably patient with him—for Kate. But he was aware of the extremely inquisitive glances she sent in his direction every time he wasn't looking, and he knew that all sorts of questions were piling up at the tip of her tongue. Matters were only made worse when he replied in monosyllables whenever Kate said anything about Stacy, thus causing the curiosity only to deepen in Kate's green eyes.

He had flown to New York from Hyannis, having summoned a taxi to take him from Devon to the Barnstable County Airport. But when it came time to leave Manhattan to go back to the Cape, he decided to rent a car. He was going to have to return to the city soon, bringing his accumulation of papers and the three-quarters completed manuscript with him.

Thus far he hadn't followed through on his plan to send segments of the manuscript to Iris regularly. There didn't seem much point in it. He'd begun to realize there was no way he was going to get this particular book finished without Stacy. She'd become too much a part of it.

By the time James returned to Devon, Stacy and Colleen were busy stocking the newly renovated store. The sand-and-sea decorative theme was beautiful, and Kate's clothes had never looked lovelier.

Colleen suggested that they ask the people who'd been working with them—and James—to come in for drinks and hors d'oeuvres the night before the Halloween grand opening. There was no way Stacy could avoid extending the invitation to James, but she hoped he'd refuse. He'd started working on the book again the moment he got back from New York and had been immersed in stacks of paper ever since.

James, however, accepted, and so on a frosty October evening Stacy set off with him as her escort. He was wearing a gray tweed suit, and he looked so handsome that Stacy felt as if she might choke every time she glanced at him.

The refreshments were served in Colleen's office. This time floral offerings had been sent by a number of merchants in town. There were enough flowers to decorate the office as well as the shop itself, and the effect was lovely.

Colleen was brimming over with happiness. So was Al, and so was Cissy. And, looking at the Reynolds family, Stacy suddenly realized that her work in Devon was over. There was no need for her to stay around any longer, not even for tomorrow's grand opening.

A small inner voice told her she'd be behaving like a coward if she ran away. She challenged the voice by answering silently that tomorrow should rightfully be Colleen's day, her triumph.

She was no longer needed here, either at Kate's Kloset or at Kate's Hideaway.

It was very late when she crept down Kate's stairs, suitcases in hand. When one of the steps creaked, she was sure James would hear the noise and come to investigate. But he evidently was sleeping soundly, for he didn't appear.

Stacy had written him a letter while still up in her bedroom. She'd let herself put some of what she felt in it, but not too much. "This is the right moment to go back to New York and get on with my work there," she'd written, "and so I'm going. I think it'll be easier for both of us not to have to say goodbye face-to-face. I shall never forget you, James. Not ever."

She put the letter on the kitchen table, setting James's coffee mug on a corner of it to secure it. The front door creaked as she let herself out, and again she was afraid James might appear, but he didn't.

When she turned on the car engine, the noise sounded like an explosion in the silence of the night. Starting down the driveway, Stacy looked back and saw a light go on in James's bedroom and knew he'd heard the car.

She drove as quickly as she could along the bumpy lane out to the beach road and, turning toward town, knew she'd put herself past the point of no return.

Chapter Fourteen

I don't understand you, Stacy," Kate Clarendon said. "It's bad enough that you sneaked away from the Hideaway in the middle of the night..."

Stacy flinched. She didn't like the word *sneaked*.

"I think that was insulting enough to James," Kate went on, "but now you want to add further insult to injury by skipping out of town before he gives his lecture."

"I really doubt James will miss me at his lecture," Stacy said drily. "I understand it's a sellout."

"I hardly think that's the point," Kate retorted coldly.

They were in Kate's office in the Lower Manhattan headquarters of Kate's Klosets, Ltd. The office color scheme was that same combination of apricot and ivory that Kate had used in her living room at the Hideaway. Even those colors reminded Stacy of James...as if she needed anything to remind her of him. He'd been constantly in her thoughts on her predawn drive back to

New York and equally so over the two days since she'd been back here.

Stacy, becoming so restless she could no longer sit still, got up and walked over to the window. This particular window looked out over a small city park, and she saw a spindly little maple tree in a protected corner, its leaves flaming with vivid orange and scarlet. The maple leaves reminded her of the drive she'd taken to Plymouth with James. It was beginning to seem as if everywhere she turned she was going to see something that reminded her of James.

She swung around and faced Kate. "There must be some situation in one of your shops around the country that needs investigating," she said. "If there isn't, then everything's so perfect my job is no longer valid."

Kate snorted impatiently. Then she said, her tone as determined as Stacy's, "I'm not going to offer you an escape route, Stacy," she said. "That's what sending you off on a troubleshooting trek would be doing just now."

"I don't understand this," Stacy said flatly. "I simply don't understand it."

"That makes two of us," Kate said. "James called me in the middle of the night after you left, and I didn't think he had it in him to be so furious. I spoke to him this morning, and he said he phoned his publisher in London and told him he's scrapping the new book and will pay back the very hefty advance that was given to him."

Stacy stared at Kate. "I can't believe that," she said.

"Believe it. It's true."

Shocked, she went back to the chair next to Kate's desk and sat down again. "Why?" she asked. "Why would he do a thing like that?"

"Why don't you ask him?" Kate suggested.

"I can't ask him. Kate, please try to understand, will you? I can't see him again."

"In short, you're going to let him go back to England without so much as saying goodbye face-to-face."

"Yes," Stacy admitted.

Kate picked up a slim gold pen and started tapping the surface of her blond wood desk. "I think," she said finally, "that you'd better tell me what it is James has done to you, Stacy."

"Done to me?"

"He must have done something to you, or you wouldn't be reacting this way. You're not a silly child. Rather, you're a very sophisticated young woman, quite in control of her own destiny, I'd say—as much as any of us can ever be in control of our destinies. But right now you're acting like an adolescent."

"Please," Stacy protested.

"You are, you know," Kate said, leaning back, her eyes narrowed. "Unless James did something absolutely outrageous, so outrageous you'd be justified in refusing to forgive him, I cannot see why you find it impossible to so much as attend his lecture with me. If you don't agree with that then, I say again, this is a case of adolescent behavior that doesn't become you, Stacy."

Stacy was stung. "Perhaps you'd like me to hand in my resignation, Kate."

"What?" Kate, on occasion, could roar, and she roared now.

"You heard me," Stacy said. "I love my job, you know that, but I refuse to be dictated to when it comes to my personal affairs. I was dictated to enough when I was married to Paul Delacorte. No one's ever again going to find needless fault with my behavior or give me orders about what I have to do or don't have to do where my personal life is concerned."

"Whew," Kate said. "This is more serious than I thought." She surveyed her assistant speculatively. "I didn't mean to dictate to you," she said slowly. "Nor do I think I was finding needless fault with your behavior. Sometimes, Stacy, my dear, we need an objective eye on a situation, and that's what I was trying to give you. To be frank with you, when I was there at the Hideaway with you and James, I thought something quite special had developed between the two of you, and I admit I was pleased. James hasn't—"

She broke off, and Stacy waited impatiently for her to continue. But Kate shook her head and said, "Enough. James had two front-row tickets to the lecture sent over, one for you and one for me. Obviously that doesn't mean you have to attend."

"James had two tickets sent over?"

"Yes. He drove back to the city yesterday and got in fairly late last night."

"He's staying with you?"

"Yes."

"Oh," Stacy said.

Manhattan, for all of its millions of inhabitants, suddenly seemed too small to her. Probably there was no place in the world big enough to house James Ashley-Sinclair and herself at the same time... because when they were sharing the same geographical space, she wanted desperately to be with him.

Some of what she was feeling must have shown on her face because Kate now spoke in a much softer tone. "Stacy, my dear, you're quite right. I've trespassed. Whatever this is between James and yourself, it's your own concern, and I have no right to butt in. Much as I'd like to,'' she finished with a slight grin.

It suddenly occurred to Stacy than in some ways, at least, Kate was right. She *was* behaving like an adolescent where James was concerned. She was appalled now when she thought of leaving the Hideaway in the middle of the night. Kate was right. She had been sneaking away.

She was surprised, in view of her behavior, that James had even considered sending her a ticket to his lecture. But it did begin to seem that, under the circumstances, the least she could do was to try to regain the normal quotient of composure she seemed to have lost. She would accompany Kate. And to be honest, she couldn't wait to see James's beloved face one more time.

The house was packed for James's lecture. Looking around her, Stacy realized that, despite everything she'd learned about him, she still hadn't fully appreciated just how famous James Ashley-Sinclair really was. The things she'd read about him, that television interview she'd seen in England, and reading his book had in no way prepared her for the reality she was seeing now.

One man was going to speak to all these people. The thought overwhelmed her.

When finally James appeared on stage, accompanied by the distinguished educator who was to introduce him, Stacy was stunned anew. At his appearance the audience rose to give him a standing ovation. She found herself clapping as enthusiastically as the rest of the people, even while she felt like a heavy stone was suddenly sinking deep within her.

If she'd needed anything to convince her that James was completely out of her world, this was it.

He was wearing a dark blue suit, a white shirt and a tie discreetly striped in blue and gold. His hair looked as if it had just been perfectly coiffed. In fact, everything about him was exactly that—perfect.

Stacy swallowed hard.

Then she became aware that he was scanning the audience, specifically the front row of the hall. When he saw her, she could have sworn that his gaze lingered and that, very briefly, an odd expression crossed his handsome face. But then the distinguished educator was taking the microphone to fill in the audience on the background of tonight's even more distinguished speaker, and finally James was standing and beginning to speak.

Like the rest of his audience, Stacy became mesmerized. She listened to the voice that was so familiar to her speaking with that British accent that had always intrigued her so much, and she knew that what she was hearing were thoughts coming from a very extraordinary man.

He paused once, and again Stacy could have sworn he was looking at her, and at her only, and that he actually seemed...worried. Why would James Ashley-Sinclair appear worried at a moment like this? Stacy decided she had misread his expression, that he probably hadn't really had been looking at her anyway, and as he continued with what he had to say she was once again gripped by the relevance of his message.

Then she realized he was using some of the material they'd worked on for his second book. A couple of the thoughts he advanced even seemed especially familiar to her, and she realized they were opinions she'd tossed out to James that he'd not necessarily agreed with at first, but which they'd then discussed....

Had James really been *listening* to her to that extent?

James brought his lecture to its conclusion, injecting humor at the end so that he left his audience smiling. The ovation he received was tremendous. He had to come back on stage again—and again. Stacy had the odd feeling that each time he stood, taking the applause he so richly deserved, he was zeroing in on her face as if trying to gauge her reaction to what he'd just said.

Finally the crowd let him go, and people began to file out. "Darling, it would be easiest to walk to the reception," Kate said. "It's at the Park Helene, which is just a couple of blocks from here."

"What reception?" Stacy asked.

They were out on Fifty-seventh Street, and Kate was tugging her in the direction of Central Park South. "What reception?" she asked again.

"There's to be a champagne reception for James," Kate said. "I was going to say, back in there—" she indicated the hall they had just left over her shoulder "—that we could have fought our way back to the Green Room to see him, but it would have been so mobbed it would have been impossible to do more than say hello to him. The reception has a relatively restricted guest list."

Stacy stopped short. "Kate, I'm not going to any reception," she said quickly. "You go ahead. I'll get a cab and go home."

Kate, too, stopped short. She looked up at Stacy her chin thrust out. "I'm not speaking to you as your employer," she said tightly, "but as someone whom I hope you consider a true friend. If you value that friendship . . . come!"

James was watching the doors of the ballroom in which the reception in his honor was being held. As he watched, he kept shaking hands and murmuring thanks to the steady stream of people who were congratulating him. He was clasping a glass of champagne in his left hand and the injured finger on his right hand was making the whole hand ache from the constant pressure that was being inflicted on it.

Where the hell were Kate and Stacy?

Once he'd found Stacy in the audience he'd hardly been able to take his eyes off her. She was wearing black, which made her skin look creamy white, and she was so beautiful that she took his breath away. He'd been so sure she wouldn't come that he'd not quite been able to believe his eyes when he saw her.

Now he saw her again, and he suddenly stopped thanking someone in midstream. "Excuse me," he said, and started shouldering his way through the crowd of people, most of whom were still waiting to get a word with him.

He caught up with Stacy and Kate just as they were accepting champagne from a waiter who was carrying a huge silver tray laden with thin-stemmed glasses of the bubbly golden liquid. James bent and kissed his cousin first. And then without missing a beat he kissed Stacy.

She'd never know, he thought wryly, just how much courage that particular gesture took.

Next he looked around for some place, any place, where he could escape the crowd and, taking her with him, find a small oasis where they could talk. He *had* to talk to her, and this was probably his only chance. He was leaving for London the day after tomorrow, and he could well imagine Stacy doing an excellent job of avoiding him until his plane had safely taken off.

He quickly saw that there was no place to go because, once again, he was being surrounded. His admirers swept in, oblivious to the small scene being played before their eyes, and in a minute he and Stacy and Kate were separated.

James tried valiantly to get back to her again, but it was useless. Now and then he glimpsed her, but then he saw Kate standing alone and finally managed to get to her side.

"Where's Stacy?" he gritted, but in his heart he already knew the answer before Kate spoke.

"She left," Kate said. "She asked me to thank you very much for the ticket . . . and to say goodbye for her."

Stacy paced up and down in her East Sixty-eighth Street apartment until the sun came up over Queens and sent fingers of golden light through her windows.

She'd behaved like a jerk again, she told herself. But last night she'd been unable to stay at the reception for another minute. James had been so near and yet so far. She knew it would always be that way.

She stopped pacing, went to the front door and picked up the daily paper. As she had expected it might, it contained a rave review of James's lecture. But she was appalled to discover that a photographer had caught a shot of James just as he was kissing her.

"Who," the caption read, "is the mysterious brunette who evidently has captivated sex expert James Ashley-Sinclair?"

Stacy shuddered, tore the picture into shreds and stuffed it into her garbage can.

James went back to his cousin Kate's apartment once he was able to escape from the reception. He'd taken off his coat jacket, removed his tie, tossed it aside and run agitated fingers through his hair so often that it was standing on end. Kate, who had never seen him like this, didn't know what to do about him.

James didn't know what to do about himself. He did know that he'd never been so miserable, and he couldn't help but feel that Stacy had deserted him when he needed her the most. That he resented.

"If she weren't such a good friend of yours, I could say a few things," James finally muttered darkly. "She has been," he added rather thickly, "bitchy."

Kate blinked in surprise. "Well, just how have you been?" she countered.

"I've tried," he said. He raised appealing eyes to his cousin. "Damn it, I've tried," he insisted. "Kate, I don't want her to view me like some damn freak."

"James," Kate said, determined to remain calm through this, "I doubt very much that Stacy regards you as a freak."

"Then how does she regard me?"

"I don't know," Kate admitted.

"Has she talked to you about me?"

"Not very much," Kate said, which was true. Stacy had been more inclined to talk around the issue of James rather than about him.

"Great," James muttered. "That's just great."

"James," Kate said, "Stacy isn't one to talk much about people—that is, she's not a gossip. Also, you must realize she'd be discreet in anything she might say about you. You are my cousin, after all."

James reared up and cast a baleful eye at Kate. "You think she felt the need to be discreet?"

"I didn't say that, James. I just meant that it's not Stacy's habit to discuss people on a personal level."

"What the hell kind of a level does she usually discuss people on?"

"She sticks to business," Kate said.

"Then maybe you should have sent her out on a troubleshooting mission, where I'm concerned," James growled.

Kate stared at him. She was finding it hard enough to believe that this disheveled, unhappy man was her usually urbane, confident cousin James. Tonight he'd added another major triumph to his list of laurels with the lecture, yet to look at him and hear him, anyone would have thought he'd failed dismally.

"James," Kate asked gently, "by any chance have you fallen in love with Stacy?"

Her cousin glared at her.

"All right," she said. "You can tell me it's none of my business if you like, but regardless of what you say, I can't help but feel somewhat responsible for this."

"For what?"

"For whatever's happened with the two of you. Stacy hasn't been herself since she got back to New York. Certainly you haven't been yourself tonight. Probably I should have had the sense not to bring the two of you together. I should have realized—"

"Just what should you have realized, Kate?"

"That you're both insufferably strong-willed. That you can both be terribly stubborn and opinionated. That you'd be sure to have a very definite reaction upon each other, whether positive or negative.

"The problem is," Kate continued thoughtfully, "I wasn't thinking that far ahead when I asked Stacy to meet you in Boston and take you down to Devon with her. I intended to be there when you both arrived—and I see now I should have been. I should have said to hell with trying to get one of the best contracts for clothes that has come my way since I got into business. I should have told Carlos to go back to Spain, and I should have headed straight for Devon. Then Stacy could have gotten about her business with Colleen Reynolds, and the two of you wouldn't have been thrown together as you were."

"It wouldn't have made much difference," James said darkly.

"What do you mean?"

"I think I began to fall in love with her the minute I looked across the Ritz ballroom and saw her standing in the doorway," James said. "I couldn't believe what was happening to me. I still can't believe what's happened to me. Love her? My God, Kate, I love her so much that the thought of spending the rest of my life without her is worse than the idea of being exiled to an ice field in Siberia."

Kate was astounded.

"Believe me," James went on, "I tried to stop what was happening from happening. I tried like hell to resist. The last thing I wanted was to fall in love with an American career woman. I didn't want to fall in love with *any* woman for that matter. But . . . when it hits, it hits, doesn't it?"

"Yes," said Kate.

"Stacy runs very scared of men," James said. "Very scared. She's put that bad marriage behind her, but it left scars. She doesn't want to risk being hurt again...and you yourself were afraid I might hurt her. You said that, Kate."

"I know," Kate said. "But that's because you've become such a . . . such a personality, James. You're formidable enough by nature—"

"If you start in with that British aristocrat bit, I won't be responsible for what I do," James warned her.

"All right. But you do have a certain manner that can be quite intimidating."

"It's a defense mechanism," her cousin muttered.

"Yes, I know that," Kate said calmly, "but then I know you better than most people do."

He nodded. "So you do."

"James . . . I truly hate to see you so unhappy."

He looked up. "Then what do you suggest I do about it?"

"I hope you realize the sacrifice I may be making in saying this to you," Kate pointed out, "because if Stacy is agreeable to what I'm about to suggest, I'll lose the best assistant I'll ever have. But why don't you go to Stacy and tell her you love her and ask her to marry you and go back to England with you?"

James looked at Kate as if she'd lost her mind. "Because Stacy would take off before I said half of that to her," he informed his cousin flatly. "There's no way she'll get out of that niche she's made for herself and give up the life she's made and the job she has with you for me or any other man—unless that man had a hell of a lot to offer her. And oddly enough, I don't. She'd hate having the kind of spotlight on her I have on me. Did you see her face at the reception tonight when people kept crowding in on me? She couldn't get out of the place fast enough. Without," James finished, "even so much as saying goodbye."

Stacy had been sitting at the desk in her office for an hour when Kate arrived at work. She'd been trying to rearrange some files and catch up on her paperwork, but she couldn't concentrate. She was wishing she'd never gone to James's lecture last night, wonderful though it had been to hear him speak. The result of seeing him in the full spotlight had only made him seem like a total stranger to her, despite that kiss he'd given her.

She flinched again at the memory of her picture in this morning's paper. People she knew were sure to see it. She was probably going to be in for considerable teasing. Ordinarily she was able to take teasing in stride and to dish back as much as was dished out to her. But where James was concerned . . .

It was a relief to have Kate call on the intercom, and she quickly tidied up her desk and went to Kate's office. Kate, she thought as she sat down in a small armchair near Kate's desk, looked tired. Probably she and James had stayed late at the reception.

She hoped Kate wasn't going to mention the lecture, or the reception, or the photograph in this morning's paper, or James.

Kate didn't.

"I just had a call from the manager of our new shop down on St. Simon's Island," Kate said. "They're having a few problems. I don't think it's anything major, but they do need advice. I thought it might be an idea for you to go down there and take a look. This wouldn't be a bad time of year to spend a few days on the Georgia coast."

"When would you like me to leave?" Stacy asked promptly.

"As soon as possible, I'd say," Kate said. "No point in delaying it."

"I can be out of here this afternoon if I can get a plane reservation."

"There's no need for that much hurry," Kate protested.

"All right, tomorrow, then."

"All right," Kate agreed. She hesitated. "Why don't we lunch together, Stacy?" she suggested. "Let's say in an hour from now. There are a few things I'd like to talk over with you."

Stacy regarded her employer warily. "Anything wrong?" she asked.

"Specifically, no. I'd just like to talk to you, that's all."

"I don't want to talk about him, Kate," Stacy said.

"Stacy..."

"No. You do want to talk to me about James, don't you? Yes, your face is giving you away. Well, that's one subject that is going to have to be taboo between us from now on, Kate. I went to the lecture as you wished, even to the reception. Now James will be going back to England tomorrow, and that's that."

"You're not giving him much of a chance, are you?" Kate asked bluntly.

"What do you mean?"

"Exactly what I said. I've always considered you a very fair person, Stacy. Yet when it comes to James, you seem to have become so overpowered by the image that you refuse to look at the man."

"Kate, we started in on this yesterday," Stacy warned. "You somewhat shamed me into going to the lecture. That was enough. Now about going to St. Simons..."

Chapter Fifteen

Stacy left New York on a cold and dank early November day. The Georgia coast, in contrast, was warm and sunny and St. Simons Island—reached via a long causeway from Brunswick—proved to be a delightful oasis.

Stacy checked in at the Cloisters, which was on Sea Island immediately adjacent to St. Simons, and waited till the following morning to approach the manager at the St. Simon's Kloset. The problems in the shop turned out to be so minor that she could easily have flown back to New York the next day. But she wasn't ready to face up to business as usual.

She called Kate to say that she'd like to linger on Sea Island for the rest of the week, taking some of the vacation time due her. Kate was agreeable.

Stacy put her mind to relaxing for the next few days, concentrating on sunning, swimming in the pool at the Cloisters and doing a little local sight-seeing. The closer the time came to her leaving, the more she dreaded going back to New York. She'd done all right in her small bit of troubleshooting here, but she just didn't feel she was up to anything major.

This was ridiculous, she told herself impatiently. She had let James Ashley-Sinclair turn her whole world upside down, and somehow she had to swing it back into the right orbit.

Stretched out in a lounge chair by the pool, she tried to think coherently about James and herself, tried to keep emotion at bay and to be totally logical about their situation.

They came from two different worlds, belonged in two different worlds. There was no way of avoiding that conclusion. In her opinion marriage was hard enough without augmenting potential difficulties by piling on added impediments, such as radical differences in background.

Why was she thinking about *marriage* in connection with James Ashley-Sinclair?

Nevertheless, she persisted. Suppose she and James had—somehow, someway—decided on trying for a real relationship. She couldn't imagine going through life in the shadow of a famous man. Especially a famous man half the women in the world had their eye on.

She had to admit that James handled his fame well. She'd seen him surrounded by fans at the Ritz in Boston and virtually besieged by fans at the Park Helene in New York. If she'd had any doubt that women, especially, found his role as an internationally famous sex expert fascinating, the New York experience would have set her right. James's fans showered the kind of attention on him usually reserved for rock stars and movie idols.

But, yes, he handled the adulation well. He was pleasant, courteous, attentive, yet he remained slightly removed from the people who were surrounding him—and they loved it.

She'd experienced that sense of feeling slightly removed from James not once, but many times, and she hadn't loved it. On the other hand, there had been other times when she'd felt closer to him than to any other person she'd ever known.

She remembered James cooking for her and making love to her and listening with endless patience to her goings-on about Colleen Reynolds. Listening, too, to what she had to say when they were working on his book.

What a nerve she'd had to venture opinions in a field in which he was decidedly at the top.

Well, he was back in London now in his own milieu. She imagined his publisher would probably make him see the light, make him realize he must finish his new book and would give him another extension on the book. In fact, he might already be at work on the book again.

If that were the case, she wondered if he was painstakingly typing himself, or if his secretary Iris was taking his dictation. Or perhaps Iris had been able to persuade him to bend enough to hire a pretty young typist. Jealousy was a foreign emotion to her, but she had to admit that's what she was feeling.

Kate called the day before Stacy was to leave Sea Island. "Would you mind very much making a detour?" she asked.

"No," Stacy said, and actually felt a sharp sense of reprieve. "What's up?"

"I think they could use a little help at the Key West Kloset," Kate said. "They're getting toward the start of their big season, and I'd like to be sure everything's as it should be."

"Any word of problems?"

"Oh, not really. But I don't want to risk a repeat of the Cap Cod situation, and resorts are always tricky," Kate said. "I thought since you were that far south..."

"Fine with me," Stacy said.

"While you're in Key West," Kate said, "use my Southern Hideaway."

Kate had bought a small renovated conch house in Key West's Old Town a couple of years earlier.

"Kate," Stacy said, memories of her arrival at Kate's Cape Hideaway with James surfacing, "I don't have a key. And I'm not about to attempt a break-in."

"No need," Kate said. "You'll find a stone planter filled with geraniums to the right of the front door. Just feel around a little in the side closest to you. There's a key stuck in the dirt."

Stacy's plane landed at Key West International Airport early on a Wednesday afternoon in mid-November. She picked up a rental car and a map and then headed for Old Town, Key West's original section.

Kate's house, she discovered, was only a couple of blocks from the house in which Ernest Hemingway had lived during his Key West residence. It was small, charming, set back from the street by a fairly wide yard. Hibiscus bushes splashed apricot and rose on either side of the house, there was a coconut palm in the yard, and bright red geraniums were blooming in profusion in the planter Kate had mentioned.

Stacy set her suitcase down on the walk, reached over and was foraging around in the planter when the front door suddenly swung open. She found herself staring at a pair of polished loafers, and a much-too-familiar British voice inquired, "Aren't you afraid you're going to get your hands dirty?"

Stacy sat back on her heels and surveyed James Ashley-Sinclair. He was wearing white cotton slacks and a pale yellow shirt, and he'd already acquired a suntan.

"What are you doing here?" she snapped.

"Waiting for you," he said affably.

She got to her feet, trying to brush the dirt off her hands as she faced him. "Kate knows you're here?" she asked him.

He nodded. "Yes."

Resentment and indignation mixed with a joy at seeing him she couldn't suppress. But the resentment and indignation triumphed. She'd never felt so betrayed.

"Why did you and Kate do this?" she demanded. "Why did you set me up like this?" She didn't wait for an answer. She picked up her suitcase, turned and went back down the walk.

James overtook her before she reached the sidewalk. He gripped her arm. "Stacy, don't think I'm going to let you get away so easily," he growled. "I've done that twice before, and I don't intend to let history repeat itself."

"Please let go of my arm," Stacy said coldly.

"Stacy, for God's sake," James snapped impatiently. He loosened his grip slightly, but he didn't let go of her. "Just what do you think you're about to do?"

"I'm going to drive back to the airport and catch the first plane for New York," Stacy said.

"No," James stated.

Stacy sighed. "Look, James," she said, "I don't know what this is all about. Evidently you and Kate have collaborated on some sort of silly scheme—"

"Silly scheme, is it?"

"I'd certainly say so. Kate pretending she wanted me to check things at the Key West Kloset..."

"That wasn't pretense, Stacy. Kate does want you to check out the Key West Kloset. Look, please don't blame Kate for this," James said urgently. "It was becoming a question of my sanity, that's why she was persuaded to let me come and use her Hideaway here."

"Kate telling me to stay here at her house," Stacy went on, as if she hadn't heard him. "Telling me I could find a key in the planter by the front door..."

"There is a key in the planter by the front door."

"Great. Too bad I didn't have an opportunity to use it," Stacy said bitterly.

"When I heard your car pull up in front of the house, I couldn't wait for you to let yourself in," James admitted.

He was still holding her arm. His gray eyes searched her face. "Is it so terrible finding me here?" he asked her.

"Yes," she said bluntly.

She wanted to add that she'd been trying with every fiber of her being to get over him—or to get enough over him so she could get on with her life. She didn't expect to ever get over him entirely. She'd already come to grips with the fact that she was going to have to learn to live without him.

"Can we go inside?" he asked her. "I'm not going to let go of you until you say you'll come inside and talk with me, Stacy. I'll make a scene if I have to. I don't care how much of a damned scene I have to make."

Stacy couldn't believe what she was hearing. Would James actually create a scene if she refused to go inside and talk to him? She took one look at him and knew he would, and that was so out of character that she was staggered.

"All right," she said. "All right. But it's not going to be a long talk, James. I want to get back to the airport."

He nodded and waited for her to precede him up the walk.

The sun beating down on the walk was blazingly hot. Inside Kate's house it was cool, the rooms shaded by slatted blinds.

"May I get you something cold to drink?" James asked politely.

"Yes, please," Stacy said rather tartly.

James left the room and reappeared a few minutes later with a tall glass full of a frothy pale pink liquid. "Pink grapefruit juice mixed with orange and pineapple juice," he announced. "With lots of ice," he added, and smiled. "I'm learning," he said.

Seeing his smile was like receiving a direct blow. Stacy felt herself go weak all over, and she warned herself sharply that she was going to be in for trouble if she didn't stiffen her spine.

"How long have you been here?" she asked James.

"I came down the day I was supposed to fly back to London."

She stared at him. "You mean you haven't been back to England yet?"

"No."

He sat down in a white wicker chair with big lime-colored cushions. He'd also brought himself a glass of the pink fruit drink, Stacy saw. "You look like you've been putting in some beach time," she said.

"I have been. There's a small beach within walking distance. You look like you've acquired a tinge of color yourself."

"I've been at Sea Island."

"I know."

"Evidently you know more about what I've been doing than I do about what you've been doing," Stacy said coldly.

"I haven't been doing much of anything except lounging around and thinking about you," James said.

The admission was so simple and so direct that it staggered her. She didn't know how to respond; as a result she didn't say anything.

"I could not," James continued after a moment, "go back to England without our meeting again. It's not that England's so far away. It really isn't, you know. But I felt to go back without our resolving a few things would only make it all the more difficult for us to get together again. It seemed too much of a milestone, my leaving the States and you. Do you see what I mean?"

"No," she said frankly.

"You'd made such a thing about our occupying two such different worlds—at least that's how it appeared to me, though I admit I reached the conclusion more as a result of your actions than by anything you've actually said. But you made me conscious enough of the symbolical two worlds so that I didn't want to go all the way back into mine until...well, until we'd done a little exploration, you and I."

"I really don't know what you're talking about, James," Stacy said. Which was not entirely true. But she was determined not to read too much into what he was saying.

James sighed. "You are making this harder than hell for me," he confessed.

He stared across at her, and she would have sworn his clear gray eyes had turned cloudy. He looked utterly miserable, and he sounded wrung out as he asked, "Don't you have any idea how much I love you?"

Stacy felt as if all the red blood cells had suddenly been drained out of her body. She went limp, she sagged, she didn't think she could have moved if her life had depended upon it.

James was watching her closely. "You seem so shocked," he said. "I'm getting the impression this is the last thing in the world you wanted to hear from me. Am I right or wrong?"

Stacy couldn't answer him.

"Stacy," he said, "the least you could do is level with me."

"It's not that simple, James," she found enough voice to say. "Maybe it seems simple to you, but..."

"I have the feeling you're going to put thousands of 'buts' between us," James said. "But I warn you... I intend to deal with them one at a time until I obliterate them. Unless you can sit there and honestly tell me you have no feeling for me, I'm going to work on destroying your 'buts,' Stacy."

She couldn't speak.

"Oh, God," James said, running an agitated hand through his leaf-gold hair. "This is even worse than I thought it would be. Maybe I've been deluding myself. I'm beginning to think I don't know what the hell I *have* been doing."

At this moment, Stacy had to admit, James Ashley-Sinclair looked like anything but a world-famous psychologist and distinguished authority on sex and relationships. He looked surprisingly young and vulnerable and distraught.

"You," he accused, "are driving me crazy. You've been driving me crazy ever since we got to Kate's Hideaway. You didn't even know how to build a fire—the smoke came belching out into the living room." He paused. "That's a rather insane thing with which to endear oneself to a person, isn't it?"

He went on. "Even before then, from the moment our eyes first met in that hotel ballroom in Boston, I was...intrigued by you, attracted to you. Then, when you were the first woman in longer than I can remember to treat me like a *person*, you had me captivated. When we started to work together, I became all the more so. I was already totally bewitched by your body and by everything about you from your smile to the way you laughed and didn't hesitate to argue with me and the way you cared about what happened to people like Colleen Reynolds. But then I became fascinated by your mind, as well. I felt that so often we were on the same wavelength...."

He looked at her. "Was I wrong?" he asked simply.

"No," she said, because she had to speak the truth to him. "No, you weren't wrong."

"Then why..." he began, and stopped himself. "Let me rephrase that. At some point something happened. There was a change between us. It seems to me that your attitude toward me started to change when you began to read my book. Was the book so distasteful to you?"

"No. The book was...is...tremendous," Stacy said honestly. "It wasn't the book. It was..."

He waited, and when she didn't finish, he prodded gently, "What was it, Stacy?"

"The book made me conscious all over again of who you were, who you are. Maybe I do tend to run scared where involvement is concerned, James. I admit that. I admit I did begin to run very scared where you were concerned. In the beginning I'd been...well, I'd been fascinated by you, but I was also in awe of you. But then when we were in the Hideaway together, and you cut your finger and—" She broke off. "I began to see you in a different light."

"Thanks," James Ashley-Sinclair said. And, when she looked at him skeptically, he added, "No, I mean that. It's good to think that even for a little while you saw me as I really am. I'm only sorry that you didn't build up a little more confidence during that interval, Stacy."

"Confidence?"

"Yes. Confidence in your own judgment. You should have trusted yourself more."

Stacy digested that and knew he was right. She should have had more faith in her own judgment. She'd seen the man behind the myth, and she should have gone with her instinct. Instead, she'd let herself be as bedazzled by him as his fans were.

"Why did you come down here, James?" she asked suddenly.

"I think I've already told you that," he said. "But, to add to it, I also came down here because I couldn't face going back to England and getting into the whole damn rat race again. The one lecture in New York was enough to prove to me that I must in some way manage my life better. I need a couple of oases, like these Hideaways Kate has. Places I can go where people don't give a damn who I am, and where I can be myself. I'm going to arrange that somehow. Given half a chance, I'm going to manage to arrange a lot of things, Stacy."

He paused. "Are you willing to give me that half a chance?" he asked her.

Stacy's mind was whirling and her heartbeat was matching it. "Just what are you asking of me, James?" she asked, her voice husky.

"I'm asking you to take a hell of a chance and make the decision to share your life with me," James said. "I'm not asking you to give up anything of yourself, not your career, not anything. I want you exactly as you are, with a couple of exceptions."

"Exceptions?"

"Yes. Especially when I'm with you, I want you to let me get down from the damn pedestal people tend to put me on. I want to walk at your side, Stacy. I want always to be at your side, as a matter of fact, but I'm well aware of the difficulties there. I'm not worried about where we'd live. If I had you with me, I would try to cut to a minimum the lectures and the television appearances and all the other things that only heighten public exposure. The notoriety will die down in time. Someone else will come along." James smiled a wry smile. "The public can be counted on to be fickle, and as far as I'm concerned they can't turn fickle soon enough. I'd like to write a lot more than I have," he added. "That is, if you were there to listen to what I want to say and to set me straight about it."

"Please," she protested.

"I'm quite serious," James said. "Once you stopped working with me on the book, all I could do was fiddle with it, and now I've given up on it."

"You can't do that," Stacy told him.

"I've done it."

"That's not right, James. You know that's not right. Your book is very much needed today. People need to hear what you have to say."

"How about you?" James asked her. "Do you need to hear what I have to say?

"You've still made no statements, Stacy," he said when again she didn't answer him.

"What?"

"I'd rather have you say you despise me than not to say anything. Can't you possibly bring yourself to make a declaration where I'm concerned? Don't you *know* how you feel about me?"

"Oh, yes," Stacy said. "I know how I feel about you."

She'd been holding back for a long time, afraid of the risk commitment involved. She'd been trying to convince herself that, finally, she had things just as she wanted them. But she knew in her heart that a great deal had been missing.

That fear of standing up and being counted, when it came to her deepest feelings, still held, though. Yet . . . she owed this much to James. She phrased her reply in the form of a question, using the same words he'd said to her just moments ago. "Don't you know how much I love you?" she asked him.

James sat very still, and if she hadn't known better Stacy could have sworn he was epitomizing the haughtiness she'd so often found so intimidating. But she did know better.

She made the first move to reach out to him, and she didn't have to wait long. James met her in the middle of Kate's pale yellow rattan rug and swept her into his arms, and his kiss went all the way to the farthest reaches of her soul.

There was no chance for either of them to speak for quite a while after that. They were too busy touching, feeling, loving.

After a time James warned, "There's a lot to work out."

"I know," Stacy murmured softly.

"I can't keep you out of the spotlight, and you'll hate it."

"I know," she said, and knew that was so, having already had a slight taste of that sort of thing with the picture that had been published in the New York paper.

"I'll have to live in England a good bit of the time. I do have responsibilities over there. But I'll spend as much of my time as possible here in the States with you. Maybe we could get Al Reynolds to build us our own Hideaway up in Devon."

"Maybe," Stacy agreed.

"I want you to continue your career with Kate because I know how much you enjoy your job. Kate wants to open a branch of her firm in London. I happen to know that, and maybe you could take charge..."

"Maybe."

"You're being very compliant," James said, moving back from her slightly and looking at her through narrowed eyes. "Which isn't like you, Stacy."

She smiled. "No, it isn't, is it?"

"Stacy, you haven't said that you're willing to go along with any of what I've just been saying. Are you willing?"

It still amazed her to think that James Ashley-Sinclair could be looking at her as he was looking at her now, anxiety etching his handsome face as he waited for her answer.

But she was even more interested in coming to terms with James, the man she loved.

"Can't we talk about all of that later?" she asked him.

"Stacy, I have to know."

"You already know," she said. "Any psychologist half as sharp as you are would know by now that the two of us are going to have to effect an astronomical transfiguration."

"What?"

"We're going to have to mold two different worlds into one super globe," Stacy said, "but I think it can be done. Meantime...couldn't we just spend a little time with each other?"

Later, much later, James and Stacy left Kate's house and strolled over to Duval Street and walked the length of Old Town toward Mallory Square.

"I think we're going to miss the famous sunset tonight," James said.

"Well, there's always tomorrow night," Stacy told him.

And the night after that. And the night after that. Forever.

* * * * *